Germany's sparkling Rhineland is the perfect place for a fresh start . . .

Warming people's hearts with true accounts of kindness is what columnist Anna Kelly does best. But no one knows the private misery she endures in her abusive marriage. Still, leaving is difficult—until a deeply personal bequest from a beloved elderly neighbor compels Anna to travel to Germany. There she begins an unexpected adventure of paying it forward that will take her far from her complicated life in Brooklyn.

Arriving in the historic and picturesque city of Mainz, on the breathtaking Rhine River, Anna settles in at a cozy guesthouse filled with colorful residents. But fulfilling her task will require the help of a translator and knowledgeable guide.

Josef Schmitt will gladly shuttle the American visitor around if it distracts him from his dark thoughts. Ever since a serious accident sidelined him at the local excursions company, he's been unable to forget the pain he caused or forgive himself. Now, accompanying Anna on her mission takes them both to surprising places—and they just may find the courage to truly set themselves free . . .

Books by Sharon Struth

Blue Moon Lake Series
Share the Moon
Twelve Nights
Harvest Moon
Bella Luna

The Sweet Life
The Sweet Life
Willow's Way
Saving Anna

Published by Kensington Publishing Corporation

Saving Anna

The Sweet Life

Sharon Struth

LYRICAL PRESS
Kensington Publishing Corp.
www.kensingtonbooks.com

LYRICAL PRESS BOOKS are published by
Kensington Publishing Corp.
119 West 40th Street
New York, NY 10018

First Electronic Edition: November 2018
eISBN-13: 978-1-5161-0357-7
eISBN-10: 1-5161-0357-2

First Print Edition: November 2018
ISBN-13: 978-1-5161-0360-7
ISBN-10: 1-5161-0360-2

Printed in the United States of America

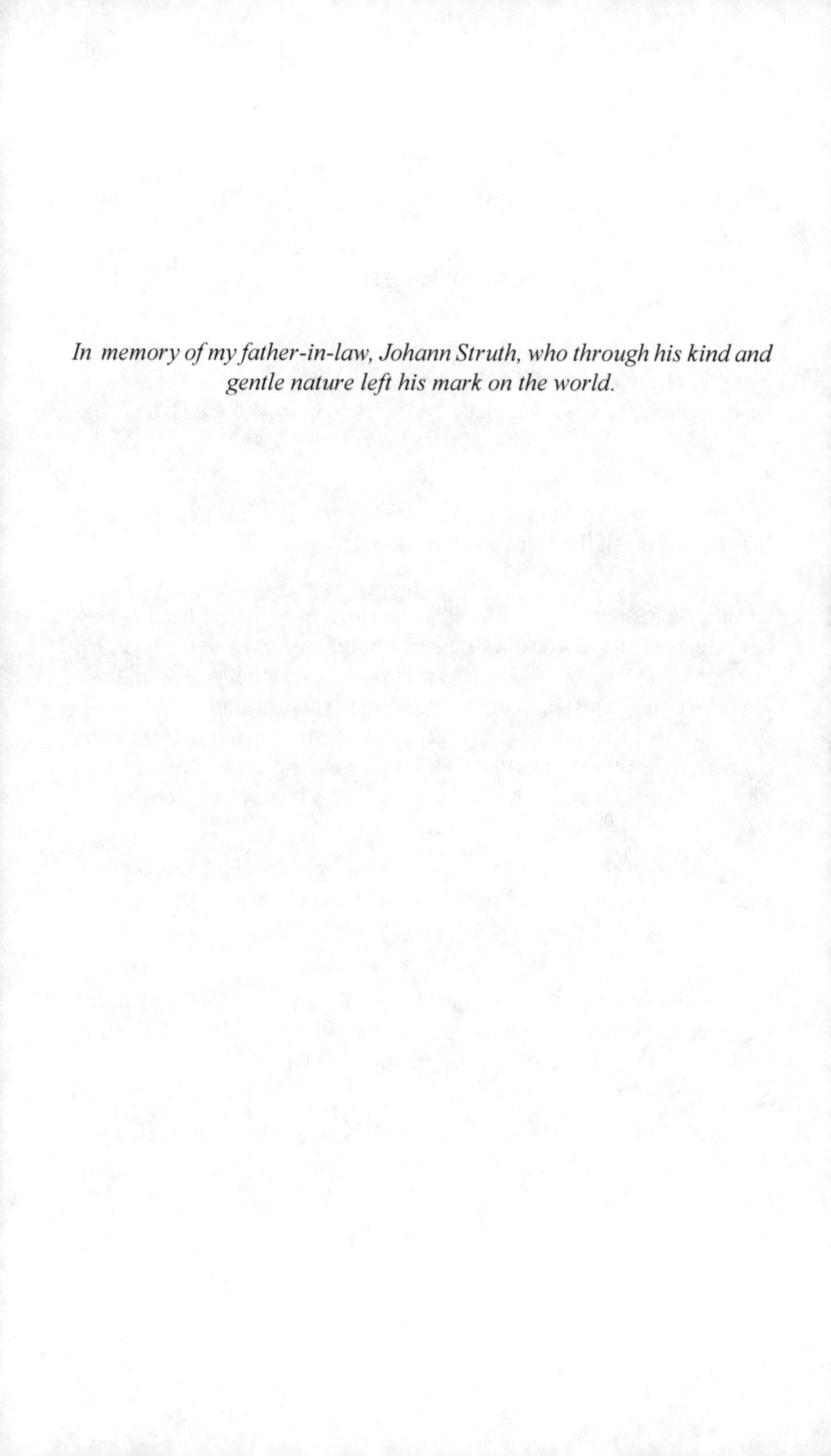

In memory of my father-in-law, Johann Struth, who through his kind and gentle nature left his mark on the world.

Acknowledgments

I've said this before, but it's worth repeating: I'd like to thank the readers of my books, who often tell me they get lost in the worlds I create and wish they'd never end. You make every second of writing (and there are a lot of them!) worth it.

A thousand thanks to Paige Christian, editor extraordinaire, my agent Dawn Dowdle, and the staff at Kensington Publishing, a place that feels like family.

Speaking of family, I'm always thankful to my supportive husband and my beautiful daughters—you guys are everything to me. But this time, I'd also like to thank some family related to me through marriage: my father-in-law's kin in Germany. Our trip years ago to Mainz, where my father-in-law was from, inspired this setting. But what made the trip memorable were the relatives who welcomed us into their homes and hearts. I will never forget any of you and Germany will always feel like a home away from home.

To my wonderfully supportive mother, thank you for being proud of me and for continuing to hand out my business cards. I am lucky to have a mom like you.

Special thanks to my writer friends, Rachel Brimble and Joanne Stewart, for being such fantastic and honest critique partners, and to Terri-Lynne DeFino for your grammar guidance.

And to my friends who always buy my books, your support is immeasurable. I love you guys!

Author's Foreword

This story is fiction, but true past events create the background to my character's journey as she explores a horrific time in Europe's history. I shed many tears reading story after story of those who escaped death, all due to the kindness of strangers who helped save them. Let us always search for our inner hero and stand up to prejudice of all kinds. Small actions can make a big difference.

Chapter 1

If Anna had known surviving would come down to this moment, she might never have married Patrick. She stood on the sidewalk outside their Brooklyn brownstone, doing her best to act natural despite the rapid thump of her heart.

He opened the taxi's back door, poked his head in. "LaGuardia Airport."

The driver popped the trunk and hopped out his door just as Patrick lifted his golf clubs. "Hold on, sir. Let me get those for you." He sprinted to Patrick's side and took the clubs while Patrick nodded his approval.

Maybe the driver hoped for a big tip after catching a glimpse of Patrick's thick Rolex watch or his well-tailored sports jacket. Her husband had impeccable style. Or maybe the driver caught a whiff of Patrick's unwavering confidence and wanted to stay on his good side. A simple lift of his thick, dark brows always commanded authority.

Patrick turned and approached Anna. His handsome face glowed with a smile masking the real demon inside, his scrutiny intense as he searched her the way a zoologist watches a caged animal for signs of distress.

She slipped her hands into the pockets of her lightweight tunic top, comfortable for this September day. But now goosebumps prickled up her arms as she contemplated what he might be thinking. The least suspicious response was to return his smile, so she did.

When he got close, he drew her to him, securing her arms around his waist. His voice softened. "I'll miss you, Anna-belle."

The nicknames, the dazzling and disarming sweetness. His charms had lured her when they'd first met and throughout their courtship. But she now knew he was a human Venus flytrap. She swallowed back a vile mix of hatred and fear. "I'll miss you, too."

He tilted his head, watched her with his unnerving stare. "What are your plans while I'm gone?"

She could practically see the gears in his mind churning. The wrong response would flip his sunny mood upside down. But she'd gotten better at this game and played it up with a flirtatious smile. "You mean besides missing you?"

His tight expression unwound, and he laughed. "Yes. Besides that."

"I plan to finish my column for work, maybe go see an exhibit at the Brooklyn Historical Society. And of course, treat myself to Thai food the nights you're gone."

He nodded, the silent approval making her tense body relax. "Good. When you go out, bring your cell phone. In case I need to reach you."

"I always do."

Satisfaction glinted in his dark eyes. She despised herself for pandering to his control, though doing so had become her means of survival.

Patrick's gaze dropped to her neck. He lifted the delicate heart charm hanging from a thin silver chain.

She wanted to shudder but held it in.

"While I'm down in Florida, I'll look for some earrings to match the necklace," he said softly.

She swallowed the urge to tell him she hated the necklace. "You're always too good to me."

He circled her in his arms, squeezing her in a tight hug. Pain pulsed in her upper arm, but she didn't dare complain. Not after he'd slammed her against the bathroom wall two nights ago because he hadn't seen her wear the necklace in a while. She'd kept her mouth shut and worn it every minute since. He leaned back and carefully brushed his lips to hers, the severe contrast to his harsh actions of that night mind-numbing.

He released her and stood back. "Wish me luck golfing. Tom and I have a serious bet going on this year's tournament."

"You'll do great. But good luck anyway."

He got into the cab and winked. "Love you, babe."

"Love you, too." Saying the words carried the bitter tang of a bite from a lemon, making her almost cringe. But she'd never be forced to say them again. "Have fun."

She waited by the steps. The driver fussed with something in the front seat, turned to Patrick to speak, and they both laughed.

Hurry. Leave! Her heart skipped a beat. Breath stalled. For three weeks she'd waited for this chance to leave town before the divorce papers were served.

The cab finally pulled away and she inhaled a deep breath. Patrick waved from the window. She smiled, waved back, and watched until the cab turned at the end of their tree-lined street and merged with the main road's busy Saturday morning traffic. She exhaled a sigh of relief and sprinted up the steps. She had a lot to do.

As she reached for the knob, the front door to the adjoining brownstone opened.

A woman dressed in a navy blazer, holding a lockbox in her hands, came out and glanced over to Anna. "Oh! Hello. I hoped I'd run into one of the neighbors." She stuck out her hand. "Maria Rossi, Coldwell Banker. I've been put in charge of selling this place for the estate."

Anna shook her hand. "Anna Kelly. I've only got a quick second—"

"I know you! You're the gal who writes a column in the *Times*. The one about people doing nice things for others."

"That's me. *Kindness Connects*."

"I love your stories. People are so cynical these days, but every time I read one of those, I think about how there are still good people out there. You know, my mother always says, love and kindness are never wasted."

"Your mother sounds like a wise woman."

Maria placed a well-manicured hand on Anna's forearm. "Oh, there was one story I adored about…"

Anna slipped on a polite face, listened, but worried about the time. The flight to Germany would leave with or without her.

Soon as she saw a spot to break in, she said, "Thank you again. I'm sorry, but I've got an appointment and don't have much time. You had some questions?"

The realtor asked about the neighborhood and if she had or knew anybody with kids in the schools. Anna hurriedly filled her in. If she and Patrick had children, she'd have been able to answer the questions more fully. They hadn't, thank God. The idea he might hurt them, like he did her, made Anna sick.

After a few minutes, Anna said, "I've really got to run. Sorry."

Maria waved. "Don't worry one bit. I've got to finish some things, then I need to get out of here, too. I appreciate the help."

Once inside, Anna flew up the stairs and went straight to the spare bedroom. She flung open the closet door and grabbed her suitcase. Back in her room, she layered the luggage with previously organized stacks of clothing she'd planned to bring to Germany. Enough clothes to carry her through the cooler month ahead. Four weeks away. Hopefully, enough time for Patrick's anger to dissolve, because she damn well knew he'd be furious.

She zipped the bag, tossed on the combination lock, and hurried downstairs.

In two days, Patrick would return to LaGuardia airport and take a cab directly to his office at Goldman Sachs. The lawyer said he'd have the divorce papers served there around lunchtime. By then, she'd already be on another continent. Far away from the physical abuse he'd want to inflict on her once the papers were in his hands. Of that, she felt certain. He'd smacked her around for lesser infractions, starting just days after they'd returned from their honeymoon.

Even though she would be leaving the country to stay safe, he deserved a note. A note would be easier than a conversation.

At the kitchen island, she found a pad and steadied a pen on the paper.

Dear Patrick,

If you're reading this, it means you're back from Florida and have realized I'm not here.

Anna ripped the page off the small legal pad, crumpled it into a ball, and tossed it on the marble island. She wrote for a living and could do better.

Dear Patrick,

For the past two years, I've begged you to get help. I understand your father hurt you, but I can no longer accept your past as an excuse for hurting me. ME! The person who always loved you, tried to help you, accepted your many, many apologies. You say you love me, but your actions speak otherwise. I no longer love you. You bully me, make me afraid, and refuse to let me to see my friends and family—

She ripped the paper off the pad and tore it in half. Too much. She'd spoken these words to him many times after he'd calm down, her speeches always soliciting remorse-filled apologies she'd blindly believed for the first year of their marriage. The second year, she'd grown skeptical, but continued to cover the bruises and lie to anybody who happened to see one. Now, she despised him.

The clock on the wall showed it was time to leave. She pressed the pen to the paper and the words flowed easily this time.

Dear Patrick,

By now you've been served the divorce papers and know I'm leaving you. Please seek help and do not look for me. If you are calm when I return, we can talk. Otherwise, you will deal with my attorney.
Anna

She propped the note next to a bowl of fruit, where they always left messages they wanted the other to see, then undid the necklace clasp and lowered his gift there. A reminder of what had happened two nights earlier. But only one thing would cause him as much pain as he'd inflicted on her.

She held out her hand, taking one last look at the antique silver band that served as a symbol of the love she and Patrick once shared. Leaving the ring would send a stronger message than words or a divorce summons.

She tightened her fingers around the band, pulled. A loud pounding on the door made her stop. *Patrick?*

Fear rushed her veins like a raging wild fire. She hurried to the foyer and looked through the peephole to find the realtor, Maria, peering back at her. She tossed her luggage and backpack in the closet, took a few deep breaths, and opened the door. Maria stood on the other side holding a worn black briefcase.

"Me again. Sorry, I know you're busy."

"No problem." Despite her racing pulse, she forced a smile.

Maria stuck out a business card. "I'm on my way out, but can I give you this in case you need to reach me? Like if you hear of someone who might be interested in the place, or notice any problems around here?"

"Certainly. I'll call if any of those things come up."

"Fabulous. You have a great day." She smiled and headed down the steps.

Anna closed the door and leaned against it. Thank God Patrick hadn't returned for some reason.

After a quick stop in the downstairs bathroom, Anna took her luggage from the closet, hiked the backpack on her shoulders, and walked out the door.

Taking long strides toward the subway station, she stared straight ahead, made eye contact with no one, and held her chin high.

I've done it. I've left him.

Horns honked. Kids hollered. Background noise as the journey she started two months ago came to an end. She'd almost channel surfed right past the afternoon talk show. *Domestic violence*, the host had said. She'd skipped to the next channel, only the phrase stuck. Wouldn't leave her head. So she backtracked and watched. Her mouth had gone dry as each woman described a life where leaving her abuser had been out of the question, due to either a desire to fix the man or plain old fear. That moment cast a spotlight on her reality.

She reached the subway station and ten minutes later boarded the car that would take her to the AirTrain in Jamaica, Queens that went to JFK. An untraceable route. Once through security, she would make a long overdue call to her sister to share everything she should have said over the past two years. The more time that passed in Anna's horrible situation, the more she'd worried about condemnation from others. Even with her sister, her closest friend.

How could she stay with a man who'd hit her, they would ask. Before her marriage, Anna would've wondered the same.

As the train rumbled down the track, she reached up and grabbed the pole near her seat. There on her hand remained the wedding band she'd been set to leave behind, forgotten with the realtor's interruption. Disappointment rattled her, but only for a second.

This changed nothing. She'd remove the ring once she got to Germany, store it somewhere safe, and cash it in when she returned to help pay for the divorce attorney.

A bad feeling settled over her. Could this be an omen the marriage wouldn't end effortlessly?

Patrick scared the hell out of her. But maybe, with her gone, he'd think about the way he mistreated her, get help for his problems, and understand the love between them had been beaten right out of her.

What if he didn't? Up until now, he'd resisted all help.

Even if he didn't get help, one thing was different now. She'd changed. She could admit she was a victim. Had filed for divorce. Even taken steps to leave him, starting with a month away to do a final deed for Isaak, the man to whom she owed this escape.

She'd return to New York as the woman she once was; someone who could stand up to a bully like Patrick.

Only she hadn't stood up to him, and she wished she understood why.

Chapter 2

"And the reason for your visit?" The round-faced Frankfurt Airport customs agent glanced up from his purview of Anna's passport.

She smiled, but his expression remained starched-stiff as he waited. "Work."

A partially true statement. Her idea to turn Isaak's request into several installments of her syndicated column had been a hit with her agent and several big city newspaper editors. Plus it justified taking the month off while they ran old columns. This story contained the kind of empathy typically found in her pieces. While her marriage deteriorated, work had served as pain medicine. Little doses of optimism in the face of her own suffering.

The customs officer flipped through the passport once more, then pushed it toward her. "Welcome to Germany."

"*Danke schön.*"

She slipped the passport into her backpack, grabbed the handle of her luggage, and followed signs written in English and German to the arrival area. As she rounded a corner, several businessmen rushed by. The gentle musky scent of Armani enveloped her senses. A chill swept along her spine and shocked her nape. Patrick's scent. It clung to everything he wore. When they'd dated, a whiff made her warm with thoughts of his tender touch. Now the smell traveled to her brain like a chemosensory warning of danger. The scent even lingered in their bedroom. A constant reminder while he was at work that he'd soon return. She glanced back, relieved that she didn't see him anywhere.

She released a shaky sigh and continued out of the terminal. In the lineup of cars, vans, and buses at the curb, she searched for the white Mercedes she'd been told belonged to Isaak's friend, who owned the guesthouse where she'd be staying.

She didn't see a car matching the description. At a bench near the pick-up zone, she sat and waited.

Isaak may have never seen the inside of this airport, having left Frankfurt under such horrible circumstances. An ache for him squeezed her chest so tight she couldn't breathe. The day they met she'd been on her patio, elbow-deep in dirt, potting fresh spring pansies, and he'd come up behind her. "Hello, young lady." He had a thick German accent. "Do you know what kind of socks a gardener wears?"

She'd glanced back over her shoulder to find an elderly man with a charming smile waiting for an answer. "Oh, everyone knows that one." She'd stood and faced him. "Garden hose."

He'd laughed. "I'm Isaak. I live right next door."

They'd seen each other almost daily, the exception being the days Patrick didn't go to work because he'd complain she wasn't spending time with him.

But she worked from home, by herself most of the day due to Patrick's long hours. And Isaak was too old leave to his house easily. So they'd bonded on a common ground...loneliness.

She had more than their friendship to thank him for. Because of Isaak, she could make her getaway today. He'd always have a special place in her heart. For being her friend. For sending her a lifeline, even after losing his battle with cancer. A lifeline he'd offered after he died, by way of a note from his lawyer.

That was the day she'd learned Isaak knew the dirty secret in her marriage.

All the hidden bruises and lies hadn't fooled him. His note said he wanted her life to change. All he asked in return was for her to help him with one thing. The reason she'd come to Germany.

She removed the envelope from her backpack, and took out the letter Isaak's attorney had handed her moments after telling her she'd inherited $50,000.

Private - To be opened only by Anna Kelly.

The letter, written in Isaak's scratchy script two days before he passed, caused her chest to swell with sadness at the subtle reminder of his life. She swallowed down her grief and read the note that had pushed her to proceed with the divorce.

Dearest Anna,

As I face my end, there is one thing in my life I regret not doing. To do it, though, would have meant a return to Germany, an emotionally difficult journey I could not face. Yet if not for one person's actions, I might not have lived to a ripe old age. A neighbor witnessed the atrocities that hurt my family and made sure I remained safe. A self-sacrificing and heroic feat, one I should have acknowledged sooner. The man's name is Gunther Hinzmann.

Two months ago, I sent a letter to Gunther to express my gratitude for his help. I sent it to the only address I knew for him, on the street where we both once lived. But it came back this week, unopened, with a note saying he was not at that address.

So to carry this out, I need assistance. I am hoping you will help me.

You are no doubt wondering why I chose you. My dear, it is because I know the secret you keep from those who care about you...

I have heard things when the windows are open or in the quiet of night. Oh, my poor Anna. It pains me to hear you mistreated by that man. You are far too sweet, kind, and forgiving. Something your rotten husband doesn't deserve.

I never spoke to you of his mistreatment because, like you, I understand how painful it is to discuss things that have beaten us down. My years in Nazi Germany scarred me forever.

Yet there comes a time when we must share our pain. And now is my time.

The things the Nazis did to my family, my people, happened over years. Through Nazi-sponsored legislation, they marginalized us. Our only family left Germany because of what was happening to Jews during those years. Not my father, though. He could be a stubborn man and refused to leave his home.

They expelled Jews from professions and from commercial life, so my father could not even work to support us. It worsened every single day. And this was before the war started.

It all changed one day. In nineteen thirty-eight, on an evening known as Kristallnacht *(I am sure you have heard of this horrible evening), my life changed forever. Our house was broken into. The fiends saw my father had been violating the law by operating a small bookkeeping business from our home to make money. They called for his arrest. My mother tried to stop them and was beaten to death. In my father's rage he fought back, tried to stop them, and they shot him. All while my brother and I hid, close enough to witness the horrors. On their way out, they set the house on fire. My brother and I narrowly escaped before it burned to the ground.*

Gunther came to our aid. He had seen what happened. We had nowhere to go. Rumor around the neighborhood was that the authorities were looking for my brother and me. Perhaps to send us off to one of the work camps we had been hearing stories about. Gunther took care of us, kept us in hiding for six months in Frankfurt. He helped secure new papers that allowed us to reach a family he found in Belgium, who offered to hide us there until it was safe to return to Germany.

My story goes on, when the Germans invaded Belgium. But now, I will focus on what Gunther did for us. Without him, my life might have turned out very different.

So I'm asking for your help, Anna dear.

I am hoping you will travel to Germany for me and locate Gunther Hinzmann. Deliver my letter to him. If Gunther has passed, then perhaps you can find his family and let them know about his heroism.

In return, here is my gift to you...

This trip gives you a chance to escape from your life here, at least for a short while. Maybe the time away will help you permanently find a way out of your situation, in a place where Patrick won't find you.

I beg of you, please save yourself before it's too late.

My friends in Mainz are nice people who will have a place for you to stay. My lawyer has been instructed to give you money for your travel. I have left with him a photo of me and Gunther along with his original address. Additionally, there is a lump sum inheritance given to you in my will. Use it to get a fresh start on your life when you return. Go someplace where you can leave the past behind.

Doing this is a risk, but life has shown me that without risk, nothing can change.

Thank you for all the joy you have given me.

Isaak

Without overthinking it, she'd told the lawyer yes. She would handle Isaak's last request and use the time away to have the divorce papers served.

The quest to find this man—or family of the man if he'd passed away—seemed overwhelming. But she could never turn her back on such heroism. This man deserved to receive thanks and be honored for what he did. Probably at great risk to himself or his family.

She tucked away the letter and removed her phone, holding her breath as she hit the power button. The lawyer had warned her that if Patrick had any suspicions the divorce papers were on their way, he could refuse to accept the summons. Legally, the document required he fully accept and sign for it, so surprise was tantamount. If Patrick had reached out, she needed to reply within a reasonable time. Hopefully, he hadn't tried mid-flight. Her pulse raced as she considered possible excuses.

Sorry, I fell asleep.

You called? I didn't hear the phone ring.

Would he buy those responses? Normally, she'd have replied to him immediately. It would be a challenge until the papers were served to do so because she planned to keep the phone off, so roaming charges didn't mount and raise a red flag.

When the phone connected, there were no messages. She exhaled a sigh. Between now and Monday, she'd be mindful to check, so he didn't get suspicious about her silence. When the divorce papers were served, then he'd know the truth. Even though a part of her hated doing something so sly to a man she once loved, her lawyer recommended serving them in public, so he wouldn't make a scene. He was probably right.

"Miss? Are you Anna Kelly?"

The German-accented voice startled her. She looked up from her phone. A slender man with thick, light gray hair starting far back on his forehead and falling in waves to his ears stared back. He wore a corduroy blazer and khakis, and a kind smile on his long face.

A fresh start meant a return to her maiden name. "Yes. It's actually Anna Abrams now."

His smile widened, making his chestnut eyes crinkle as he offered his hand. "*Wunderbar*! I'm Joachim Von Essen." He motioned toward a white Mercedes with the words *Villa Von Essen Gästehaus* on the side door. "Shall we go? The staff is getting breakfast ready. Are you hungry?"

She'd been so nervous on the flight, she'd barely eaten. Joachim's friendly greeting and nice smile relaxed her for the first time in over twenty-four hours. "As a matter of fact, I am."

Anna followed behind him to the car, excited to be here and start her task.

* * * *

"This is a miserable existence, Claudia. You might as well lock me in a room and not feed me if you feel that way." Josef Schmitt shot up from the chair and left his boss's office.

"*Mein Gott*," she said loudly. "It isn't my fault you cannot return to the field and work the adventure tours."

"I know it isn't your fault." He clenched the cane and stabbed it against the oak floor on his way to his desk, knowing full well he was behaving like an angry jerk. "It was the doctor's orders."

And he was damn sick of doctors. He'd go nuts if she didn't let him work with a tour soon.

Just as he fell into his chair, Claudia came out of her office carrying her favorite mug with the words *You Can Call Me Queen Bee* displayed on the white ceramic.

She reached him, her eyes meeting his and refusing to yield. "You know, you can be a real baby when things don't go your way."

"Oh, really? I was thinking more like a jerk." He rested the cane against his desk.

She laughed, a soft belly laugh making all the anger inside him melt. "I would argue it's a little of both."

"I'm sorry. It's just frustrating."

She lifted his mug. "I know. I'll get you a refill, but you must promise to stop being so difficult."

"I'll try, but I never dreamed at forty-one I'd be stuck walking with a cane and pushing paper in an office."

Across the room, Klaus glanced up from his work and pushed his wire-framed glasses against his nose while passing a look of disdain at Josef. "And what is so wrong with office work? I love my accounting job." He motioned to Adele, who worked intensely on their new website. "And Adele's happy."

Adele possessed the focused concentration of a bloodhound on a scent. Her eyes never left the computer screen as she nodded.

Josef offered his co-worker a smile. "I'm sorry. There's nothing wrong with this type of work. It isn't for me. That's all."

Klaus's face softened. "I know." He returned to the scattered papers on his desk.

Claudia stopped at the coffee pot and filled the two mugs, then plunked one down in front of him. "There are some benefits to your leg problem."

"Name one thing."

She leaned over and whispered, "You've got me waiting on you. I don't bring coffee to any other employees."

He laughed. His childhood friend always knew how to soothe his moods. "And they say you have no compassion…"

"Who says that?" Her rich blue eyes widened, and her brows lifted. As the owner of Wanderlust Excursions, with staff located all over the globe, she ruled with an iron fist. "You'd better tell them I do. After all, I have you here at the home office until you are back on your feet. Not sitting home watching Netflix."

"And I appreciate everything you have done, but this"—he waved a hand to the stack of papers he needed to address—"scheduling hotels and guides. I am glad to do it, but even a small assignment to get me out of the office some days would make me happy. Even with this cane, there must be a way I can get back out there again."

"There isn't. And what I gave you is the work I need done."

"Fine, fine. I'll do it, and I appreciate you finding me work. But in addition, maybe I can also create some new programs?" Three years ago, when Claudia put him in charge of creating their adventure division, he'd never been happier. "I saw yesterday the caves of Cinque Terre tour is doing so well that there are two guides doing them now, and both are booked solid. Plus, my Conquer Iceland tour is full for the whole season."

"And your bonus reflected my appreciation for all those things. But now—"

"Plus, the Norway trip is six weeks away. I should be on site. I mean, you can't just assign anyone to handle rappelling in the Valdall canyons, or zip-lining—"

"*Halt*." Claudia closed her eyes and pinched the bridge of her patrician nose, which was almost too large for her petite frame.

Give him a line and he'd push it, but he also knew when to stop talking and listen.

Drawing in a deep breath, she released her fingers and her gaze fell on him. "You haven't recovered fully from the accident. For now, the doctor said you should restrict your activities. If I sent you out on one of the adventure tours in any capacity and you got hurt…" The office phone rang, and she paused. "My point is, this is my company and I will not risk further injury to your leg while on the job." She lifted the phone on an empty desk next to Josef's. "*Hallo*? Wanderlust Excursions."

While she turned her back to talk, Josef dug deep, trying to think of something he could do around here to make his days more palatable. She was right about his injury. It didn't stop him from wanting things to return to normal.

Claudia hung up and turned to watch him, lips pursed.

"What?"

"That was Regina Von Essen."

"How is she?"

"She sounds busy." Claudia stared at him, head tilted. "She needs… well, I'm not sure if… It seems they have a job opportunity. Joachim, of course, thought about you."

Claudia's hesitation defied her usual directness. "And?"

"I'm wondering if you are interested."

"Will this get me out of the office?"

"Yes, but you should understand the full scope of the work."

"It has been just about six months since I got out of the hospital. I'm sure it will be fine."

"Someone needs a guide—"

"Then I'm your man." He slapped a palm on his desk. "With one of your drivers in the van, I can easily cover a full day of touring."

She frowned. "I'm not sure this will work. Maybe I'll see if my friend up the river at Rüdesheimer Travel is interested."

"Come on, Claudia. I can walk and talk to people."

"But this isn't an assignment as a tour guide, Josef. There's an American staying at the guesthouse for a month who needs a driver and translator while here in Germany."

A driver. The word settled on Josef's skin like acid. On his last drive through town, his heart pattered erratically and perspiration moistened his temples. He'd slammed on the brakes each time movement in his peripheral caught his attention, and drivers behind him beeped their anger. Then his brain froze toward the end of his drive, as images of the car accident bombarded him from all angles. Not that he remembered the crash, but he'd seen pictures in several French newspapers.

"I know you've been taking the tram to work," Claudia said softly. "It's okay to be afraid of driving after such a thing happens."

"So? I take the tram because it's easier than finding parking," he lied, but the bigger lie was the agony worming through him every single day.

A woman had died while he drove, and he couldn't remember a damn thing about what happened. He'd survived the accident, but Lily had not. But here was a chance to return to normal…

"Really, Claudia." He tried to sound strong. "I can handle driving."

Claudia remained silent long enough to make him uncomfortable, then said, "I know you'd try. You're the most fearless man I know. But there'll be a passenger, a paying client."

If she knew the level of his angst and the horror each time he got behind the wheel, she wouldn't have offered the job. Shadowed images from the accident stalked him like invisible demons, instilling fear in his bones and reminding him that whatever caused the crash was lost in the black hole of his mind.

Who was he kidding? He was half the man he used to be. Self-hatred chomped away at his soul. He'd finally been handed a chance to get back on his feet, and instead he toyed with the idea of raising a flag of surrender.

"On second thought, this doesn't sound very exciting. Maybe I should pass." Liar. He was terrified.

Claudia nodded. "*Gut.*" She took the cordless phone from the base. "I'll pass the opportunity over to Rüdesheimer Travel."

The panic of missing an opportunity settled in his bones. This job could be the thing to bring normalcy back to his life. Help him overcome those nasty demons greeting him each morning. He reached out, touched her arm. "*Nein.*"

Claudia stopped dialing, looked at him. "It's okay if you are not ready."

"I know." He drew in a sharp breath. "I need to do this."

She blinked a few times then nodded. "Okay. Call Regina and let her know, but at any time if the driving becomes too much, you will say so. Understand?"

"*Ja, ja*, boss." He grinned, so she'd see confidence, not the apprehension he felt inside.

She eyed him suspiciously, then returned to her office.

He drew in a deep breath that traveled to the nerves rippling inside his gut. By taking this assignment, he hoped to fix himself, but was he putting someone else's life at risk? God forbid he flipped out or panicked on the highway. If only he knew what had made him swerve…

But how could he ever gain confidence in himself again if he didn't try? His entire life, he'd never shied from challenges. Just like his father. Now, his knees wobbled at the prospect of driving a woman around Germany. All because cars were his kryptonite. But so what? He'd be careful, even practice driving before the job started. He *could* do it!

He dialed the Villa Von Essen, and agreed when they asked if he could come over that afternoon to meet the new client.

After he hung up, he shuffled paperwork. The office phones rang, and his coworkers talked amongst themselves, but the sounds were muted by the thump of his pulse in his ears. A lump grew in his throat along with a fuzzy image of Lily, dead in the passenger's seat of his car.

Was it a real memory or imaginary? He didn't know. But as the driver, he took full responsibility for her death, and he'd never forgive himself.

Chapter 3

Anna stood on the small balcony off her room and watched a passenger ship drift down the sparkling waters of the Rhine when a woman dressed in a short skirt hurried down a path on the side of the guesthouse building. Her hip-high leather jacket flapped behind her.

A man appeared on the ground below. "*Tschüss,* Karen," he yelled.

The blonde spun around and her long mane sashayed like a wedding gown train. "I already said goodbye, Florian," she said with a pleasant British accent. "You're going to make me late for work."

"But you forgot something." He trotted over to her, wrapped her in his arms, and kissed her with the passion of Rhett Butler leaving Scarlett, then they talked quietly, still clutched in their embrace.

A kiss like so many she'd shared with Patrick early in their courtship. Where the heat of his gaze left her with no doubt they'd have a happily ever after. Over the course of their marriage, Patrick never stopped offering her romantic moments like the kind these two lovebirds shared. His abuse, however, added to her confused feelings toward him. After a while, she'd forced herself to respond to his overtures like an actress playing a role, just so she didn't upset him. Even in their bedroom.

The couple parted. As the man turned to head back inside, he glanced up and peered at Anna through his thick, dark-framed glasses.

"*Guten Morgen*." He smiled warmly, and his handlebar mustache twitched at the twirled corners.

"Good morning."

"I bet you are the new guest from America."

"I am."

"My name is Florian. I run the Von Essen Restaurant and Biergarten. See you at breakfast?"

"I'll be right down."

His long legs carried him across the patio, and he disappeared through the restaurant doors.

She quickly freshened up, changed into clean jeans and a pullover, then left the room.

Taking the burgundy-carpeted staircase to the main entrance, Anna followed the sound of voices along with the smell of food down a hallway decorated with pictures of castles on the river. Just as she passed through an arched opening marked *Restaurant & Biergarten*, loud voices traveled down the hallway from where she'd just entered. A disagreement, but she couldn't understand since they spoke in their native tongue.

A couple entered the room but didn't notice her and kept arguing. The man's face was long and slim like his body, his nose prominent as an eagle's beak. He towered over the short woman at his side. Yet it was the woman who stood out. The top layer of her silver curls had been dyed pink. Not passive pink, but eye-blinding, earth-shaking pink. The no-nonsense tone of her grainy voice, combined with the sour expression on his whiskered face, suggested she might have the upper hand in their passionate discussion.

He spotted Anna first and said something to his companion, who glanced at Anna and stopped talking.

"Good morning," Anna said quickly. "I'm new here."

The man extended a hand. "Otto Braun. Joachim mentioned a new guest would be here today."

Anna reached out to shake, but Otto took her hand and brought it to his lips. His salt-and-pepper mustache tickled her skin while his coal-black eyes made contact with hers. "Welcome to Mainz. This is my wife, Ruth."

Ruth elbowed her husband. "Stop flirting, you old fool. Do not mind him," she said to Anna. "He is an old man, wishing he was young again."

Otto blurted out a loud laugh. "That is rich coming from you after what you did to your hair yesterday. Was that not a desperate cry for youth?"

She lifted her silver brows. "Of course it was. That is the point I wanted to make. Society does not even notice an old woman like me. I changed my hair to make a statement."

"It's a gorgeous color." Anna envied the woman's gusto and wished she'd had the guts to speak as directly to Patrick from the start of their marriage.

"*Danke*, dear." Ruth's dark eyes sparkled like a mischievous teenager's, her attitude defying the gentle crepe of her skin. "There is a saying…

better to be absolutely ridiculous than be absolutely boring. At my age, I will go for ridiculous."

"But, darling…" Otto put one of his long arms around her and kissed the top of her head. "You did not need to change your hair. You are never boring and always beautiful to me."

Ruth lifted a hand to the gray bristles of his cheek. "And you, *liebe,* are a charmer. No wonder I fell for you even after I'd sworn off all men."

The love between them was evident in the way they looked at each other. If only the disagreements between her and Patrick ended so amicably, Anna might still be home.

Otto stepped forward. "Come and meet the others." The couple linked arms and headed to a rectangular table with quite a few people already seated.

She was introduced to the long-term houseguests, more names than she could remember. As she got seated, Joachim hurried out from behind a swinging door, carrying a clear coffee carafe. He'd run off when they returned from the airport, mumbling something about how his work at the guesthouse never ended.

His eyes landed on Anna. "I see you met the others," he said while pouring coffee into an empty mug at her place setting. "Good news. My wife just arranged for a guide to meet you this afternoon."

"Oh." So soon? She wasn't quite prepared to talk to someone, but maybe the person could help her figure out how to begin the search for Gunther. "Thank you."

She reached into her back pocket for her phone to check for messages from Patrick. High-pitched barking stopped her, and all conversation at the table. Heads turned to the patio entrance.

"*Nein*!" barked a plump, older man holding two leashed, longhaired dachshunds.

The dogs quieted and the man entered, taking inventory of the table from behind wire-rimmed glasses sitting crooked on his bulbous nose. Two red suspenders pressed to his plaid shirt secured his large gut.

"*Guten Morgen*, Max," said a few of the guests.

He grumbled a reply in German and walked around the table with a frown on his face as he headed to an empty seat near Anna.

Ruth put out a hand to stop him and said something.

He looked at Anna, frown set in stone. "Hallo, Fräulein."

"Hello." The dogs stared up at Anna, their chocolate eyes friendly and eager, like they had something urgent to tell her. She reached down and petted their heads, but it was their owner she wanted to see smile. "Who have we here?"

"Please meet Ricky"—he pointed to the black-haired dog—"and Lucy."

Lucy's reddish-brown fur and Ricky's black mimicked their namesakes. Anna greeted the dogs by name, making their long, thin tails wag. Patrick had never wanted pets, though she'd once dared to ask for a puppy or kitten to keep her company while working at home. A stern shake of his head had answered the request, and she hadn't dared to persist.

"Hmph." Their owner's gaze swept over the scene with an assessing eye. "Seems they are glad to meet you." He took a seat nearby, stared at Anna for a moment, then smiled. "Can you pass me the sausage? Lucy and Ricky are starving."

She handed off a large platter and gave him a smile back, satisfied to see him less grumpy. He took a hefty serving for himself then broke one into pieces and gave it to the dogs then turned away from them and considered Anna for a beat. "My name is Max."

"Nice to meet you, Max. I'm Anna."

Plates were passed, food shared. Anna relaxed, despite the hectic pace. Guests conversed using both German and English, the small group acting as comfortable as family. She listened politely to the conversations she didn't understand, thankful for dispersed bits of translation from Ruth.

By the end of the meal, she'd learned Ruth and Otto were also writers and taught classes on the subject at the nearby university. Max tended to speak to others in conversations that included his dogs, and everybody whispered with curiosity about Florian's latest romantic interest, Karen, who attended the university and worked in a local dress shop. And much to Anna's surprise, they all knew she'd come to find a man who'd saved her friend from the Nazis. No doubt because Joachim told them.

They operated like a family, and families didn't have secrets. This group of kindhearted and curious strangers was no exception.

* * * *

Anna sat on the side of her bed, still groggy from her short nap. Enough sleep to keep her awake for the day and get her body in sync with German time after the overnight flight. She reached to the pretty white nightstand next to her bed, took her phone, and turned it on. Her first day in Germany and Patrick's final day in Florida. Tomorrow morning kicked off the workweek, and he'd return to New York. She'd be holding her breath all day, anticipating the delivery of those papers.

She stared at the phone, waiting, her nerves raw as she wondered if he'd tried to reach her. He liked to keep her guessing about when—even if—he'd call. Sometimes when traveling, he'd be gone for days without a word. Other times he'd call multiple times a day.

All that popped up was a text from her sister asking if she'd landed. She replied, *I did. Will catch up soon.*

The conversation she'd had with Jenna while at the airport left her uneasy. With Anna's marital problems out in the open, Jenna confessed she'd thought Patrick often acted "too nice" with Anna, to the point it didn't seem genuine. She wasn't wrong. Abusers behaved that way, to throw their victims off-balance.

But one other thing Jenna had said left Anna shocked.

"You were smart to disappear before he got served," Jenna had said. "Men like him have been known to kill their wives, if angry enough."

Several times in the past six months, Anna had threatened to file for divorce. Each time, Patrick begged her not to leave. Pitiful displays of crying and promises, at first. A few months ago, though, when he'd woken in a horrible mood and she'd turned into his punching bag, she'd threatened again. That time, he'd turned ugly, angrier than she'd ever seen him. She'd worn turtlenecks for two weeks to hide the bruises on her throat. From that day forward, bringing up divorce carried a new risk.

What if Patrick's rage had room to grow?

For too long she'd taken a chance that the once sweet, reasonable guy who'd worshipped the ground she walked on remained inside his soul. But maybe he never really existed.

Shame crashed against her chest over all the times she'd softened from his apologies instead of walking out the door. Where was the spirited woman who'd spent her first thirty-three years embracing what life had to offer? How had the adoration of one man stolen every part of her self-worth? Or was she broken before Patrick, and he'd detected her weakness and taken advantage?

Damned if she knew the answers, but she was determined to restore her damaged pieces. The pieces of her Patrick had crushed, choked, and beaten into submission.

Chapter 4

Josef swiped his car keys off the coffee table and opened the front door to leave the apartment. Two steps out, his throbbing leg sent him back inside. He grabbed the cane off his bed and left again.

The car accident had left aches in places he'd never once thought about before. Most of them had disappeared, but not the pain in his leg, the worst of his injuries. The surgeon had made a big fuss about him using the cane to ease his discomfort and aid in healing.

He often wondered if he subconsciously forgot it on purpose. The object reminded him he was no longer the spry guy who'd lived for the thrill of physical challenges. Each time he used it, he morphed into an eighty-one-year-old with a bad attitude.

On his way across the apartment complex's grass courtyard, he chanted in his head, *What does not kill me makes me stronger.* He said the phrase over and over until some of the anguish simmering since Claudia had offered him this assignment lifted.

Six months ago, when he'd left the hospital, he'd said the mantra at least ten times a day. Improvement with his injuries was slow, though, and he'd given up on the internal pep talks until now. He needed to shake off the dust, show both Claudia and that nitpicky doctor he deserved to be out touring again.

"Sinbad. *Komm her Miezekatze*. Meow. Meow."

Mrs. Freudenberger shuffled down a sidewalk in front of the apartments, still dressed in her bathrobe and slippers, though it was mid-afternoon. She leaned over to look beneath a bush and her white curls bounced upside down.

Not again. Josef glanced at his watch. He'd given himself plenty of time to test his driving abilities on the way over to the Villa Von Essen, hoping the lighter Sunday traffic would ease his transition behind the wheel.

He walked toward his neighbor. "Can't find Sinbad again, Mrs. Freudenberger?"

She stood upright, and her anxious face brightened. "Oh, Josef. My cat is gone. Do you see him anywhere? He's always off on an adventure." She smiled and patted his arm affectionately. "Like you."

He laughed. "Lucky cat. My adventure days are on hold." She tilted her head and her eyebrows furrowed, even though he'd explained to her about his accident the last few times he'd helped her find her pet. "Did you look carefully in your apartment?" He offered an elbow to help her get back home, where he'd found the cat last time. "He seems to like hiding under your living room chair."

"Oh, I'm not sure if I checked there." She put her hand on his arm, and he tucked it close as they slowly walked toward her open apartment door.

Josef felt certain he'd find Sinbad inside. The cat was no more of a wanderer than he was these days.

Once inside, he kneeled next to the chair, lifted the gold fabric skirt, and found two glowing eyes staring back at him.

"Hello there, Sinbad." Josef stuck his arm underneath, guided the large tabby to the edge, and lifted him out. As he handed the feline over to Mrs. Freudenberger, he glanced around. Dirty dishes on the kitchen table. Milk left out. Unwashed pots on the stovetop.

"Where's the woman who comes each morning?"

For a minute she looked confused. "Oh, I guess she's late."

He got out his phone and called Johann to let him know his mother had a problem. Luckily, her son worked five minutes away and said he'd be right over.

Josef turned to find Mrs. Freudenberger sitting on the sofa and watching the television, Sinbad curled on her lap like a multicolored ball of yarn.

"Johann is on his way over. He'll find out why your helper did not show." The clock ticked, escalating his anxiety over his drive to Villa Von Essen. "Will you be okay if I leave?"

She glanced at him for a split second before returning to her program. "Oh yes. My show is on."

But he couldn't move. He slipped his hand in his pocket and wrapped the metal key in his fingers. An involuntary shiver coursed through him, the object invoking as much fear as a drop of plutonium.

There was still time to take the tram to the Von Essens' to meet his new client. The idea withered almost immediately. Soon enough he'd be in the car and driving this person places. Claudia had said the client might need to travel distances. On the highways. A tremor rumbled through him.

No tram. He needed to practice in the car. Alone.

He stepped to the door. "Enjoy your show, then. Bye, Sinbad." The cat ignored him, but his neighbor tossed him a wave.

Josef walked out of the complex, gripping his cane, feeling as vulnerable as he imagined his aging neighbor did with her fading memory. Getting old wasn't easy, but better than the alternative of not being alive.

Like Lily.

Guilt flowed through his veins, cold as an icy stream in winter, leaving him numb, drowning in sadness over her death once again. Though he'd known her less than a day, she'd spent the last moments of her life with him.

If only he could somehow have a do-over, change the domino of events that put them in that car. Maybe he would've come home during his week off instead of staying in Avignon, France, where his last tour had ended. Or when he and Lily started kissing while they'd danced at the club, he might have changed his mind about asking the pretty stranger back to his hotel. The next morning, what if he'd said no when she suggested they drive to Nice to hang out with her friends, instead of happily joining her?

A simple change of plans, and Lily would be alive.

He stabbed the ground with the cane. Angry stabs. Harder and harder the closer he got to the car. What was he so angry about? The doctors' prognosis about his injury? Or at himself, for not knowing what he'd done to cause that accident?

He reached his car and got inside. Holding his breath, he turned the key in the ignition. The engine purred, and he thought of Lily's Fiat. Closing his eyes, he tried to awaken those last moments before impact, when his world went blank…

Nothing. Again.

The wheels of his mind were stuck in the mud. He sighed.

Time to go to the Von Essens' guesthouse where he'd be greeted by the usual suspects, always happy to see him—and he them. They'd corner him, beg to hear a story of Josef's travels. So he'd slip on the mask of confidence they all loved to see. The one that got him through the day when he ran into old friends. Where he'd act a part and re-live his prior adventures while clinging to the hope he'd soon return to his old life.

But first, he had to drive there. An adventure of a different kind.

He drew in a deep breath and exhaled slowly while placing his hands on the wheel. *Thump. Thump. Thump.* His pulse, pounding in his ears. A foreboding sound. Like he should escape from the car and run while he could.

He concentrated on breathing and shifted his focus. A few years ago, he'd taken a leap with a bungee cord. The same pounding had gone on inside him. An excited pulse. Not terror, but exhilaration. Drawing from that feeling, he gripped the gearshift with determination, kicking his resolve into high gear. He could do this. It was merely a car drive!

He gently placed his foot on the gas pedal and slowly backed up. After taking a deep breath, he shifted into drive. His arms tensed, and he clung tight to the wheel, blood racing as if the car were about to plunge into the Grand Canyon. He lifted his foot off the brake and pushed the gas pedal, easing out onto the street with more trepidation than he'd ever had in his life.

* * * *

The neighborhood streets around the guesthouse were lined with trees, apartment buildings, single-family homes, and plenty of shops. Homier than the busy part of the city Joachim had driven them through on the way from the airport. Anna stopped at a bakery, purchased a delicious sandwich filled with meat, cheese, and veggies for a late lunch, and enjoyed eating while walking alongside the sparkling river toward the guesthouse.

When she arrived, she searched the main floor for Joachim or his wife, Regina, to ask if her guide had arrived. Anna walked toward the sound of laughter in the dining room. Several of the hotel's guests sat at one of the round tables, listening to a man she didn't know. A sideboard near the table held a cake, coffee carafe, and china cups. The afternoon *Kaffee und Kuchen* Joachim had mentioned during breakfast.

The stranger wrangled the attention of all the men she'd met a breakfast, who seemed spellbound by his words. Even Lucy and Ricky sat quietly next to Max, their eyes focused on the speaker.

Anna stopped at the entryway to listen, drawn to the passion in the stranger's voice. He orchestrated like a conductor, his large hands with long fingers moving with exaggerated actions, and subtle lifts and drops of his light brown brows animated his face. At times his square jaw jutted out to emphasize words she couldn't understand. His short brown hair carried a hint of red, also visible in his mustache and close-trimmed beard. She stared longer than polite at his eyes, the blue-green hue enhanced when they sparkled as he laughed at something Max said.

The relaxed posture of his long, slender body spoke to his confidence. A man who, no doubt, adored this audience. Any audience. That same kind of self-assurance had drawn her to Patrick the night she'd seen him performing karaoke at a bar in Seattle.

As he continued talking, the man glanced to the doorway and their eyes met. He went silent as his gaze flicked over her face for a beat then traveled her body.

He smiled. "*Hallo, willst du hereinkommen*?"

She straightened. "I'm sorry. I didn't mean to interrupt."

"You are not." His brows furrowed, a split second where he seemed confused, then he said, "I asked if you would like to come in."

"Anna, please join us." Joachim waved her over and pulled out an empty chair at his side. "Josef, this is the young lady who needs your assistance while in the country." He glanced at Anna. "I get you some cake." He stood and hurried over to the sideboard.

She smiled at her guide while he stared at her, his eyes lingering with a look she could only describe as uncertainty.

He finally pushed out a stiff smile. "Hello, Anna."

She nodded. "Josef."

Joachim placed a slice of cake and fork in front of her and returned to his seat. "Finish the story, Josef."

"Yes. In English, for Anna, *bitte*." Max leaned forward and ran a hand along his dogs' heads. "Lucy is waiting to hear what Borneo is like."

Lucy *did* seem interested in Josef. The piece of cake on a plate in front of him probably explained why.

He smiled at the dog and leaned over to give her a good scratch behind the ear. "Borneo was beautiful. A lush island, with some of the richest equatorial rainforest in the world." He sat back but kept an eye on Lucy. "Did you know it is the third largest non-continental island in the world?"

Anna was a little relieved the dog didn't answer, but Max said, "*Nein*, I did not."

Josef took a bite of his cake as he looked at Max. "What about Ricky? Does he have questions?"

Max glanced at the other dog. "Just more details, because at his age, he will never see Borneo."

"Then the details you will get." Josef smiled, kindly, as if he enjoyed playing along with Max. "My trip to Borneo was a special assignment, given to me in my third year of working at Wanderlust Excursions. This trip was for a group of German politicians who wanted a different kind of vacation. The excursion owner is a childhood friend and she knows I love anything new and different, so she gave me first shot at running the tour. A different path for our company, but one that opened the door to the adventure tour division I expanded…"

So this was her guide. A man who'd been to Borneo, who was the go-to guy at Wanderlust for action-oriented tours? Why would he want to haul her around? Spend days in the car driving to locations for research, or to meet possible men who matched Gunther's description?

As he finished his story, the coffee carafe was passed around. She listened to the conversation at the table, more questions about the trip, spoken in a mix of German and English. Every so often she'd glance Josef's way to find him watching her, his perusal filled with curiosity. Or was it suspicion? Was she just paranoid because she'd spent the past two years of her life guessing what her husband might be thinking? Fearful he might strike her over the slightest misstep, innocent as it might be?

Florian complained about having to get back to work and left for the kitchen. Joachim collected cake plates. Otto and Max lingered a little longer, but when Josef finally stood and walked his plate toward a bin near the kitchen door, the other two men got up but didn't leave.

Josef moved slowly, his frame tall and lean, his jeans a little loose and his long-sleeved pullover fit snug to his broad chest. To her surprise, he limped.

Before returning to the table, Josef lifted a wooden cane leaning against the wall and returned without using it. He rested it on the tabletop, then slowly squatted down to pet Max's dogs.

Before coming here, Anna had considered German a harsh language, certainly not a romance language like Italian. But there was nothing severe about the exchange as Josef talked to the dogs. Each strong consonant—for the language definitely emphasized those—was cushioned by his gentle tone, and the dogs wagged their tails in response.

Max joined the canine conversation, and they went on like that for a minute before Josef took a seat and continued conversing.

She felt awkward, even a little ignored, so she stared out the patio windows. Would he be this indifferent to her during their drives? Did it matter? Or maybe they were chatting in their native tongue because it was easier, what they did more naturally. It didn't mean they were intentionally ignoring her. Two years with Patrick had groomed her to hone in on subtle nuances of interactions that she often internalized. Even her sister once said Anna had become overly sensitive.

The men went silent, then Josef glanced Anna's way. "I was just telling Max my sister was thinking of getting a dachshund."

"Oh." The uncomfortable feeling lifted. "They are nice dogs."

Max finally grunted as he rose from his chair and turned to her. "Maybe you would help me walk the dogs later, Anna? My knee is under doctor's care right now."

"I'd be happy to. I need to stay awake."

He nodded and walked off, Otto saying goodbye and leaving right behind him.

She turned to Josef. He watched her, a flash of discomfort zipping across his eyes.

"So where do we begin?" She took the seat Max had just left. She smiled brightly, enough to soften even the hardest soul.

He ran his hand along his chin and his lips wavered with a slight smile. "Some specifics on exactly why you need my services would be a good start."

"Well, I'm searching for a man. All I know is his name and where he lived back in 1938, but he's no longer there."

"I see. Have you done any additional research?"

"I'm afraid not." She debated telling him that her hosts had reached out to him too early, but she didn't want to sound as though she hadn't appreciated the effort.

"Then you may need me to drive you in a search of public records?" He raised a brow, but with far less enthusiasm than he'd shown during his talk about Borneo.

"I guess. To be honest, I'm not certain how to go about finding someone in Germany with only dated information. I tried a little after breakfast today but didn't get very far. I think I'm just tired."

"I see." Tension tugged at his jaw, making the lines of his handsome face harden.

"Oh, wait. I have an envelope upstairs with a photograph of the man. Should I get it?"

"Sure." He stood and grabbed his cane. "I'm going outside for a smoke while you do."

He slipped on his jacket and walked carefully on the tile floor toward the patio doors.

He didn't seem thrilled to be working with her. Heck, she wasn't sure if she'd want to work with him. He was like two sides of a coin, one friendly that loved playing to an audience, the other tense and a bit direct. Even somewhat moody. Same as Patrick. But why? She hadn't done anything to him.

A knot formed in her belly as she hurried up the staircase. She'd never done anything to provoke Patrick, either. Yet she'd felt his fury more times than she could count. She wanted to crawl inside herself, never get into a car with this man. What if he hurt her, too? Even crossing the Atlantic couldn't get her away from horrible men.

Panic enveloped her as she neared her door. She stopped, took a deep breath, stopped her ridiculous thinking. Assuming that because a man was lukewarm toward her he might hurt her only proved she was overly sensitive. Obstacles like this could haunt her for the rest of her life. It gave Patrick control, even when he wasn't around.

But only if she let it.

She'd get in Josef's car and try not to take everything so darn personally. Patrick's treatment was personal. But she should give others a fair shake. Like Josef. If he became intolerable, then she'd find another way to search for Gunther. A new guide.

No, that would be all wrong. The act of a scared woman.

Instead, she'd become the woman she wanted to be. One who asserted herself and asked people if something was wrong. Didn't retreat into her shell in the presence of a moody man. And above all else, demanded to be treated with respect. The way she should've in her marriage, after the first time Patrick's rage appeared.

Chapter 5

A ghost. He'd seen a bloody ghost. Or so he'd thought. For a few minuscule seconds.

Josef leaned his cane against the wall of the guesthouse, reached into his jacket pocket, and removed a cigarette.

After lighting it, he took a drag and vowed to quit again. Soon. The nicotine flooded his blood stream but didn't calm his nerves.

He'd looked up to the doorway, and there she'd stood. Lily. His body had gone cold, but the second she spoke, he'd been jolted back to reality. Lily was French and spoke English with a very strong accent. This woman appeared to be one hundred percent American. Of course, upon closer look, she'd borne only a slight resemblance to Lily. Hell, he'd known the French woman less than twenty-four hours and images of her in his mind blurred more with each passing day.

The American stared at him as he'd tried to gather his better senses and continue talking like nothing had been wrong. Only the worst was yet to come. Joachim had introduced her as the traveler he'd been hired to drive around. He'd sat there, stunned. Plunked right into a nightmare come to life. He could barely get behind the car's steering wheel alone, but put a woman in the passenger's seat who happened to resemble Lily….

Verdammt!

He took a long drag from the cigarette and blew out a slow stream of smoke. Both women had the same heart-shaped face surrounded by dark, loose, wavy hair. They had pretty eyes, black as opals and mysterious as the unknown. But Anna had a pert nose, turned up ever so slightly. Lily's was straight and Grecian. And she'd been taller, her hair a bit longer. Hadn't she?

He laughed at his foolishness. A ghost. What next? Zombies and werewolves?

He wouldn't have accepted this job if he'd known they looked similar, though. Or maybe he would have. The boredom found in office work had left him restless. Mornings lately he had to force himself to rise from bed. So what if he had to chauffeur a ghost around town?

But the idea sent a little chill up his spine as he considered the awful drive over here.

He inhaled another drag, slowly letting the smoke swirl in ringlets that eventually broke apart and drifted away, much like his memories of what had occurred in that damn crash.

Uncertainty pummeled him as he paced the patio. How could he get into a car with her—Anna? If anything happened, he'd end up living his nightmare all over again.

Maybe he should call it quits, end this charade before it started. He searched for ways to back out. Before he could get too far, though, he realized this opportunity could be a gift in disguise.

Driving a woman who looked similar to Lily might stir the details about the accident his mind had blocked. Those irretrievable moments right before impact that held all the answers to one big question: Why had he swerved? And if driving Anna kicked off any memory, this nightmare of blaming himself for Lily's death might end. He could move on, not wake each day asking himself the same answerless questions. Of course, the return of his memory might show his culpability in her death, but he couldn't feel any worse than he did now.

He stamped out the cigarette in an ashtray on a table. The near-constant ache in his leg flared on his way inside. He patted his pockets only to realize he'd left his pain medication at home. New over-the-counter meds, less potent than his prescription, but the doctor insisted he wean himself off the harder stuff during the day.

Anna had already returned to the table where they'd been sitting. He approached, dismissing the ache with each step and vowing to sound optimistic about this assignment.

"Have you visited Germany before?" He sat at the table, across from her.

She looked up, hesitation in her eyes. "No. First time. The Rhine is pretty."

"You should take a boat ride upriver to see the castles."

"Joachim mentioned them." She smiled, loosening the tension of her expression. "He said there are quite a few to see."

"He is correct." As he rested his cane on the chair next to him, she glanced at it. The heat of embarrassment ripped through him. The damn cane always made him feel "less than," worse when he was in the presence of a pretty woman.

He folded his hands, trying to get some control over the discomfort shooting to his knee. Once it started hurting, the pain spread fast and furious until he took his meds. "I am told you need a driver and translator. May I ask where you think we will be going?"

"Like I said before, the man I need to find lived in Frankfurt in the late 1930s but has since moved. Maybe Frankfurt has some resources that track where people move. I guess I can try to find out."

"Did you know the city was bombarded very badly during the war? The home he was in was most likely bombed."

"I didn't know. I guess that could complicate things." She ran a bright red fingernail along the edge of the envelope lying in front of her. "Your Borneo trip sounded very interesting. It must be a change doing more local work."

He shrugged. "I am only helping in the home office for a while." His neck warmed. The latest saga of his life was far too humiliating to discuss with a stranger.

"You speak very good English."

"My mother is German, but my father's from England. We learned both languages growing up." He motioned to the envelope, eager to get home, take his pain pill, and put a cold pack on the increasing burn in his thigh. "What did you bring to show me?"

She pulled out a photograph, and he noticed a silver wedding band on her left hand. In Germany, married couples wore them on their right, but someone on a tour once told him it was different in America. So she traveled without her husband?

"His name is Gunther Hinzmann. Finding him is a favor for a friend. If I learn Gunther has passed away, I hope to find any of his living family." She placed the picture in front of him and pointed to a man in the black-and-white photograph. "This is him. I noticed he's wearing a uniform. Do you think he was a Nazi soldier?"

The heat of his injury escalated, as if someone stuck a hot metal rod in his thigh. He bit back the urge to complain as he studied the picture. "Even if he were a soldier, the German armed services were known as *Wehrmacht*. The Nazis were a political party, though the SS and Gestapo were policing forces of Hitler's. In America you wouldn't call soldiers by their political affiliation, right?"

"No, we wouldn't." Her cheeks flushed. "I didn't know."

"Yes. Of course you would not know."

She blinked at him, turned back to the photo. Had he said something wrong? A sharp zip ran along his thigh, leaving dull pain in its wake.

"I would not expect you to understand this country's politics. Many outside of our country do not realize this, but not all Germans became Nazi party members."

"So they didn't make people join?"

"They tried. One day, my *Onkel* Fritz got a visit from a party leader asking him to join. The story goes, my *onkel* yelled at the representative, said he would never join them, and proceeded to boot the man in the ass as he tossed him out the door." Josef chuckled at thoughts of his strong-headed uncle, but his laughter faded as he remembered the outcome. "Later that night, he got a call from the town magistrate saying he had been ordered to issue arrest warrants for Fritz. The magistrate suggested if he had a passport, he should get out of the country. Sadly, he spent the next three years living in exile in Austria, with some family there."

"For not becoming a member of a political party?"

"Yes, partially. I suppose booting the guy in the ass while he said no had more to do with it."

Her brows furrowed and she frowned, her expression filled with anguish. "What an awful time."

"*Ja.* A complicated time." Her empathy reminded him she wasn't the enemy. He was his own enemy. "Anyway, the man here is not in a soldier's uniform, though I am surprised. Most men his age would have been serving." He studied the photo carefully for a moment. Both the man and the teenage boy at his side had the same expressions on many photographs of the time. No smiles. Dark, dull eyes. As if the pain of what had been going on in their country had stolen their spirits.

With a more detailed look, he understood why the young man remained free of service in the German army. "Ah, I see why he did not serve. Look."

Anna leaned over the table. Josef pointed to the narrow space between the two people, who stood close. "This man, Gunther. His shirt arm is folded up to his elbow but partially hidden from view. He appears to be missing an arm. That may have prevented him from entering military service. This uniform could mean he was drafted into State Labor Service, or another state-run agency. Who is the teenage boy with him?"

"My neighbor, the one who asked me to find Gunther."

"I see." He considered asking more, but did he really want to know? He had enough of his own issues to deal with. Like this ache, pulsing like hot lava down his leg. Worsening with each tick of the clock.

He peeked at his watch. An hour past the time he needed his pain pills. No wonder he hurt. "And where was this picture taken?"

"In Frankfurt."

He glanced at her, finding her staring at him with discomfort in those innocent eyes. The ache in his leg swelled further, raging like an angry lion and fully waking his near-constant irritability. What he needed was to get out of here. Go home and ice the injury.

"Isaak is trying to find him now because—"

"And you said you have searched the internet?"

Her lips clamped shut at his interruption, and she paused a moment before continuing. "Yes. I don't know much about the German records, though, and had sort of hoped—"

"Well, I will drive you wherever you want to go and translate, as my firm promised." The throbbing invaded his knee, spread to his lower leg. Time to leave. He pulled out a business card and slapped it on the table. Next stop, home. "Call me here when you have a plan."

She dropped her gaze to his card. Steadily, she raised her chin until meeting him square in the eye. "Did I do something to offend you? You cut me off rather suddenly. If you're not interested in this job, please say so now and I'll find someone else."

He swore her hands trembled and her breath sounded clipped. She crossed her arms over her chest and stared back with a blank expression, but her frozen-as-ice posture screamed of her displeasure. Yet she showed determination. The kind of determination Josef respected, and it made him rethink their conversation, including his possible terseness that occasionally slipped out because of his pain. His sister had pointed it out just the other day.

He'd offended a client. But mostly, he'd offended this woman, who shook as she confronted him. "Anna," he said, nicely as he could. "Please accept my apology."

He searched her eyes, looking for signs of forgiveness, but she said nothing. Only watched him with the gaze of a high-stakes poker player, hiding her hand, and leaving him uneasy enough to consider the way he behaved around her more seriously. "What had you wanted to tell me before I so rudely interrupted?"

She pursed her lips and stared at him for several long seconds. "My friend who sent me here passed away recently. Isaak had been searching for Gunther to say thank you himself, but ran out of time before he could find him. As a last request left with his lawyer, he asked me to bring Gunther or his family the message."

"I see." Contempt over his miserable behavior grew. He owed her more than an apology. In spite of the shooting sting from his hip to his toes, he struggled to soften his voice. "My leg hurts and makes me not act like myself at times."

"Oh. I see. Well, thank you for telling me." The muscles of her face relaxed as she started to thaw. "We could try again tomorrow, when I'm not so jet-lagged from traveling and, hopefully, your leg won't hurt. With any luck, I'll have a plan in place by then. Or at least a first step."

He nodded, strangely relieved. As he took his cane from the chair and stood, he said, "How about we meet at 9:30?"

"Perfect." She gave a pencil-thin smile that quickly vanished.

He walked away, trying his hardest not to limp, but knowing he did.

Just as he reached the door, she said, "Josef?"

He turned, raised a brow.

"I'm here for a month. If any day we plan isn't good for you to work with me, don't hesitate to say. We have plenty of time to find this man."

A beam of sunlight from the window made her dark hair shimmer, making the resemblance to Lily even more pronounced. Quick flashes bombarded his brain. Lily's smile. Her laughter. Her tender kisses as they drove on that fateful last ride. All making every nerve ending in his body hurt even more.

"Josef?"

He blinked, and Lily's image vanished, but Anna watched him, her brows furrowed.

"I will. Thank you." He pivoted and headed for the exit as fast as his leg would allow.

* * * *

"May I join you?"

Anna looked up from her menu, happy to find Ruth standing by her table. The guesthouse restaurant was open to the public for dinner and strangers sat at the small tables. Though alone at home much of the time, being in a foreign country by herself made her long for the comfort of the familiar. Ruth's smiling face set her at ease. "Please do. Where's Otto?"

"His book group meets the second Sunday of the month." Ruth sat across from Anna at the table for two near the patio window. "I have papers to grade tonight, but everyone needs a dinner break." She motioned to the menu in Anna's hands. "All Florian's dishes are good, but I recommend the Rouladen."

Anna had been eyeing the dish, consisting of bacon, onions, mustard, and pickles wrapped in thinly sliced beef. "I'll give it a try."

Ruth studied her menu. "Otto said Josef met with you this afternoon?"

"Yes. I guess we needed to meet, but it may have been premature." A little charge ran through her limbs. She'd stood up to him and received an apology. He'd seemed surprised and shown genuine remorse. But her actions proved to her that she had to assert herself when necessary. "I haven't done much research so didn't have a place for us to start. Honestly, I'm not sure how to go about locating this man."

Ruth closed the menu. "After we eat, show me what you have. Maybe I can help."

"I would really appreciate that. Are you and Otto from this area?"

"We lived across the river in Wiesbaden until ten years ago, when we retired. Once we sold our house, we purchased a small house in Munich, close to our daughter." She laughed. "That got boring real fast, even with our writing and two grandchildren. An opportunity to teach part-time at the university came up for Otto, only for the fall semester. We found the Von Essens', tried it out. It is much better than a hotel, *ja*?"

"Oh yes. It's very homey."

"Soon the university asked me to do two classes, on the same schedule as Otto. Every year, right before Christmas, we return to Munich. The change of routine is good for us."

A cute blond waitress, with straight bangs and a petite frame, came to the table, took their orders, and left.

"Lovely girl. Florian used to date her." Ruth shook her head. "He is like no other German man I have ever met when it comes to the opposite sex."

"How so?"

"Well." She frowned, accentuating the age lines around her mouth. "German men do not flirt like an Italian, or romance like a Frenchman. Their romance is subtle. For us women, getting to know them is a gradual process. They are a bit like peeling an onion, exposing themselves one layer at a time." She crinkled her nose and laughed. "Maybe that is a bad simile. Onions can make you cry. Then again, so can men. But our Florian, he is a romantic soul who shares his adoration for the women he dates with the joy of a puppy."

Patrick certainly had layers. Complicated ones. And once stripped away, they led to his damaged, rotting core. Anna gave Ruth a perfunctory smile. "I think your onion simile is perfect."

"Are American men easy to get to know?" Ruth asked.

On Anna's second date with Patrick, he'd pried open the book of his life, talking about his abusive childhood. Her heart had gone out to him. Now she could see it had been manipulation.

"It depends. I've dated both kinds of men, but in general American men take a little time to get to know, too."

The waitress dropped off a breadbasket and Ruth reached for a piece. "Sensible, I think. Some say love conquers all." She arranged her napkin on her lap. "I can tell you it does not always."

"Otto seems to be a romantic."

Ruth snorted. "In his old age he has become very gallant. At least when he is not arguing with me." A soft smile crossed her lips. "Though he did make me fall for him against all odds." Her eyes drifted to Anna's hand. "What about your husband? Is he a romantic?"

Anna's tongue tied into a knot, and her cheeks burned as she glanced down at the ring. She'd meant to remove it. While here, she wanted just to be Anna Abrams. Not a woman who'd left her abusive spouse. Not a woman handcuffed by the shame of staying with her abuser. "Uh, sometimes."

Ruth nodded. Anna hoped her discomfort wasn't as obvious as it felt. "And he could not join you on this trip?"

"No." She shrugged while fumbling for words. "Sometimes we all need a break."

Ruth watched her for a second, then focused on her bread, slowly spreading the butter. She lowered her knife and bread onto the small plate to her side. "You know, I was married to another man before I met Otto. A whole three years, four months, and six days. I was too young and foolish to leave the marriage sooner, but I finally did."

"I can't imagine you having trouble leaving. You seem so confident."

She offered a thin-lipped smile, her eyes squinting with bitterness. "I've always had spunk, perhaps too much confidence for my own good." She chuckled. "And Karl knew that when he married me, but for some reason after we married, he wanted to control me."

Anna understood control. Patrick had dominated the mood in their household, leaving her in a constant state of insecurity. Was Ruth's experience the same? "What do you mean? That is, if you don't mind talking about it?"

"My dear, it was so long ago, I am happy to discuss. Our problems were small things at first. They barely seemed consequential, but in hindsight were meant to show he had power over me. How I dressed or decorated the house. Maybe the place was not cleaned to his high standards." She snorted a sarcastic laugh. "God, he could be so arrogant. At first, it seemed picky. Yet it did something to me. I started feeling guilty if he wasn't happy. I'll never forget the day he called me stupid because I made a mistake on a bank deposit. I said nothing about the way he spoke to me in order to keep the peace. But it was shortly after that he raised a hand. I don't even remember why, but I told him I'd leave him if he dared to follow through." Ruth's mouth bowed and anger burned in her eyes. "About six months later, I found out he was cheating on me." She shook her head and her jaw tightened. "That is when I left the bastard."

Anna's cheeks blasted hot. She dropped her gaze to the white linen, lifted her glass of water with a shaky hand, and took a sip.

As Anna lowered the glass, Ruth's hand slipped over hers. The light wrinkle of her pale skin and age spots seemed frail on the surface, but her confidence and courage transcended the decades. "Marriage can be very difficult."

"Yes." Anna's story played on her lips. The details that sent her running to a lawyer, fleeing New York. Embarrassment kept her from sharing with those close to her. Their opinions mattered. But maybe talking to a stranger would be easier. A stranger who'd shared her own story and understood how it felt to have a man mistreat you.

"You do not have to talk about the details," Ruth said quietly. "Are you thinking of leaving him?"

"The divorce papers will be served to him tomorrow." Unexpected relief flooded her tense muscles and loosened her lips. "My lawyer suggested I avoid being around when he receives them…considering some of the things he did to me in the past." Her cheeks stung with humiliation thinking about her next words, but if she made this confession, maybe she'd begin to feel strong like Ruth. "He mistreated me. Then my neighbor died, and I got his request to come here to help him. So the time seemed right for me to leave. But I wish I'd done so sooner. To have been brave like you."

"My dear, it took me time. Besides, you did leave him, Anna. You *are* brave."

"I worry it was a little cowardly to run, not face him."

"Nonsense. In Germany we say *Aller Anfang ist schwer.* It means every beginning is hard. Besides, some women don't go as far as you did." She motioned to Anna's hand. "And the ring, you still wear it because…?"

"Only because I forgot to leave it behind with my note. Then, I'd planned to take it off when I got here, but got busy."

Anna stared at the ring. A symbol of love she no longer felt and a bond that no longer existed. Talking to Ruth opened a door and skimmed off a layer of the humiliation she carried for staying with Patrick for so long.

She lifted her gaze to Ruth. "Since we are talking about it, now might be a good time to put this where it belongs." She worked the ring until it came off her finger. "There." Anna reached for her purse beneath the table and plunked the ring inside the wallet pocket. While only symbolic, removing the band put her back in control of her life. "It's off."

"Another big step." Ruth patted her hand and gave her a huge smile. "You have the power, Anna."

Anna's chest swelled with pride. A new sense of freedom. Another move in the right direction.

Ruth leaned forward. "This conversation is between us. The others here do not need to know."

Anna squeezed her new friend's hand and embraced the feeling of liberation.

Chapter 6

The breakfast crowd had disbursed but Anna stayed behind. Alone in the dining room, she studied a map of Frankfurt on her laptop. Ruth's suggestions had at least given her a place to start.

But she was distracted.

Monday morning had arrived, at least in Germany. Patrick would return from his golf weekend to head straight into his downtown office to start his workday. With the six-hour time difference, the papers would be served around 6 p.m. in Germany. It would be a long day of worrying.

Her belly trembled as she pictured him opening the documents, the swift anger swelling on his handsome face, turning him from nice to nasty in seconds. A small breeze had been known to fan his flames. This would start a forest fire.

She forced herself to concentrate on the map and push the images of him from her head.

During dinner the night before, Ruth had suggested Anna visit the neighborhood in Frankfurt where Gunther had lived and ask around to see if anybody remembered the Hinzmann family. The city had been destroyed during the war, but Ruth had said people rebuilt and it was worth a shot. She also pointed out Gunther's birthdate would help with online searches, so Anna should check churches near the home for baptismal records. Last night, she'd gone online and found several places of worship near where Isaak and Gunther once lived.

She scanned the Frankfurt map, verified church information, and tossed the list into her purse. After closing her laptop, she gathered her things and headed to her room. Josef seemed punctual, and she didn't want to keep him waiting.

After brushing her teeth, she changed into lightweight white pants and a short-sleeved shirt. She'd been warned it was unseasonably warm today. Her shoulder ached as she pulled off one top and put on the other. She smoothed the front, went to the dresser mirror, and turned to make sure her bruise remained hidden.

She'd become an expert on the life cycle of a bruise. As one healed, the body absorbed the leaked blood and the injury changed color. Early pink or red quickly changed to blue or dark purple—the painful stage. Pale green followed, meaning healing had begun, and a brownish-yellow meant her skin would soon return to normal. All facts she wished she *didn't* know.

She pressed her finger to the purple mass extending down from the top of her shoulder to her upper arm and winced, the impact of hitting the solid bathroom tile still a vivid memory. As she smoothed down the sleeve, the bottom edge covered the bruise. She'd wear this one.

While she packed up her purse, she wondered which manifestation of Josef would arrive today. The showman, who came to life with tales of his adventures, or the pained soul who hid whatever it was that ailed him.

A man with dual personalities, who lashed out and apologized, was what had sent her running here. Was she crazy to get in the car with him, or was this the test she must pass to move forward? Fear had kept her chained to Patrick. If she let it stop her now, then he again won.

Besides, Josef seemed different. He'd reacted with a quick apology when she confronted him. Nothing like Patrick. Life had always taught her how each person's story served as a two-sided coin. There was the side they showed and the side they hid. She did the same.

Keeping that in mind, from now on she'd stand her ground when necessary. The way she had with Josef yesterday. Standing up to one moody German wouldn't cure the damage she'd incurred during her marriage, but everyone had to start somewhere.

The sound of voices outside made her go to the open window. Josef stood next to a sedan parked along the street and talked to Florian and his girlfriend. The lovebirds faced him, their arms intertwined, bodies pressed so close they could wear the same pants. Anna smiled.

She slipped on black canvas flats and hoop earrings, grabbed a light jacket in case the warm day got cool, and hurried down to the lobby.

Regina, Joachim's wife who also ran the guesthouse, arranged delicate yellow flowers in a vase near the entrance. As Anna hit the bottom steps, Regina glanced over and smiled, the corners of her rich blue eyes crinkling as she did. "You are off?"

"Yes, for a while."

"*Tschüss*," Regina said merrily.

"*Tschüss*," Anna replied, having learned yesterday the phrase was a less formal way the Germans said goodbye.

She headed out toward the car. Josef's gaze drifted over Florian's shoulder and their eyes met. He waved and continued his conversation.

As she neared the car, Florian said, "Good morning, Anna. I see Josef is your chauffeur today. I think he should be wearing an official outfit and cap. You have my permission to boss him around if you would like."

Josef's brows arched, then his lips curled with a smirk. "Boss me around? This from a man who watched *Steel Magnolias* last night because his girlfriend made him."

Karen edged herself even closer to Florian. "And he was duly rewarded."

Florian smiled at Josef. "It is what I do for love, my friend." He turned and kissed Karen on the cheek. "Come on, sweetheart. Let us get my errands done for the lunch service."

Josef's smile vanished as they walked away. He removed his keys from his pocket and walked around his car. "Where are we headed today?"

"Frankfurt."

He jingled the keys, glanced at her for fraction of a second, tension visible in his jaw. "The door's unlocked."

She hopped inside and buckled up. He didn't get in right away but stood outside the door, staring straight ahead in deep thought. After a minute, he got in and started the car, staring out the front windshield, his concentration seemingly on nothing.

It was as if a storm cloud had moved in, casting a dark shadow over his face. "You okay?"

"*Ja, ja.*"

He sounded irritated, anything but okay. Her nerves tightened, but she'd give him space. It could be his leg bothering him again. As long as he kept things professional, did it really matter if he treated her like he had his friends?

He grabbed his phone, left sitting on his dashboard, and poked at the screen. "What is the address?"

Anna reached in her purse and pulled out the pad containing her notes. "Staufenstra—Staufenstra…"

He leaned over to see the paper and almost smiled. A sense of relief crossed her stiff shoulders. "The letter where you are stuck is called an *eszett*. It makes a sharp *s* sound." He hissed like a harmless snake and again offered her a quick grin. "That's all. Pretty easy, *ja*?" His gaze skipped to hers. "The address you need is *Staufenstraße*. Staufen Street. What number?"

She told him and waited quietly as he entered the location into his GPS. Now he was nice. Offering a smile that seemed sincere enough, if brief. So maybe he wasn't all bad.

He exhaled a breath and took the steering wheel with both hands, his grip tight. After glancing over his shoulder, he eased from his space. They inched down the street. His body leaned slightly forward, every muscle taut, his attention hyper-focused. The way an old man might drive.

"What is at this address?" His eyes didn't leave the road, as if they were navigating rugged terrain, not a quiet residential block in the small city.

"It's the address where the man I'm trying to find lived as a boy. Ruth suggested I ask a few of the neighbors to see if they remember the family. She thought if we start with the address we have, someone in the area may have lived there back in '38."

He nodded.

"After that, I thought about checking out the local churches for his baptismal papers, get his date of birth."

"I see."

As they neared an intersection, a large mixed-breed dog stepped off the sidewalk, dragging his owner out into the street. Josef slammed on the brakes and muttered something in German. He angrily waved them on, then shoved up the sleeves of a long-sleeved T-shirt, complaining about the heat as he ran a hand through his short hair. He blew out a loud breath, then continued to drive in the same tense manner.

The car merged on the autobahn at a crawling pace, making other drivers honk as they flew past him. Anna remained quiet, thinking about everything that had happened since he'd stopped his relaxed conversation and joined her at the car to leave.

Soon they cruised on the multilane road, not quite going the speed limit, but enough to keep the other drivers satisfied. They sped past clusters of neighborhoods, companies, and wide fields, one with wind turbines lined up like soldiers, the massive wings slowly spinning. At one point, she caught him glancing her way, lingering on her face for a second too long, and they started to drift. A driver in the next lane blared his horn, and Josef's hands twitched on the wheel, correcting the car.

They approached an exit ramp, and he put on his signal. Their turtle-slow departure resulted in more angry toots. He'd get eaten alive in Manhattan traffic. His behavior suddenly became clear. He didn't dislike her. The car—and driving—scared the hell out of Josef. If anybody could spot fear, she could. So why would he have accepted a job driving?

As they waited at a red light, about to enter the more modern city of Frankfurt, he cleared his throat.

She glanced his way, surprised to find him watching her. "Yes?"

"I am sorry again if I was rude yesterday." Josef's Adam's apple slid along his throat. He sounded sincere and even a little sad. "Are we okay?"

His eyes looked tired and sympathy for him tugged at her chest. "Yes." She smiled. "Of course."

The light changed. He gave a nod and accelerated. They drove quietly. Her gaze drifted to the steering wheel, noting the earlier white-knuckled tension had eased from his highway experience. Soon he pulled into an empty space along the street and shut off the car.

"The address you want is up ahead. I will show you."

She got out and stood on the sidewalk, looking around at the relatively quiet city street. Most buildings looked like apartments. Nicely landscaped and well cared for.

Josef opened his door, leaned in, and came out with his cane. As he came around the car, he motioned to her arm. "What happened?"

She glanced down to find that her sleeve had shifted, leaving her bruise exposed. Heat warmed her cheeks, but she quickly gathered her wits and smoothed down the sleeve. "Oh, I fell getting out of the shower a few days ago. Hit the tile. Lucky I didn't get banged up worse. It really hurt."

"I bet it did."

He watched her for few seconds before starting to walk. She followed, wondering if he believed her. She always thought that after lying to people when they saw her marks.

After passing a few houses, he stopped in front of one. "Here is your address."

She stepped past him and stared up at a multilevel stucco home. The upper levels had balconies that were adorned with wrought iron railings. "Must be an apartment building, maybe built after the war." She glanced back at Josef for confirmation, but he was reading his phone.

His eyes shifted up and an annoyed expression crossed his face. "What?"

At first, she stiffened, as she would've if Patrick showed even the teeniest bit of annoyance. Then, a little piece of her snapped. With her back to him, she didn't know he'd been reading a text. Were her wires so crossed on reading men, she could no longer filter right from wrong responses? She forced her chin high and said forcefully, "I'm sorry. I didn't realize you were reading a message."

He frowned. "I, well, yes…"

She smiled so he didn't feel bad. It wasn't him, as much as paranoia ingrained in her mind. Trained every single day for two years to think the worst of any reaction besides a cheerful smile. It might be best to let Josef deal with whatever was bothering him and reach out in this neighborhood on her own. "Why don't you wait in the car while I look around?"

"You do not need me to translate?"

"If I do, I'll come get you."

He shrugged. "Sure." He limped away, scowling at his phone and typing furiously with the cane tucked under his arm.

She almost felt the pain of each step he took. The nervous driving. His mood shifts. They had to come from the same place. And yet, for the first time in her life, she wondered: Did having problems justify treating others poorly? Patrick took the concept to an extreme, and she'd let him.

When he reached his car, he leaned against it, still staring at his phone.

She turned away, determined to stop thinking about Josef. Moodiness had ruled her home life. But she wasn't home, and this driver wasn't Patrick.

She strolled past the house, peeking over the waist-high fence into the front yard. A woman holding a watering can stepped out of the front door, pausing on the landing to quench the thirst of some potted geraniums at the top of the steps. She appeared to be in her sixties, at least from a distance.

Anna plastered on a smile and yelled, "*Guten Morgen*."

The woman glanced back, smiled a little. "*Guten Morgen*." She continued to water the plants.

"Sprechen Sie Englisch?" Anna asked, trying out what she'd practiced from her phrase book.

The woman straightened and studied Anna. "A little."

"I'm visiting from the US and trying to locate someone who lived at this address a long time ago. Back in 1938."

"Oh. This house was built after the war. I have been here *zwanzig*...um, twenty years." She put down her can and came over to the fence. "Who do you wish to find?"

"A family named Hinzmann. Specifically Gunther Hinzmann."

"Hinzmann," she repeated as she plucked off the heads of a few dead flowers from a bush. "Hmmm. It doesn't sound familiar."

"Do you think anybody in the neighborhood might remember someone from so long ago?"

She frowned. "Many moved during the war." She shook her head. "But I am afraid that name I do not know."

"Well, I thought I'd try. *Danke* for your time."

The woman smiled. "*Bitte*. I wish I could help more."

Anna turned away, taking note of the other houses nearby. She could go to a few in this general vicinity, even though all appeared to be post-war construction. Who knew… She just might get lucky.

"Why are you looking for this man?" the woman yelled.

She returned to the fence. "I live in New York City. My neighbor came from Germany and grew up on this street. He was Jewish, and the man I am looking for helped him escape capture from the Nazis. I have a letter to deliver, to thank this man."

The woman tipped her head, considering Anna. "I am Erika. Would you like to come in? There are many families in this building. Perhaps someone might remember. We could knock on some doors, try to find out."

Anna glanced to the car. Josef still leaned against the driver's door with a cigarette in one hand, his phone in the other. "I'm heading inside," she said loudly.

"And you do not need me right now?" he yelled.

"No. I'm fine."

He nodded and even gave her a brief smile before returning to his phone.

She followed Erika up the wide stone steps to the main entrance, more optimistic than she'd been a minute ago.

Chapter 7

I do not need a therapist. I need a better doctor.

Josef hit send a little harder than necessary due to irritation at his sister's suggestion. A therapist? How would that help his leg?

The simplest things set off his irritation these days, like the dog and owner he'd almost hit on the way over. At least he and Anna arrived in one piece. Driving wasn't climbing a mountain, but sure felt like it.

He took one last drag off his cigarette, tossed the rest onto the ground, and stomped it out. How would he cope with having Anna in his car for days? Possibly weeks? Every time he looked into her dark eyes, the ghost of Lily reappeared. It took over his mind, ate away at him.

Claudia always raved because his reviews from his passengers were stellar, with customers applauding his zest for adventure, easygoing humor. A few of the single females on his tours privately told him he had charm. He imagined if Anna wrote a review about him, she wouldn't say any of those things. Yesterday, when his leg hurt, he'd upset her to the point she was shaking. Though he'd apologized and she'd accepted, his behavior only added to the general sense of self-hatred seeping through his soul since Lily died.

The way she and Lily blended in his head could be partially blamed for his erratic behavior around Anna. Especially shameful considering her thoughtful mission here to get an important message to a man for his heroism.

Risky efforts back in those days could cost a person their life. Most of his older family members hated to talk about the war. When they did, they'd speak quietly, their voices cracking as grief swallowed their expressions.

They'd share how nobody believed the National Socialist Party would gain so much power, but when they did, good people watched in horror because men with guns kept them silent. A lump gathered in his throat. Living through such a time was unimaginable. He needed to show due respect for the search Anna undertook. Now if only his aching body and overactive brain would cooperate.

He drew in a deep breath of fresh air, suddenly hating the scent of the cigarette clinging to him. Ten years away from them. Since the accident, though, nothing mattered. He felt crappy, both inside and out.

Ping! He glanced at his phone screen. Helga again.

I suggested a therapist because I care about you. You've been through a lot.

He sighed. Helga always had his back. What were sisters for? The love he had for her melted away his irritation and he replied.

And I love you for caring so much. I will think about it. Gotta run.

He got into the car, unrolled the window, and put on the radio. Tipping back his head, he closed his eyes and relaxed into the bucket seat.

What would he say if he saw a psychologist? He yawned. Last night the pain in his leg woke him every half hour because he was trying to cut back on the stronger medicine. He yawned again. If only he could turn back the moment they got into Lily's car, opened the sunroof, and drove while the warm sun beat on their skin. He yawned again. Details blurred as his body melted into the seat…the radio had been on at one point… music, a pop tune. Lily sang, her voice lifting with the high notes. He got lost in the melody, the smoothness of her pretty voice. He could almost remember…almost…almost…almost…

BOOM! BOOM! BOOM!

His eyes flashed open. Heart pounding, skin damp with sweat, he shifted in the seat, trying to gather his bearings. The bass beat of a Bruno Mars song pounded from his car speakers—the noise that woke him and in the process stole a thunderous roar in his subconscious. Another dream. He reached for the details, but they scuttled away like crabs on a beach. An hour had passed since he'd closed his eyes. He sat upright, drank from his water bottle, and a few minutes later his body returned to normal.

The door to the house Anna visited opened. She walked out with the woman and a little girl maybe four or five years old. The woman hugged Anna, who then squatted down and said something to the girl. She handed Anna a small bunch of flowers.

They all walked to the gate. Through the open windows, he heard them shouting assurances that they'd see each other again before Anna left the country. One hour with these total strangers and they parted as if she were a long lost relative.

Smiling, she approached the car then got inside. "That was a delightful visit."

"*Gut.*" The realization hit Josef he'd have to drive again. He took a deep breath, gradually exhaled. *Steady boy.* "What did you find?"

"The woman who lives there, Erika, took me around the apartment building with her granddaughter." She held up the flowers. "Sweet little girl. She picked me these from their back gardens. Anyway, on the second floor I met an older woman who lived on this street during the war, but her family came back and rebuilt afterward. She wanted to go see the flowers in the back of her property, so I offered to take her for a walk. Poor thing needs help. An aide only comes twice a week to check in on her."

Anna shook her head and frowned. "She reminded me of Isaak, before he got cancer. He'd get by, but sometimes still needed a hand…"

Her voice was filled with genuine tenderness for people, some she knew well, others she barely knew. But she really *did* seem to like helping. True altruism. Though he sometimes helped his elderly neighbor, he mostly thought about his own problems.

Anna personified goodness. All wrapped up in her petite frame, her perky nose, her whimsical waves. Toss on tights, wings, and a magic wand and she could be cast as a real-life fairy godmother, traveling the world and doing virtuous deeds for others. At least that's how it seemed.

He let the thought linger, its taste almost bitter. So what did that say about him?

"…and she thinks she remembers Gunther's family, although she was young at the time. But when I mentioned I'd be going to churches to search for baptismal records, she named two where she felt certain they may have gone. One of them even has a remembrance to people affiliated with their church who were victims of the Nazis."

His mind drifted. By anybody's measure, Anna would be called selfless. Hadn't she flown to another country to help her friend from New York? The other day, he'd witnessed her offer to walk Max's dog because of his leg. And just now, she took an older woman she barely knew for a walk in the garden. But what about him? Would he have done all those things? Probably not. At least not in his current state of mind. Or had he always been a man who mostly thought about himself, missing important moments in life?

She paused and searched his face. "What do you think?"

He snapped back to the conversation. "So, you want to visit these two churches for baptism records?"

"I do." She glanced down at a piece of paper. "Here's the first address."

He entered the information into the GPS and readied himself to get back on the road. This time when he eased his foot on the gas, some of the prior tenseness had gone. Nothing like the ease he had driving before the accident.

Anna sat and stared out the window.

He drove in the direction of the first church. The accident didn't occupy his thoughts. Instead, he couldn't shake the image of Anna as she hugged two strangers goodbye. Not a casual hug, but an eye-closing, I-really-mean-it hug. So warm, he'd felt the emotion from where he sat in the car.

Had he ever embraced someone that way? Since he couldn't remember, it must be a no.

* * * *

"And this is a *halbtrocken* Riesling? Half-dry, so I can taste sweetness?" Anna lifted the glass Florian had just lowered to the patio table, thankful for a drink as the time the divorce papers were to be served had passed thirty minutes ago without even a peep from Patrick.

He nodded and launched into a brief lesson on sugar levels and the German wine industry while she sipped the cool, sweet vintage and it steadied her nerves.

"Very nice," she said, lowering the glass, glad to have Florian's company for a few minutes to take her mind off her stress. "I'll use this to toast my success today. I got a birthdate for the man I'm trying to find."

"*Wunderbar!* It is a good start. I will be back." Florian headed off to wait on another group that entered the restaurant patio.

She inhaled the early evening air. Six-thirty here meant the time was twelve-thirty in New York. A half hour past the scheduled time for delivery. Maybe she'd have some dinner soon, and a few glasses of wine. Try not to think about Patrick. Instead focus on the accomplishments of a successful day in her search for Gunther. Finding his birthdate at the second church she'd visited would help her internet search. With any luck, she'd find him quickly and still have time for seeing some sights before she returned home.

With each tick of the clock, her imagination went wild with worry. Did the server have a problem, or had Patrick refused to sign? She picked up her phone, double-checked to make sure it was roaming…and it was. If anything went wrong and he didn't take the papers, then what would she do?

Come on. Think positive. He'd no doubt try to reach her at the house first, her cell phone second. If he called the house and got no answer, would he leave work immediately to find her?

She turned back to the view, spotting a tourist boat while she swallowed a gulp of her wine. What she'd give to climb aboard the vessel, float to where the river ended in Switzerland, never have worry about Patrick finding her there.

But, in theory, he'd never find her here, either.

Not unless the lawyer told him where she'd gone, which he wouldn't. She'd avoided using their personal credit cards or ATM. A debit card funded by Isaak's estate paid for things while here.

So the only real connection to Patrick she still had was her cell phone. Since she used it minimally, she hoped he couldn't track down her location from the device. Even if he could, she hoped he'd never go through such an extreme measure to find her location. Until he got those papers and she could size up his reaction for real, everything was speculation.

She pulled her laptop closer and typed in an ancestry site recommended by Ruth, entering Gunther's full name and birthdate. After a half hour of searching, she'd written two pages of names. Once several were eliminated, she had a list of eleven worth meeting. As she scanned through them, she took minor differences into account and ordered them by strongest to weakest likelihood of being the man she wanted. The top four were in the towns of Marburg, Müden, Wörrstadt, and Gau-Bickelheim.

A map of Germany showed the towns within an easy day's ride, with the man in Marburg the most perfect match. Perhaps she'd suggest they start there. With any luck, she'd find him first try.

Her phone rang. Patrick's name flashed on the display. She froze, counting the rings until it went into voice mail, hoping he'd leave a message telling her all she needed to know—that he'd been served. The ring continued, practically screaming at her to answer. When it stopped, she still couldn't move.

She closed her eyes. Wimp. He couldn't hurt her from the telephone.

Ping.

A message. She drew from the same inner strength that somehow made her file divorce papers, hit play, and lifted the phone to her ear. "Anna, how dare you do this to me! Call me. Now! I mean it. NOW!"

Fury burned in his voice, terrifying as a lion's roar. Her hands trembled as she deleted the message, but the phone rang again. Patrick's name crossed the display. She hit a button to send it directly into voice mail and tossed the phone onto the table, trying to look calm despite the hysteria raging inside her head. Three more times he called. Each time she sat still as a pole, staring at the phone while her gut quivered.

Finally, the calls stopped. She lifted her glass, slowly sipping the soothing drink, gathering up courage. After she downed the last drop, she lifted the phone, played the messages. "You'd better answer me, Anna. I don't want to track you down, but I will. And then you'll be sorry."

The rests were hang-ups. She nearly dropped the phone when a text message pinged.

Damnit, Anna! ANSWER ME! If you don't, I'm coming home!

Her hand trembled, his tone conjuring up reminders of what he could do. A swift blow to the head, kick to the gut, or hard slap to her cheek. Wrapping her arms around her shoulders, she tried to comfort herself, as she'd done so many times before. Had she stayed in New York and served those papers, this was the rage she'd have been subjected to. She wanted to crawl inward, hide, bracing herself for his…

"More wine, Anna?" Florian approached, watching her carefully through his thick black glasses. "Are you all right?"

"I'm fine." She forced out a smile. "Just got a strange message from home."

"Ah, I see." His handlebar mustache dipped when he frowned. "Many of us from the house are going to a wine festival in Stadtpark later. You will join us? It should take your mind off your troubles."

Patrick would no doubt have gone home by then and be on a campaign to reach her again by phone. No sense in waiting around for those calls. Besides, how could she search for her old self if she wallowed in her fears? Sulking in her room would only mean Patrick still controlled her life. But going out and enjoying herself would be a way to feel in control of herself.

Plus, it was nice of Florian to invite her. She was lucky Isaak sent her to these people. "I'd love to go."

"Fantastic! Come to the kitchen at eight. You can walk over with me and Karen."

"I'll be there."

After Florian returned inside, she shut off the phone, turning off all Patrick's anger. At least for now. The papers were served. She could rest knowing her journey to leave Patrick was well underway.

Chapter 8

"Were you scared, Uncle Josef?" Tobias, the youngest and most vocal of his nephews, stared at Josef and waited for an answer, wide-eyed like his brothers, Jan and Benedickt, who sat on the lawn next to Tobias.

Josef shook his head. "Not a bit. Iceland has volcanic activity going on all the time. It was one reason I took a tour group there."

Benedickt puffed out his chest. "When I grow up, I want to give tours like you."

Josef rose from the ground and ruffled Benedickt's hair, proud to see the excited gleam in his ten-year-old nephew's eyes. His boyhood antics always gave Helga a reason to worry, and Josef had no doubt about Benedickt's sincerity in pursuing an adventurous line of work.

Helga plunked a dinner plate on the nearby patio table, making a little too much noise and casting Josef an annoyed glance. "Enough filling my sons' heads with stories of dangerous places. They should be happy to find a nice office job, like their father. Boys, go to the kitchen and help *Oma* bring out the food."

On his way to the closet to retrieve some folding chairs, Josef bypassed his cane, and endured the dull pain in his leg with each step. Ignoring it made him feel normal again, even if just an illusion. While he opened a chair at the table, his sister arranged utensils around the plates.

"You should use your cane," she said as she placed the last fork down.

"There are a lot of things I should do but choose not to. Like taking a daily multivitamin." He tossed her a grin.

"Ha-ha," she said tonelessly, but then cracked a teeny smile. "I'm serious. If you don't listen to the doctor, then how will you get better?"

"I listen." He placed another chair at the teak table.

She snorted a sarcastic laugh. "Like the game of football you played with the boys before finally getting off your feet ten minutes ago."

"We were just batting the ball around. What kind of uncle would I be if I didn't play a few rounds?"

"You're a great uncle, no matter what you do." Helga gave his shoulder a squeeze as she walked past him. "You know, speaking of work—"

"Who was speaking of work?"

"My son was. Christian says there is a job at his company you might like."

Not this again. Josef was proud of his brother-in-law's rise to CFO at the large office, but the place held little interest to Josef.

He eased into one of the chairs, giving his leg some minor relief. "And what is this job your husband recommends?"

"Right up your alley. Relocation advisor."

"Watching others move around the world while I sit at a desk job for a large pharmaceutical company?" Josef laughed. "I don't think so."

The boys entered like a small stampede, each carrying a bowl. Josef's mother brought up the rear. For the first time he saw she was only a head taller than Benedickt. The boys were growing up fast.

Helga took a seat. "The firm most likely has more opportunity than working at Wanderlust Excursion's home office."

"I'm not looking for any opportunity at Wanderlust's office." He shifted so Jan could put his dish on the table. "The job is temporary, until I can get back on the road."

"You should consider it, Josef." His mother raised a brow. "Christian says his company is a nice place to work with good job security."

She looked quite serious with her cardigan buttoned to the top and simple cross necklace. Josef wondered how she'd ended up with his father, but maybe opposites did attract.

"And they pay very well," his mom added while passing the salad to him.

"Money isn't everything," he mumbled.

His sister and mother shared a glance he pretended not to notice. "Tobias, can you hand me the bread basket, *bitte*?"

Bowls were passed, and plates were filled. While they ate, the boys argued over who amongst them was a better ball player. He didn't know how his sister managed to keep three boys, aged six to ten, in line as much as she did.

When the boys finished, they asked to be excused and scrambled from the table the split second their mother said yes.

Josef watched them kicking a football around the yard, wishing his body didn't hurt so he could jump in the middle and join them again.

"Are you bringing a date to your brother's wedding?" His mother's voice was filled with innuendo, her ongoing quest to see him marry not a big secret. "It's just around the corner, you know."

"I can't think of anybody to ask at the moment." Josef clapped as Jan outwitted his brothers and got custody of the ball. "Good job, Jan!"

"What about Annette's daughter, Louisa?"

When Josef had been in high school, more than once his mother had hinted to Josef about her neighbor's daughter. "She's married, *Mutti*."

"Not any more. Last year, she divorced."

He hadn't heard. Louisa always turned heads, at least when they were teenagers. But she'd never been his type. Even back in their school days, they mixed in different circles. She lacked an interest in the world and adventure.

Yet as he enjoyed this evening on his sister's homey patio, it struck him that maybe this lifestyle had some merit. Would a commitment to ground him at this stage in his life be so bad?

Gabriel's upcoming wedding needled Josef with reminders about getting older and having no commitment to a woman or children. A notion he'd never given much thought until the accident. Endless days lying in bed gave him plenty of time to mull over life, death, and everything in between. And his sister's home in a family-friendly neighborhood always made him feel comfortable, even made him miss the lack of stability in his own life at times.

Up until now, marriage had carried the appeal of being stuffed inside a box with only air holes to breathe. That damn car accident had forced him to face the frailty of life and highlighted his choice to run from one country to the next seeking escape. From what, though? His new steady diet of being around family made him admit he might be missing something.

"In case you're wondering, Louisa has moved back to her mother's house," his mother said, deftly keeping the conversation going. "So, she lives in town now."

"I'm sorry to hear about her divorce. She was always a nice person, but she doesn't need an old man with a cane at her side."

Helga blurted out a laugh. "Oh stop! One, she is your age. And two, you will get better. Compared to when you first came home, you've improved in leaps and bounds."

"I suppose, but I'm not perfect yet."

Helga poked his side. "And you were perfect before?"

He pulled away, laughed. "You know what I mean. Able to do the things I love to do. On another topic, Claudia gave me an interesting assignment. An American visitor has hired me to help her while she's here."

"So you will take her on the sights of Rhineland?" His mother raised her brows. "How will you manage with your leg?"

"The sights around here aren't so dangerous I cannot easily maneuver them, but she isn't here as a tourist. She is here to find a man who helped her friend during the war." He explained what he knew about Anna's search.

Both women asked several questions he could not answer. He chuckled but only to hide how foolish he now felt at having asked Anna so little. But his leg had hurt. And the next day, driving took all his concentration. "You two are like the press. If she wanted me to know, she would have told me."

Helga chuckled. "It's called having a conversation. Or you were too busy thinking about yourself to ask?"

The remark had some truth to it and stung, but he kept the mood light and gently elbowed her. "Watch it, or I'll take back my offer to take the boys for you so you can go to the spa with Regina."

She tossed back her head and laughed. "*Ja, Ja*. I take everything back."

His mother patted Josef's shoulder. "Be nice, Helga. Josef is like his father. Just focused on other things."

Ten years ago this past spring, his father had passed away. His mother still talked about Dad with great reverence, but a man who served himself first did not deserve such appreciation for eternity. Josef both admired and detested his father, leaving him conflicted even long after losing him.

Helga stood while raising a brow at Josef. "Maybe my brother can help me clean up, so *Mutti* can have some time with the boys."

"Oh, Helga, let him relax." His mother gave Helga a disapproving shake of the head. "With his leg, he shouldn't be doing anything."

Helga rolled her eyes while stacking her sons' plates. "Oh, yes. We must spoil King Josef."

Her tone mocked in a playful way, but deep down, Josef heard more.

Helga turned to him and winked. "Good thing I love you so much."

Josef usually laughed off these exchanges, only this time the exchange didn't seem so funny.

Maybe it was the talk about the likeness to his father. A man whose job as a reporter for the BBC had taken him to dangerous parts of the world. Assignments he happily took, as if he didn't have a family back home, waiting and worrying about him.

But when Dad came home, Josef followed him everywhere, hung on his every word. The man loved an audience. By God, he defined *self-absorbed*, and yet Josef aspired to be just like him.

And he had.

The sacrifice? Commitment. A family of his own. With freedom, he pursued adventures knowing he'd never burden a wife or children with his absence. So he'd turned into a single version of his dad, but at least nobody at home ever felt disappointment each time he left.

The pattern of his life had made it easy to mostly think about his needs. Seeing himself in this light made his stomach turn.

His mother lifted her plate and started to stand, but Josef put a hand on her shoulder. "Relax and watch the boys play. I'll help Helga clean up." He stood.

"You are such a good boy, Josef."

He took her plate and stacked it on his. "No. Not really, *Mutti.*"

She frowned.

He smiled to lighten the moment for her. "But I am lucky I have a sister who keeps me in line and mother who loves me so much."

He walked towards the kitchen door carrying the plates but kept hearing his mother's words. *A good boy.* No, good boys turned into grown men who drove carefully, with regard for other people's lives. They took better care of those around them…

Blame sank into his chest, pulling him into a darkness he'd visited often in the past six months. As he walked into the kitchen, Helga stood at the sink washing out a pot. He went to her side and lowered the plates.

"I'll dry." He pulled a dish towel out of a drawer, his sadness lingering like a storm cloud. He fought it, tried to hold himself together.

She handed him the pot she'd just cleaned, carefully looking him over. "What's wrong?"

The string holding all his emotions snapped. "I'm a mess, Helga."

She scrubbed a platter and didn't look at him. "You've been through a lot. You need to give yourself a break."

A lump hardened in his throat, but he fought tears. Why couldn't he give himself some slack? If only he could turn back the clock.

Quietly, he said, "I cannot stop thinking about the woman in the car with me."

Helga stopped washing and let the platter sink into the water. "Lily?" she asked softly.

He nodded and the lump dissolved, but a tear ran along his cheek. "If I hadn't crashed the car, she'd be alive."

Helga wiped her hands on his dish towel then embraced his shoulders. "But, Josef, it was an accident."

"Maybe. I have no memory of what happened. Not one damn thing. And now, a woman I barely knew is gone."

"And it's eating away at you. You look tired. I can tell you aren't yourself."

He dropped his head to hide tears sliding along his cheeks.

Helga drew him into a hug. Neither spoke. Josef stared at the tile floor but all he saw was the darkness of a single instant.

Finally, Helga leaned back and placed a hand on his forearm. He slowly looked up.

Helga's eyes glistened. "Sometimes we are handed a bad circumstance. Like a test. We have to search deep to understand why whatever we faced has us so troubled and what we can do to make it better."

"And what does that mean for me?"

"Dig deep, Josef. What's really going on right now?"

"What you just said out there is true. I *have* been indulged by the people around me most of my life. It may be a family joke, but it holds some truth."

"Yes, a little. But I tease—"

"No. I've always run a little too hard, a little too fast, with no regard for anybody but myself. Maybe I'd been doing that the day of the crash, too. Lately, I'm beginning to see the man I am and…" He looked to the counter because he didn't want to see the agreement in his sister's eyes when he made this confession. "I can be very selfish. Like Dad."

"You are not selfish. Whenever I've needed you, you've come to my aid. And yes…" She lowered her voice. "A bit like Dad. But there are good things about that. When you walk in a room, everyone wants to be at your side. You're friendly and interesting. Same as Dad."

Same as Dad. A man blinded by his own interests, who couldn't sustain any relationships because he'd forced himself to remain on the go. Recklessly pursuing adventures, not real-life moments with people he cared about. He lacked depth. The kind of consideration that most people gave to others. Like using caution while they hold the life of another in the palm of their hands

Josef had become all of the above. More tears spilled, and he closed his eyes.

Helga touched his shoulder and he jerked his gaze toward her. "When I said you were like him, I'd meant it in a good way. Everyone loved Dad, like they do you. But I can tell you're not happy."

"Because I would do anything to change what happened. Even give up…never mind."

Helga frowned. He braced himself for a lecture to pull himself together, much like the one she'd given him at his hospital bedside in France, when he'd woken from the surgery on his leg.

Only this time, her face softened and she sighed. "You would have liked to have died, too?"

"Not *too.* Instead of." He grabbed the dish towel only to realize nothing needed to be dried.

"Ah, I see. So you dying would make any of this better?" She shook her head. "*Mein Gott*, Josef. It was an accident. Even the police said so."

"They don't know what caused it. They are guessing. Maybe I could've prevented the accident if I'd been more careful."

"You mean like our father?"

The words slammed into his gut like a sucker punch. His father's death in Baghdad back in 2007 was unforgiveable in Josef's eyes. Was the blame owning him since the crash coming from the same place?

He lowered the dish towel. "What happened to me is totally different."

"Like I said to you the other day, maybe you're seeking help from the wrong kind of doctor."

Tobias banged open the screen door leading into the kitchen, heading straight for his mother.

"*Mutti,* I need a glass of water."

"How do you ask?"

"*Bitte?*"

She nodded, retrieved a glass, and filled it from the tap.

Josef needed to get out of here, get his sister's suggestion about a shrink out of his head. "How about I referee a game for you boys before I leave?"

Tobias's eyes lit up. "*Ja*!"

Josef slipped out the kitchen door and didn't look back, but Helga's words about needing a therapist whispered in his ear.

Chapter 9

Anna walked behind Florian and Karen through a tree-lined path displaying banners for the wine festival in Stadtpark. Lively jazz music played in the distance, and the scent of grilled meat and smoke permeated the air.

She tried to enjoy the festive atmosphere, but Patrick's last text rang in her ears. *That's it! I'm coming home!* She pictured him in the brownstone, screaming her name and getting no answer, only to find the note and necklace she'd left on the counter. No doubt he'd race upstairs in a rage, see if she'd taken her clothes and suitcase. Her mouth went dry just imagining it, but without her there, he'd need another outlet for his anger.

They turned a corner and a clearing opened to the festival grounds. Strings of bright, white bulbs outlined tents stationed over long rows of picnic tables on the park's well-manicured lawn. Additional lights in the surrounding trees and bushes glowed brighter as the sky darkened.

"There they are." Florian glanced back at Anna then detoured toward one of the tents.

They neared a long table where many people she'd met at the hotel were already seated, including a new couple who'd arrived from the US that morning. Even Max had come, trusty canine companions at his side.

Ruth waved to them, her flashy pink hair a beacon amidst a sea of neutral colors. She pointed to an empty space between her and Otto, who waved his hands while he talked passionately with another guesthouse resident.

"I saved you a seat," Ruth said loudly. "Florian told me you were joining us."

"Thanks." Anna settled onto the bench.

Otto, without missing a beat in his discussion, pushed an empty glass in front of her and filled it from one of the open bottles.

Conversation flowed. The atmosphere was relaxed, happy. There always seemed to be at least two bottles of wine being passed around while they nibbled on garlic bread, bratwurst, and currywurst.

"So tell me, Anna." Ruth refilled her glass. "How did your column become syndicated in so many papers? That is no small feat."

As she finished telling Ruth about her search for an agent, Anna heard loud laughter and looked up. Josef stood near the end of their table, talking to Joachim and Regina while several of his friends surrounded him. A second later, his friends headed off to another table, but he stayed behind. The rugged crags of his face softened as he smiled at something Regina said. A nice smile when he used it. He stood with his legs firmly planted, his hands tucked in the pocket of an unzipped khaki military jacket, making the broad shoulders on his slim frame seem wider, and a black T-shirt clung to his ribs.

"Josef!" yelled Otto. He held up a glass. "*Wollen sie einen Drink*?"

Josef pointed with his thumb toward the group he'd arrived with. *"Nein Danke."*

Josef's gaze panned the table and fell on her briefly. He gave her a quick nod, finished his conversation, and walked over to his group.

Ruth leaned close to Anna and quietly asked, "How did Josef do as your guide today?"

"Fine. I mean, he wasn't really a guide. More like a chauffeur and translator, though only twice did I need his translating services." Anna ended it there. Josef appeared to be friendly with many at the guesthouse, and she didn't want to cross any line by sharing her personal observations about the man.

"Otto was happy to see him back at the guesthouse for the job with you. He's kept to himself lately."

"Oh?"

"Yes. I first met Josef a few years ago, during one of our stays at the guesthouse. He liked to watch football in the biergarten with Joachim and Florian. Joachim told me he wasn't always around much because of his job traveling, but I found Josef relaxed, quite likable. But this year, he has changed."

"How so?"

"There is less life in his eyes, less spirit in his step. Joachim said he was hurt very badly in the car accident. It seems to have taken a toll on him."

So he'd been in a car accident. It explained both his limp and his nervous driving—if they were related. After witnessing his stress firsthand, she wondered why he would have accepted this assignment. But he must've had a good reason. Maybe he was trying to face driving again. Face his fears. Wasn't that what she was trying to do? Perhaps she and Josef had more in common than she'd first thought.

Otto turned to Ruth and asked her something in German. She gave him a sharp reprimand for interrupting, but after a quick apology to Anna, he continued to talk to his wife.

Anna gave them some privacy and people-watched.

Her gaze drifted to where Josef sat, and she surreptitiously watched him. One minute, he'd be engaged with his friends, smiling as if he didn't have a care in the world. Then she'd catch a dark spark rushing past his distant eyes, gone in a flash when someone in the group called his name and he looked their way with a wide grin. This was a man with problems.

Sympathy tugged at her heart. Whatever ailed him, he wore it on his sleeve.

Her attention stayed on the changing faces of Josef, stirring an always present need she had to make things better. The same need that drove her to never give up on Patrick, until living with him became unbearable.

But Josef wasn't Patrick. Maybe he needed to talk to someone. She considered approaching him. Before she could, he quickly rose from his seat and walked off without a word to his tablemates.

A short, spikey-haired blond woman sitting across from him watched as he left. She stood and followed him.

Good. He had a friend, possibly a girlfriend. He didn't need Anna's help, yet she kept an eye on the path where Josef and the woman had disappeared.

A few minutes into her vigil, she forced herself to stop. Josef had been hired to drive her around. Nothing more. Not even a minute later, though, her gaze drifted back to the footpath. The idea he had problems bothered her like an unscratched itch.

Her parents had raised her to be concerned about other people. They were very active in mission work at their Presbyterian church, and their daughters had done the same. But thinking about those days, she became aware how focusing on the needs of others often meant ignoring her own problems. Especially the year her parents not only opened their hearts, but their home, to a stranger. Six months. Six long, stressful months. A knot tightened in her stomach. That time in her life had changed her, left her with a message: if someone was less fortunate, her needs didn't matter. Had she let that rule her life with Patrick, too?

When members of her party starting singing, she let go of the memory and smiled as she listened until they were finished, and then she asked Ruth where she could find the ladies' room.

Following signs reading *Toiletten*, she ended up in an open area overlooking the river where the bathroom building awaited. Once she finished, she walked to a railing along the path of the river. People mingled nearby, many carrying wine glasses and leaning on the railing like her. Lamppost lights cast a spotlight on the Rhine, making the black water glisten like a fine gem. On the opposite shore, Wiesbaden's bright lights outlined the buildings.

She took a deep breath of the crisp air and stepped away to return to the festival grounds, nearing a man and woman who talked in the darkened shadows.

The man shouted, "*Nein*, Claudia." He continued to talk loudly in German, then abruptly turned away from the woman and walked out into the light. She followed and both stopped right in Anna's path.

She froze.

Josef stood still, head down, shoulders slumped, seemingly unaware of her presence while he mumbled words Anna didn't understand. The woman he'd called Claudia moved to him, put an arm around him, and spoke quietly.

Anna didn't move, stalled momentarily by curiosity. Just as Anna shook it off and managed to take a step away to give them some privacy, a noisy group came up behind her.

Claudia dropped her arms, then both she and Josef looked up. Josef's gaze met Anna's. She took in the agony etched on his face, so real that his deep torment infused her heart.

His brows furrowed. "Yes, Anna?" His eyes shifted, then went back to her, no doubt embarrassed to see her there. "What is it?"

Her cheeks burned. She wanted to ask if he was all right, but he obviously wasn't. She felt like a fool staring at him, and felt horrible for eavesdropping. "Nothing. I'm sorry. I didn't mean to interrupt."

She hurried past them, her heart beating wildly as she found the path. What had she witnessed? A breakup? Or some other matter? It didn't matter. She owed him an apology.

* * * *

"Who's she?" Claudia stared down the path where Anna had just disappeared.

"The American you asked me to drive around." The obvious pity on Anna's face remained embedded in his brain. As if she'd caught him on display, naked and unable to hide his flaws. How would he look her in the eye again? He walked back to the railing and stared out at the river. "Was she there long?"

Claudia came up to his side. "I don't know, but she does not speak *Deutsche.*" Her voice softened. "Forget about her. I'm glad you finally told me everything bothering you. I had no idea you couldn't remember what happened during the accident. You haven't seemed yourself, but I figured it was because of the pain in your leg."

"Both things have left me miserable. You're a good friend for listening."

He didn't need a therapist. All he'd needed was to open up to his childhood friend, who always understood him. Lately, even when with his friends, he'd felt alone with his anguish. Tonight's confession didn't fix his problems, but speaking about his worries helped eased some of the pressure inside his head.

"Let's go back," he said.

They walked the path in silence. Claudia glanced his way. "Are you sure you're comfortable driving the American around? I can find someone else."

"No need. The job takes my mind off my worries."

"Okay."

As they neared the table, Claudia's husband waved to them, held a bottle, and pointed to the wine tent. "Looks like we need another bottle of wine. Be right back." She headed toward the vendor area.

As Josef continued to their table, he glanced to where Anna sat talking to Ruth. Her big eyes never once strayed from Ruth's face. The more he thought about it, she was nothing like the fun-loving French woman. Certainly more serious, carrying a touch of vulnerability. Now he'd come along and shown her his worst side. Self-loathing bubbled inside of him. He didn't like being this way, feeling like he'd lost control of his impulses. If only he could turn back the clock. He wanted a do-over for so many things in his life, but especially that ill-fated drive in France. He even wanted one with Anna, too.

A do-over.

A chance to make things right.

Was it fate that the gods above made damn sure he walked straight into a woman who reminded him of Lily? Anna wasn't Lily, but she did need help. And therein lay his opportunity.

A chance to let go of his own problems and help someone else.

A chance to stop being self-absorbed…

To stop being like his father.

Could he change? Maybe. Maybe not. The best thing that might happen was his life might improve. The worst thing was—nothing. He already lived in his own private hell.

Anna rose and walked in the direction of the food vendors. She stopped, looked at a sign, and continued to the next trailer, doing the same thing.

He moved fast, not sure what he'd say when he reached her. Once at her side, he casually said, "Hello."

She turned from the menu. "Oh. Hi."

He smiled, though every muscle in his face fought it. "Decide what you want?"

"I wanted a plain old pretzel." She laughed. "Only now has it dawned on me: I can't read German, so I'm not getting too far finding one."

"The word is *brezel,* but you could probably ask in English. They might understand." He studied the white board. "This vendor doesn't have any, but there are sausages, Hungarian langos—"

"What's that?"

"Fried dough, served with sour cream and cheese." He spotted a man walking away with one. "See?"

Her eyes opened wide with interest as she watched the man pass by.

He laughed. "Better than a pretzel?"

"They don't even deserve to be discussed in the same sentence."

"How about we get in line? I'll get one, too."

As they waited, he turned to her. "Had you needed to speak to me before?"

She glanced his way. "Oh, no. Well, yes. No." She blew out a breath. "First, I must apologize. I didn't mean to interrupt—"

"It is no problem. What did you want to tell me?"

She hesitated, but only for a second. "Any chance we can plan to get together tomorrow? Now that I have a birthdate for Gunther, I've found several matches online with his name. The locations aren't in the area. More like day trips."

So he would have to drive on the highway again. Farther this time. "Sure. How about in the afternoon? I need to help Claudia in the office in the morning."

"Afternoon works. Who's Claudia?"

"My boss. She was with me earlier, when you saw us talking." His cheeks warmed as he remembered how she'd looked at him when he was upset. "Would after lunch be all right?"

"Perfect."

They neared the head of the line, making small talk about the festival. Outwardly, he stayed calm. Inwardly, though, turmoil seized him as he considered doing longer highway rides. All while he'd have to stick to his commitment to be pleasant to her the entire day. Nice. Not selfish, moaning about his aches and pains.

But what did he have to lose by showing Anna some kindness? He'd lost himself in the accident, and that was his most valuable possession.

Chapter 10

Anna's laptop blurred behind her tears. She shut the lid and crossed her arms onto the patio picnic table, taking a moment to absorb the emotional details of the stories she'd read. Stories similar to Isaak's, occurring both before and during the war. Each one ripped her heart a little more. Good people who'd suffered because of hate and bigotry. Anger boiled in her veins toward the perpetrators of such violent actions, even though it happened so long ago.

No wonder Isaak, as well as many others, never returned here. Yes, the political party leading the charge had lost power and the country was restored to normal. But memories were hard to erase. Something she understood first hand.

These stories hit her hard, deep in her soul, because they made her think about rarely discussed ancestors on her father's side of the family. Not that the history was a secret. Just that nobody alive today knew much about the names or faces going back that far.

But one thing was clear; the Abrams clan had a Jewish bloodline going back several generations. And knowing this was part of her genetic pool fused a connection to the people in the stories she'd read that she couldn't shake away. And a deeper connection to this quest she made for Isaak.

The family details were sparse. Her great-grandfather had arrived in the US from Poland with his parents. They'd taken on a Christian name and faith but lived in Poland as Jews. Neither her father nor uncle knew more because that was all their father ever shared.

But Anna wanted to learn more.

Had prejudicial treatment caused them to go to the US as non-Jews? Probably. What family had they left behind? Poland had suffered under the Nazi regime, too. Had anybody on her family tree faced persecution because of faith?

The idea sank deep, churning inside her heart and head. More than a distant story. It was personal, as though a Nazi had stepped right inside her door. And knowing that might have happened to a long lost relative… Well, it hurt.

An urgency to find Gunther rattled her core. As she sat here staring at the river, her mission in Germany developed a personal connection somewhat distant, and yet powerful enough to matter.

She turned to the sound of footsteps. Dr. Walker, a British resident at the guesthouse who taught theology at the nearby university, approached her with a smile peeking out from behind his graying beard. She'd sat next to him at breakfast yesterday morning and found him to be a very well-traveled and knowledgeable man.

"Good day, Anna. A smashing one, isn't it?"

She forced a smile, her prior thoughts still resting heavy in her heart. "Yup. Perfect fall weather. Although my mind is elsewhere. I was just reading accounts of people who were saved from Nazis by the good graces of others. Incredible stories at such a heart-wrenching time."

Dr. Walker's lips pressed tight as he frowned. "Yes. Horrible, and yet hopeful that not all mankind had gone mad."

"Yes. One story told about an Israeli man who still has a picture in his house of the *Wehrmacht* soldier who'd saved him. But the soldier was later arrested by Hitler's police and executed because of aiding the Jews." The heaviness of the outcome forced a sigh. "Details about the Holocaust aren't new to me, but now it has the face of Isaak, a man I cared a great deal for."

"Tragedy is different when it becomes personal."

"It sure is." She shared what she knew about her own lineage.

Dr. Walker shifted his messenger bag on his shoulder. "Many Jews who migrated to Poland from Germany were still oppressed there for their Judaism. I suppose that's why it wasn't uncommon for many to change their names to more Christian-sounding ones after moving to safer places, like America. Your dad's ancestor might have done the same."

Anna nodded, wondering if any of her family had been forced to move to the ghettos of Poland or wear stars on their clothing to show their faith. Or had died because of religious persecution during the war. The thought hit her like a punch to the chest. What if someone like Gunther had saved one of them? She'd certainly want them recognized for it. She vowed to do everything in her power to get Isaak's message to Gunther.

"I guess I'll be off." Dr. Walker took a step and stopped. "While you're here, you might want to visit some of the Holocaust memorials nearby. There's one in Frankfurt and another in Wiesbaden. A visit can be quite powerful."

"I'll try. Thanks."

He glanced at his watch. "Time to run. Cheers."

"Cheers."

She thought about the conversation, wondering if she should email her father. Her parents had no idea about the divorce or her visit to Germany. With a little white lie, sent via email, she'd said she planned to travel the east coast to conduct interviews for her column, all in the hopes they wouldn't call the house looking for her.

Once things with the divorce were on track, she planned to return to Whidbey Island for an extended visit to her parents' home and figure out the next steps in her life. A much better time to talk about her family tree would be while she enjoyed a nice long visit with them. Alone. The kind of visit Patrick had always discouraged.

* * * *

Boom!

Darkness. Silence. Further he fell into the darkness, unable to move any part of his body...

Boom!

Josef's eyes flashed open. His temples throbbed. Sweat clung to his skin.

He rolled to his side. Outside his cracked-open bedroom window, the noisy trash collectors did their usual Tuesday morning pickup. He flopped back onto his back as the reoccurring nightmare skirted the edges of his brain.

He shut his eyes, gathered the dream. The end never changed. Always dark and quiet. Before that inescapable ending, he'd been flying through the air, his arms outstretched like a bird's wings as a breeze cooled his skin. Bright sunshine. Laughter. Lots of laughter.

Today there was something new.

An image of Anna's pretty, heart-shaped face had perched in the bright sky. She watched his flying antics, her expression filled with concern, maybe confusion. The same way she'd looked at him when he confessed about his memory loss to Claudia. To make it worse, the dream gods showed him

Anna's face slowly turning into Lily's, with the French woman asking in her strong accent, "How could you have done this to me, Josef?"

He kicked off the duvet cover, glanced at the clock, and dragged himself to the bathroom. Noon. He never slept this late. Too much wine had guided him last night, made his thoughts foggy enough to confess to Claudia and later talk to Anna.

He scrubbed in the shower. Each time he shut his eyes, Anna's confused face returned. "Go away!" he screamed. His plea bounced off the shower surround and echoed in his ears.

After he dried off, he skipped the need to tidy his beard and mustache and tossed on jeans with a slightly wrinkled button-down shirt for the short day ahead. After a meeting with Anna to firm up some plans, he'd head off to the office for a few hours. They'd talked last night, but he could barely think straight right now, let alone remember what he'd said.

Once in the kitchen, he got the coffee maker going. When their group broke up last evening, Claudia had told him not to come into the office this morning. Thank God. Besides sharp stabs in his temples, his leg throbbed from walking too much. He downed something to kill the pain and grabbed a roll to eat with his coffee.

Several days' accumulation of mail sat on his peninsula. He sifted through the pile while eating. About halfway down, a long white envelope with a Montpellier, France return address filled him with dread. Why would Lily's parents be contacting him again?

He'd met them at the hospital, a day after learning their daughter had died. Despite the sadness on their faces and the depth of their loss, they'd been kind to him. A kindness he didn't deserve.

He drew in a deep breath, tore open the back flap, and removed a newspaper clipping from the French publication *Midi Libre*. He knew only a little bit of French, but after translating a few words on his phone, he determined the article discussed a fundraiser in Lily's memory. Monies raised would go to the local hospital's children's center where she'd worked as a nurse.

Next to the article was a picture of Lily in her nursing uniform. He took a closer look. Perhaps he'd been quick to compare her to Anna. There were similarities, but a soft aura surrounded Anna's heart-shaped face, like she might smile or laugh at any second. Lily's determined gleam held the hardness of a woman who didn't take no for an answer.

He removed a checkbook and an envelope from the kitchen drawer, wrote out a check to the fund, and addressed the envelope to Lily's parents. The donation wouldn't bring their daughter back, but it was the least he could do. He returned to the drawer and took out a folder, sliding in the latest article related to the accident.

His memory folder. The earlier articles showed things he didn't remember from the crash. The first few months after leaving the hospital, he'd stare at them daily and beg the images to retrieve something—any little thing—from the recesses of his mind.

He flipped through the pile and removed the most detailed article. The headline read:

L'accident sur A8 prend la vie de la femme de Montpellier

His throat constricted as it always did when he studied this one. No matter what language it appeared in, he understood the headline: *An accident on A8 takes the life of a Montpellier woman.*

Beneath the headline a photo of Lily's mangled eight-year-old Alfa Romeo showed the small car crumpled like an accordion into a thick tree trunk. Next to a photograph of Lily, the paper had used his publicity photo from the tour company's website, taken on a day when he'd had an easy smile, spirit in his eyes. He missed feeling like that man.

He focused on the destroyed car, boring his gaze into the mangled mess until a chill skipped up his spine. How had he even made it out alive? How had he completely forgotten every single second before impact?

Concentrate. Concentrate! He squeezed his eyes tight and willed the photo to stir his stubborn memory banks.

After a minute passed with still nothing, Josef opened his eyes, swallowed back his disappointment, and scanned the article to the line that told about him being admitted with life-threatening injuries. It also said no signs of alcohol were found in his blood.

But what had he been doing? They were out late, had come back and climbed into the bed, too caught up in their passion to think of sleep. Sure, they got a few restless hours, but she woke suggesting the drive to Nice. A shower and cup of coffee appeared to wake him, but not fully. Had he fallen asleep at the wheel?

He sat back. All these months later, he was no closer to answers.

He dropped the article and gathered his wallet and keys off a table near the door. After swiping up his phone, he left for his meeting with Anna.

As he eased into the car's driver seat, the usual panic skipped through his limbs but only half as bad as last time. Yet after five minutes of driving the city streets of Mainz, his hands hurt from gripping the steering wheel.

He took a deep breath and loosened his hold, making the last part of the drive a little more relaxing.

He reached the Villa Von Essen, parked along the curb, and went inside while lifting his sunglasses onto his head.

"*Guten Tag*, Josef." Regina stood at the reception desk, filing papers into a box. She twisted her lips while examining him more closely. "Late night at the festival?"

"Do I look that bad?"

She laughed. "You look fine. Just a little, um, perhaps tired. Looking for Anna?"

He nodded.

"She was eating lunch on the patio last I saw her. Why don't you check?"

He headed to the outside patio but didn't see Anna. Max Fleisher sat at one of the picnic tables without his dogs. The older man faced outward with his elbows leaning back on the tabletop, his large belly jutting out.

"Good morning, Max."

"*Hallo*, Josef." Max waved him over.

"Where are Lucy and Ricky?" Josef asked when he got closer.

"Anna is walking them. My knee is bothering me and she offered. The doctor gave me medicine for the swelling, but it may take time to heal." Max's mustache twitched as he smiled. "God bless Anna. I will be sorry when she leaves. Such a sweet girl, and very helpful."

Sweet. Helpful.

The decision he'd made last night to be nicer to Anna struck like a thunderbolt. And why was that again? Oh, right. To prove to himself he wasn't a self-centered jerk.

Josef patted Max on the shoulder. "I'm glad she could help you with them. If you need anything from me, you let me know."

They chatted about the weather, the wine festival. Josef watched the sidewalk, hoping to see Anna soon.

Five minutes turned into ten. At the fifteen-minute mark, he stood. "Well, looks like your dogs are getting a good walk, Max. I may go do some errands. Can you ask Anna to call or text me when—"

"Sorry I'm late."

Anna jogged toward them, the two dachshunds in full gallop as they approached their master. The cheeks of her fair skin glowed, and dark curls bounced with her gait.

She reached Max and handed him the dog's leashes. "I don't know how you do it, Max." She squatted down and scratched behind the ears of both pups. "They tuckered me right out."

Her white-and-gray striped skirt fanned the ground. Josef noted the small of her waist where a pullover sweater outlined her curves.

Max leaned closer to the red-haired dog and mumbled something. He glanced up at Anna. "Lucy says you are much faster than me."

Anna laughed and tossed back her head, more relaxed than Josef had seen her since her arrival. "I think she's much faster than both of us."

As she started to rise, her hem got caught beneath her flat shoe. She lifted the skirt and Josef's gaze flickered from her smooth calves to her slender thigh. A bruise a few inches past her knee made him pause, think about the one on her arm.

She rose to full height, dropping the skirt to knee-level and smoothing it at the hips. "Max, let me know if I can help with them again. I enjoyed the exercise."

"We will set up a walk schedule then." Max grunted as he lifted himself off the bench. "How does that sound?"

Her smile didn't waver. "Sounds good to me."

Though Josef knew Anna had things to do here, she didn't balk at the idea of being on Max's schedule. The commitment he'd made last night mocked him. No way could he turn back on his vow. He'd do it and report back to Helga so she would stop calling him self-absorbed.

"Do you need help getting inside?" She went to Max's side and took his elbow.

He waved her away, his chest puffed out, most likely not wanting to take assistance from an attractive young woman. "No, no. I am okay. I'll just go slow. Come on, Lucy, Ricky. Tell Anna *Danke*!"

The dogs only looked up at their owner, wagging their tails. Max smiled and winked at Anna, the gleam in his eyes that of a much younger man.

Anna watched them walk off, a smile stuck on her face. Kind as an angel, with a natural ability to care for others, she made his decision to be nice to her seem almost greedy. The end goal had been to prove he could do for others altruistically, but his whole motive now looked self-serving. What the hell was wrong with him?

And yet last night, the plan had seemed so perfect. Going the extra mile for her had felt right.

She turned to Josef. "Sorry. I lost track of time. Those dogs are adorable. Growing up, my family had a few dogs. Now…" She frowned and met his gaze. "Now I live in a city. So—well, I just don't have one."

She looked away, but he couldn't miss the sadness in her expression.

He cleared his throat but was unsure what to say to make her feel better, so he uttered, "How about we get started?"

“Oh, sure.” She went over to one of the other picnic tables holding a laptop and slid onto the bench seat. She patted the seat to her side. “Sit, so I can show you what I’ve found.”

He did as she asked. Without looking at him, she navigated to an ancestry website, explaining how learning Gunther’s birthdate opened up her search.

“I have a long list of possible matches but narrowed it down to the top four most likely to match the man I’m looking for. I’d like to work out a schedule to visit them with you.” She turned, looked him in the eye. “If I get lucky, maybe the first will be the man who knew Isaak. Then you’re done with me.”

“Well, I do not think of this as a chore. I—”

A slow smile crossed her lips. “I’m teasing you. But if it isn’t him, I’ll feel better if we have a plan in place. I know you have other things to do besides driving me around.”

“It seems I have given you the wrong impression. I have not been myself lately. Well, maybe I have, but perhaps I have offended you, or made you think I do not want to drive you to these places.”

She smiled, genuine but brief. “Not at all, Josef. Really.”

Of course he sounded awkward. Idiot. He felt awkward, like he was trying too hard. “What I mean is, I find myself interested in this story.” Yes, much better.

“Oh. I see. Well, that’s great.”

“Yes. And it is hard to talk when driving. But since we are not in the car, maybe now we can talk. I realized I did not even ask you your neighbor’s story, why he needed help from Gunther. I would be interested. That is, if you want to share.”

She glanced down at the computer keys for a long moment. Finally, she looked up and into his eyes. “Yes. I’d be happy to. Gunther and Isaak were neighbors in Frankfort, as you know.”

He nodded.

“Isaak’s life changed on *Kristallnacht*.” She pressed her lips tight and appeared to be gathering her thoughts. Her voice quieted. “That evening, my neighbor’s family’s home in Frankfurt was destroyed.” She shared the details, the pain on her face palpable. Once finished, she drew a deep breath. “Gunther helped the boys hide for a while in town. But things were getting worse in Germany, so he finally got them out of the country to Belgium. I’m not sure how he got to the US.”

Josef sat quietly, stunned by the story, his heart bleeding for the family he didn’t know. “I am so sorry. For your neighbor. For not asking.”

"It's okay. Really." A tear slipped from the corner of her eye, and she swiped it aside with a brush of her fingertips. "Sorry. It's such a sad story. Every time I think of it, I… It's unimaginable."

Her sadness filled him with a sense of urgency to find this man. To make sure Gunther understood how valued his actions were. Children losing parents, losing their home, their country. Having to hide instead of attending school or play outside like normal kids. How had such madness owned the followers of the Nazi party? Finding Gunther meant doing something good. Josef needed to be part of doing something good, to step away from his own problems.

Quietly, he asked, "So, what is our first stop?"

She showed him her list. "The man I found in Marburg seems the most perfect match on paper. Is it far?"

"An hour and a half drive." His nerves teased him again. *Damnit.* He could drive that far. He *would* drive that far. Because the man who'd saved those boys deserved to get his thanks. And while it might help Josef on his path to self-redemption, his issues were no longer his primary goal.

"Tomorrow morning around nine we will leave," he said. "We will spend the day on this, do whatever you need."

And he smiled, as though he wanted nothing more than to do this for her. Because, in a way, he really did.

Chapter 11

Anna watched Josef pat the pockets of his blazer and frown.

Now what? He'd picked her up a few minutes ago, thirty minutes late and acting a bit, well, edgy. At least compared to how he'd been yesterday afternoon, when a gentler version of him had arrived at the guesthouse.

He stopped at a traffic light, shifted in the seat, and checked each back pocket. "Damn it," he mumbled.

"What's wrong?"

"I forgot my wallet. We have stop at my place."

She nodded. So they'd get to Marburg a few minutes later. "It's okay. We're not on a time schedule."

He nodded and flipped the radio to a pop music station, seeming content with their silence. When they reached the parking lot of an apartment complex, he pulled into a space and turned off the car.

After opening his door, he said, "I will be back."

She almost teased him about sounding as gruff and direct as Arnold Schwarzenegger's character in *Terminator* with his "vill" and "baach." But given his somber mood, and other more pressing matters, specifically against her bladder, she said, "May I use your bathroom?"

He glanced back over his shoulder at her, stared for a beat. "Sure. Follow me." He got out, shut his door, and started to walk rather fast for a man using a cane.

She hurried to catch up with him while looking around the homey complex of garden-styled apartments with a nice central green housing a few benches and flower beds.

They stopped at a ground-level apartment with a dying potted plant on the step, and he pushed his key into door. Someone yelled his name.

He glanced back over his shoulder. "*Ja,* Mrs. Freudenberger?"

She spoke to him and he listened carefully, nodding, his face softening with concern as she spoke. He replied to her and looked at Anna. "Go on in. The bathroom is down the hall, first door on the right. I will be a few minutes."

She watched him walk off, slipping on a genuine smile as he took the older woman by the elbow and listened to what she had to say.

Whatever drove today's mood shift, he still managed a smile for his elderly neighbor. She wondered if anything had happened, or if he just was quiet today for no particular reason. Yesterday's conversation had left her feeling like they'd started to have a friendship, but part of being a friend was understanding an "off" day.

She entered his apartment. Nice hardwood floors and contemporary furniture. Modern and comfortable, with knickknacks speaking to his passion for travel, like some beautifully painted prints of Tuscany on one wall, a small, wood-carved replica of a Viking ship on an end table, and a photograph of the bull run in Spain.

Passing by a marble-topped peninsula, she put down her purse. On her way down the hallway, she studied simple framed photographs of Josef in action: climbing a wall, standing with his fists raised on top of a glacier. After finishing in the bathroom, she headed back into the living room.

"Josef?"

When he didn't answer, she turned to get her purse. Newspaper clippings scattered on top of an open folder caught her eye. *Midi Libre.* Sounded French. One showed a photograph of a gruesome car accident.

She slipped her purse strap over her shoulder but couldn't tear her gaze from the destroyed car. Beneath it were photos of two people. Her gaze drifted to the man. Josef. Hair a bit longer, no beard or mustache, and the same piercing eyes. The other photo was a woman. Was this the accident Ruth had mentioned?

She tilted the topmost article to get a better look at the headline. *L'accident sur A8 prend la vie de la femme de Montpellier.*

An accident in Montpellier? Had the article contributed to his silence this morning?

The front door clicked open and she jerked her gaze up. Josef entered looking first at her, then the counter, then back to her again. "Did you find what you needed?"

"I did. Everything okay out there?"

Anna's heart raced. She wasn't the type to snoop and couldn't imagine why she'd done so just now. But lately, nothing she'd done was in character.

He frowned. "Yes. My neighbor is getting forgetful. I don't think her family realizes how bad the situation has become. I got her settled, but I will call her son on our way to Marburg."

"She's lucky to have a neighbor who's looking out for her."

He shrugged as he walked past her. "Let me get my wallet."

She stepped over to the window, far from where she'd been snooping. But she wondered about the woman in the article. She glanced back to the counter, wishing she could've read a little bit more about what had happened. Not that she could read French. But if the woman had been hurt or even killed in the accident, it explained his behavior. Coupled with his limp, he probably felt crappy both inside and out. Maybe he needed to have a reason to smile. Take his mind off his troubles.

He came back out, stuffing his wallet in his back pocket. On his way past the peninsula, he stopped and tucked the articles into the folder and pushed it against the wall.

He turned around. "Ready?"

She straightened like a soldier and saluted him, keeping her face stiff and formal. "Roger that."

His lips flicked, as if he wanted to crack a smile but couldn't. "Ladies first."

She marched out with her shoulders stiff and chin out while tossing a final salute and a wink. Outside, she glanced over her shoulder and she caught him watching her, certain she saw curiosity in his eyes and the desire to smile. Enough to give her confidence to keep trying with him.

* * * *

Anna leaned toward the windshield to look out the window. From the corner of his eye, Josef took note of her baggy khaki pants and long-sleeved striped shirt. Toss on a beret and she'd look like a colorful mime.

He shifted his gaze back to the highway. Best he stayed focused. He'd overslept because of the painkiller he'd taken, and his leg ached from the second he got out of bed. Though he'd been late picking Anna up, she hadn't complained. But the painkiller had left him tired and in no mood for conversation. A day when shuffling papers might have been better. Yet Anna chatted away with him, seemingly unaware of his short answers.

His hasty plan of being kind to Anna had fallen apart before it could even start. Damn this pain. It mangled his mood. In a better frame of mind, he might have laughed at her cute little salute as they'd left his apartment. *Is it not enough I'm helping her find this man?*

Of course it wasn't.

"Whoa. What the heck is that place?"

He took in the view of the cityscape and tried to soften the harshness he felt inside. "That is Marburg."

"You mean, the place we're headed?"

This time he glanced over and raised a brow. "That is where you told me to drive to, *ja*?"

She laughed. "*Ja.* I did."

The twinkle of merriment in her eyes made his cranky interior crack. He smiled. His shoulders miraculously relaxed just a little as he sped along the highway headed for the city skyline wrapped around a hillside.

Anna watched out the front window, eyes wide, as if this place were something remarkable. Not another old German city. "Is that a castle?"

"Yes." Okay, he had to admit, this city was an impressive sight. Rising in layers along the hillside, the new city served as the base, topped by the old part of town. Everything culminated at the hilltop, with the University Cathedral and the castle topping off the peak. Like the cherry on a sundae.

"It is Landgrave Castle."

"I'd love to see it."

"The castle is in the upper town. Our destination is on the outskirts of town."

"Oh." Her shoulders slumped and she leaned back in her seat.

Her disappointment made him feel bad. Maybe he would take an extra dose of the non-sleepy pain meds and see how his leg felt once they finished with their visit and how they were doing on time.

They drove in silence for about a minute or two. She glanced at his cane, resting between the bucket seats. "Your cane is so unusual. Do you mind if I look more closely?"

"Not at all."

She reached for it. As she ran her delicate hand along the rich ebony wood to the smooth brass handle, he noticed she no longer wore her wedding band.

His mind whirled with possible reasons she'd removed it: her fingers were swollen or she'd simply forgotten to wear it. She never mentioned her husband in their conversations, oddly.

He was about to ask what her husband did for a living when she said, "The tiger head on the handle is so detailed."

"A man in northern Italy made it. Belonged to my father." Josef remembered when his father had brought it home after being hurt on an assignment. "My father said he picked that one because tigers are fearless, like him."

"What did he do?"

"A reporter for the BBC. He often went to the Middle East. Iraq. The injury that caused him to buy that cane was caused by a roadside bomb."

"He was lucky he only got hurt."

"Yes." A decades-old force clutched his heart, not enough for tears but enough to remember the sadness. "Later, he wasn't so lucky."

"You mean he got killed there?"

He nodded, but the resentment he had for his father's choice to put work above all else always hit Josef like a smack to the center of his chest.

"I'm so sorry. He must've been very committed to his job."

"*Ja.*" What drove his father down such a path? True fearlessness or running from something, like family responsibilities or deeper issues?

The dichotomy in Josef's own life again rose to the surface. How badly he wanted to be like his father, but resented his father at the same time. How had he spent most of his life oblivious to the intricacies of their relationship, and now he thought about it too much? Bah! Why did this have to hit him now?

As he focused on the road, Anna carefully rested the cane back where she'd found it. He glanced over, his attention briefly settling on her empty ring finger.

Their eyes met, and she stared at him for a split second before turning and looking out the window. They continued toward Marburg in silence, but the air carried the weight of a hundred questions between them.

* * * *

Anna glanced at the GPS, the knots in her stomach twisting tight. "Just a few more minutes until we get there. I feel a bit anxious."

"Anxious?" Josef briefly looked her way then back out the windshield. "Why?"

"What if this isn't him?" Yesterday's revelations about her missing roots possessed her all night. She'd ended up back on her computer at midnight, reading stories of Americans like her who'd learned about long-lost relatives from Europe who left behind not only their family and friends, but faith, too. One article she'd found told of a woman who'd searched out the roots of her once-Jewish family by taking a trip to the town where they'd lived in Poland.

He shrugged. "If not, we will try the others. It could take a few tries. You were given very little information to begin your search."

"I know. I… You're right."

She sat quietly a few seconds, wondering why today felt different. Yesterday's research and talk with Dr. Walker had left her with some powerful feelings. Isaak's story collided with some missing chunks of her own life. What if the course of history had changed? What if her ancestors had left Poland but entered America as proud Jews, who brought their religion and customs to a new land? She'd have been raised differently, perhaps even found another bond with Isaak in their common faith.

She glanced Josef's way. He concentrated on easing off the highway exit. Would he want to know about her life, or even care? Then again, maybe a little openness on her part would make him feel more comfortable with her.

"Yesterday, I was thinking about my ancestors from Poland. They immigrated to America, probably at the turn of the century."

He stopped at a traffic light off the ramp and turned her way. "Oh? So you are of Polish lineage?"

"On my dad's side. I've been told the family who moved to the States were Jewish, but they must've changed their faith when they left Europe. That's all I know about them."

"I imagine those who leave for America do so for many reasons. But always for a fresh start."

"Yes. I mention it because I think that's why I feel like I have more at stake with this visit." He lifted his brows, seemingly interested, so she continued. "I keep thinking what it must've been like to be Jewish around the war. Or even before it. My readings have shown Jews were persecuted over centuries."

"Yes." He shook his head. "It is hard to understand such prejudice. I am sure when you think about your family, it makes this more personal."

Their eyes met and his softened, showing empathy for what she'd disclosed. "Yes. It does."

The car behind them tooted. He glanced up at the changed light and slowly took off. "But you still need to be patient. It may take a few tries to find Gunther. More than a few."

"That's not what I want to hear."

"Maybe not, but it is… Oh, what is the word?"

"Annoying?"

He frowned. When he glanced over, she smiled so he'd know she was joking and, to her relief, he laughed. "No. Realistic."

They turned down a street and parked in front of a simple one-story house with peeling paint.

"We are just outside of the city." He shut off the car. "We may find fewer English speakers in these parts. I will introduce us, explain why we visit."

"Sounds good."

They approached the front door and knocked. Within a minute, a woman with long gray hair opened the door.

She didn't smile but gave them a no-nonsense eyebrow raise and said something in German.

Josef smiled. Anna had no idea what he said, but within seconds the woman smiled back and nodded.

After they talked for a minute, he turned to Anna and said, "She doesn't speak English. May I show her the photo?"

Anna passed it over. While they discussed matters and looked back and forth between the photograph, she strained to figure out what they were saying to no avail.

Josef finally turned to her. "She is getting a photograph of her father but says this is not him. He is in a nursing home. Aside from the man's missing arm, her father served in the *Wehrmacht* the year this was taken."

A wave of disappointment crashed at Anna's feet.

The woman returned holding a dated picture of another Gunther Hinzmann, working in his family bakery after the war ended. He definitely wasn't the man they were looking for.

Josef glanced at Anna. "Do you have anything else you'd like to ask her?"

"No. Please tell her I appreciate her time."

Josef translated and the woman nodded.

Anna smiled. "*Danke schön*."

She walked towards the car ahead of Josef as the weight of disappointment pulled down her mood.

At the car, she leaned against the hood to wait while he carefully made his way along the slate walkway.

Josef neared the car and stopped in front of her. "Nobody said this would be easy."

"So? That doesn't mean I can't be disappointed."

He raised his brows. "No. You can. But I'm going to stay positive."

With his floundering moods, she never would have expected such a comment. Though she wasn't sure where it came from, she accepted the dose of optimism. "And I suppose you'd be right."

"I am. It is our first try," he added. "We will have luck maybe next time. Besides"—he motioned over his shoulder toward the city and turned back to her—"it frees up our time to go see the castle."

"But you sounded like you didn't want to go before."

"I cannot walk much, but will do my best."

She smiled, and his eyes softened. Had simply handing a little bit of her trust Josef's way earlier relaxed them both? "Are you sure?"

He walked to the driver's door, watching her with a playful sparkle in his crystal blue eyes. "Better get in or I will leave without you."

Chapter 12

Josef stood near the doors to the *Oberstadt* lift in the commercial district of Marburg, an easy way to reach the old upper city. Midday traffic zoomed by past him, but he kept watch on Anna until she reached the entrance to the road leading to the same place.

He yelled out, "Are you sure you don't want to take the lift?"

She twirled around, smiling bright. "Positive. I want to see the city from the ground up. So all I do is follow this street uphill, right? I'll get to the same place as if I took the lift."

"Eventually. Yes."

She shot him a thumbs-up.

Before she could even take a single step, he shouted one final warning. "Do not get lost."

She tilted her head and plopped a hand on her slim hip. "Like I would do that on purpose."

"I meant, do not wander."

Tours required he monitor his flock of passengers like a herding dog tracks sheep. He took his job seriously. Anna brought out a different type of protective. One he struggled to define. "The road leads into the market square. Meet me at the fountain."

"Got it." She didn't look back as she stepped away and disappeared around the bend.

He tapped the lift button. When the doors opened, he boarded with a few people who looked like students from the nearby university. Once at the top, he exited and followed a hallway taking him to the *Obserstadt*'s cobblestone streets, as though he'd traveled in time when compared to the modern paved roads on the street below.

On his way to the fountain of St. George, he took slow steps, using care on the smoothed, uneven stones. He admired the crooked, half-timbered houses and medieval atmosphere of the old city, last seen by him on a weekend away during college.

He arrived at their meeting point. Mounted high on the horse, St. George held a spear aimed straight at a dragon, struggling for release while pinned beneath the horse's hooves. The mythical beast's ferocious face proved he still had some fight in him. A fate Joseph understood. He'd be damned if this pain got the best of him. Not yet.

He leaned against the fountain's edge, resting his cane there and lighting a cigarette. He'd wanted one in the car, but hesitated because he'd never seen Anna smoke, so he didn't light up. Just as well, because he'd have to quit again. Someday. After his leg healed.

Tourists wandered in the area, snapping photos and stopping in the local shops. The students were easy to pick out in the busy square, usually simply hanging out with their friends. Lively, young adults, unencumbered by the many burdens adults faced later in life. He longed for those days.

"I made it." Anna approached, smiling, perhaps over her accomplishment.

"So you did. How was your walk?" He pushed himself away from the edge and went down the steps.

"Nothing short of amazing. It's like stepping into a fairytale."

As he neared her, the smoke from his cigarette drifted her way and she stepped back, away from it.

He took one more drag and tossed the cigarette into an iron ashtray stand. "Do you not approve of cigarettes?"

"I'm just not a fan, for myself." She shrugged, gave him a quick smile.

He went up the steps and grabbed his cane. "I had quit for a long time. Recently, I started up again."

"It happens. Hopefully when you're ready to quit again, you will have the same success." She tucked one side of her hair behind her ear. "Thank you for taking me into town. It's awesome."

"You are welcome. You're right about this place. It does feel like we're in a fairytale up here, compared to the newer parts of town. The Grimm brothers actually went to the university here."

"Are you kidding?"

"Do I kid?"

"Not from what I've seen."

She laughed and he did, too, because he'd forgotten how to laugh at himself lately. "Touché."

Her smile faded, but merriment still showed in her eyes. "I'm teasing, you know?"

"I know."

Seeming satisfied, she turned in a circle, her eyes going wide as she took in the square. "So this is the upper town. I feel like I'm back in the seventeen or eighteen hundreds and should be wearing a long hooped dress, with a fancy hat decorated with ribbons and feathers. And you." She scanned him from top to bottom. "You should be wearing a jacket with tails and a top hat, and you've already got a classy cane."

He blurted out a laugh. "Not once have I thought about this as classy."

"Because you weren't using your imagination."

The shift in her mood and excited glow in her eyes was everything he'd wished to see by offering her this side trip. A fact he didn't realize until this very moment. "Mine is boring. I would rather see what you envision."

"I suppose we might have ridden a carriage into—" A loud chime rang through the air as the gothic town hall clock noisily struck the noon hour. She turned to the sound just as a trumpeter statue beneath the clock began to rotate and toot.

"Would you look at that," she whispered and pulled her cell phone from the pocket of her baggy khakis. After she snapped a few pictures and waited for the full twelve toots, she turned to him. "Where to now?"

"Lunch?"

"Sure. Then the castle?"

He laughed. Her energy had a hold on him. Contagious, persistent. And endearing. "Yes, some of the town, and then the castle." He motioned up the street. "This way."

At first, she walked at his side, kept his pace. But soon she wandered ahead, disappearing into shops and looking at merchandise while waiting for him to catch up. At her third stop, he found her looking at guidebooks and asking the old man who ran the place if they stocked any books in English.

"Englisch? Nein. Nur auf Deutsch."

Before Josef could translate, Anna grabbed the German guidebook off the stand, pulled a five euro note from her pocket, and handed it over to the shop owner.

As she slipped the purchase into her bag, Josef came up behind her. "You know you just bought a German book?"

"I know." She pivoted around and tossed him a coy smile. "I figured you'd help me read it."

"Oh, did you now?"

"Yup." She looked up and down the street with a grin on her lips. "Where should we eat?"

He pointed down the road. "We're not far from a place I remember from my last trip here."

Turned out, the place was no longer in business. Another place nearby looked good so they took seats at an outside table, and a few minutes later ordered food. While waiting, she flipped through her new book. He enjoyed watching her reactions to the photographs with little exclamations of "Oooh, so pretty" and remarks like "I can't get over how old everything is."

"Look at the organ in the..." She twisted her lips and narrowed her eyes. "Elizabeth-kerch? Did I say that right?"

"Almost. *Kirche* means church. The *ch* and *r* are soft sounds."

She tried a few times and he corrected, but she hung in until saying it perfectly.

She turned the page in the guidebook. "Oooh. The castle view looks incredible." Positioning the book to face him, she pointed to a caption beneath the fortress photo. "What does this say?"

He leaned closer, suddenly very aware of her creamy skin, her lightly floral scent. He cleared his throat and focused on the words. "'Origins date back to around 1000 whereby the Landgrave Castle was counted among the first hill castles in Germany and the starting point for the development of Marburg.'"

"That's old. Back home, anything built in the sixteen hundreds is ancient."

"You are a young country."

She nodded, took back the book, and continued flipping through the pages.

"So, what does your husband do for a living?"

She slowly lifted her head and her cheeks blasted crimson red. "Investment banker. Why?"

"He did not accompany you on this trip. I figured work must keep him busy."

"Yes. I suppose it does." She stared at her open book, so still he was sure she wasn't reading it. Her head slowly lifted and she looked him in the eye. "I didn't want him here and—I can't believe I'm telling you this—but I left New York to get away from him." She paused, blinked back at him for a few seconds. "Two days after I arrived here, I had divorce papers served to him."

Missing ring explained. "Oh. I am sorry."

"Thank you, but no need to be sorry." She closed the guidebook. "It was for the best."

"Were you married long?"

"Two years." She drew in a breath and he waited. "The marriage had—well, he was—it wasn't working out. He had some issues."

The bruise he'd seen on her arm. Her reaction when he asked about it. Another on her thigh. Had her husband hurt her?

A loud wail came from the street.

He turned just in time to see Anna spring from her seat and run to the side of a young boy, maybe around five or six, who'd fallen off his bike. The child lay on his side on the street's smooth stones.

Anna crouched down next to him, helping him into a seated position. "Gosh, I'll bet that hurt."

The young boy's face contorted as tears sprang from his eyes. He spoke to her in German, pointing to his scraped elbow. She responded in English, and though they didn't speak each other's language, the smooth tone of her voice somehow settled him down.

"Where is your mother?" she asked, and he just stared at her.

Josef stood and went over, smiled at the boy. "*Wo ist deine Mutter?*"

The child pointed down the road and answered.

Josef looked at Anna. "His mother owns a shop down the road and is working."

She nodded and gave the boy her attention. "Can you bend it?" She moved her arm at the elbow a few times. The child tried with success. She nodded. "Good."

She motioned for him to come to the table and take a seat. While searching through her bag, she babbled in a soft voice about how she'd fallen off her bike at his age, too. The boy listened, staring curiously at Anna and no longer crying. She removed two antiseptic cleaning wipes and cleaned near the scrape. The boy winced as she carefully dabbed the cut.

Josef soaked in the warmth of such genuine care. For a child she didn't even know. A reaction that seemed, for her, as natural as breathing. He leaned close, made a little joke to the boy, who laughed.

"What's so funny?" Anna wrapped the dirty wipes up in a napkin.

"I just told the boy I think you are like Marburg's own Saint Elizabeth, of the *Elisabethkirche*."

"Why?"

"She dedicated her life to the sick. The reason they built her a church."

"Oh, really?" Her gaze swung between the boy and Josef. "She sounds like a decent person."

Their food arrived. She gave the boy a hug and told him to be careful.

"*Danke, Fräulein,*" he said and smiled.

"You're welcome."

He lifted his bike, hopped on, and took off down the road, good as new.

Anna cleaned off her fingers with another wipe. "Where's this Elizabeth Church?"

"In the main city. We can stop in on the way out, if you like."

"I'd like." She smiled, and his chest lifted with a kind of joy he hadn't felt since his accident.

As they ate, he enjoyed watching her tackle the *Flammkuchen*, devouring the German version of thin-crusted pizza with gusto. The sensation inside his chest lingered, enough so that it couldn't be ignored.

In between bites, they talked about the town, cuisine, and how much she liked being at the guesthouse. But his thoughts were preoccupied with the way Anna had helped the boy. She possessed goodness, neatly wrapped in a protective layer. Guarded and fragile. Fragile and strong. Strong enough to have left a bad marriage.

* * * *

Anna kicked off the covers, crossed the dark bedroom, and pushed open the French doors. The night air rushed inside and cooled her warm skin.

She sat on the mattress edge and reached for her phone. One a.m. She'd gone to bed over two hours ago. Marburg had left her exhausted, yet she still couldn't sleep. Too many questions plagued her since coming back to the guesthouse. Mostly about Patrick's state of mind since he received the divorce summons two days ago.

Keeping her phone shut off didn't stop her from worrying about his anger. It merely avoided the inevitable.

Josef's questions at lunch about her marriage had come out of nowhere. So did her response. She felt a connection to him, though. They both stood in plain sight to the world, concealing their woes with self-made barriers. An occasional lowering of the gate let others in, but only at their discretion. He'd shared about his cane, his father's death and dangerous job. At times with angst on his handsome face. A man with a history and limp, who definitely had a story to tell. So she'd given him a partial truth about the wedding ring and pending divorce. Talking about her physical abuses, though, would be a step too far.

The phone's weight drew attention back to her hand. A simple push of a button and she'd know if Patrick had cooled down or continued raging, but either answer might allow her to sleep. The neon glow of the screen cast an eerie light on her mission, but she ignored the ominous warning, went into settings, and flipped roam to the on position. Soon, her phone bleeped with notifications. Phone calls. Messages. Texts.

Anna held her breath and closed her eyes, the drumbeat of her heart pounding in her ears blending with the pings. When they stopped, she opened her eyes. There were several more missed calls from the day the papers were served, while she'd been at the wine festival. There was also one made an hour ago from her sister.

Before calling Jenna back, she read Patrick's text messages.

How dare you leave me!

You'll be sorry!

I swear, if I get my hands on you, you'll regret it. Answer me, Anna!

I'm sorry.

I'm sorry.

I'm sorry.

Forgive me, Anna. PLEASE

I promise to get help. I love you.

She could practically hear the pleading tone in his voice, see the tears in his eyes, just like every single time he'd spoken those words to her in the past. If she were there, after promising to get help, he'd tenderly take her hand in his and squeeze it as one would a fresh egg, as if his strength were sapped. Pathetic. The madman who'd possessed his body vanished as quickly as he'd arrived.

But even his messages left her mentally battered and his words of love hurt.

Bzzzzz. Bzzzzzz.

The cell phone vibrated in her hand. Jenna's name flashed on the display.

Now what? A pit formed inside Anna's gut as she hit the answer button. "Hi, Jenna."

"Thank God you answered. I've tried a few times but didn't want to leave a message."

"I saw. Was just about to call you. I turned roaming off because I didn't want to hear from Patrick. He left a tirade on my phone."

"I imagine he did. He's very upset. We were just sitting down for dinner an hour ago and he showed up at my door."

A mix of dread and disbelief walloped Anna. "Oh, God. What'd he say?"

"He was in rare form, at least compared to the man I've seen in the past. At first, he acted polite. I asked him to come in. But when I denied knowing where you were, his politeness disappeared. He started screaming. Chuck left the kitchen table and came to the foyer. He forced Patrick back outside, talked to him a while. Seemed to calm him down, and then he took him to a nearby hotel for the night. He didn't trust Patrick staying in our house."

Chuck. A great husband. Genuine, good-hearted, and the type of guy to hand you the shirt off his back. "I'm so sorry, Jenna. Please tell Chuck I'm sorry, too. Patrick is out of his mind! I pictured him smashing pictures around our house, or maybe burning my clothes. Never did I dream he'd go to Texas."

"Yeah, imagine my shock when I opened the door. He'd called the house twice before this. Of course I told him I didn't know where you were."

"Besides outraged, how'd he seem?"

"Tired, but I couldn't garner any sympathy for him. My God, Anna, what's wrong with him? This isn't the man who came to family functions or walked down the aisle with you. But it did remind me of how strange I thought he was acting at Christmas."

"Well, getting him there was a struggle." He'd agreed to the holiday visit on a good day back in early November. As the trip had neared, he'd complained they wouldn't be alone for Christmas and twice threatened to cancel the tickets. Anna stayed quiet, always on her best behavior so he had no reason to make her miss the family holiday. But as the day to leave neared, he'd been tense and his anger easily provoked.

"I noticed Patrick was constantly at your side," said Jenna. "Had an arm around you or held your hand. Almost…" Jenna sighed. "Possessive."

"I know. A week before our Christmas visit, we went to his Christmas party. He started an argument the second we got in the car to go home, insisting one of the waiters was flirting with me. When we got home, he punched me in the stomach, knocking the wind out of me."

Her belly shook, as if it happened days ago, not months. The pain. His anger. The terror as she lay on the bed gasping for air, anticipating another strike. What a fool she'd been for not fighting back. For not admitting this was a problem sooner. For not leaving him then.

She took a steadying breath. "I'll bet he didn't want me to be alone with any of you during the holiday visit. Afraid I'd tell you."

"Oh, sis." Jenna's voice cracked. "I wish you'd told me what he was doing sooner."

She swallowed down the hard lump in her throat. "I don't know why I stood for his mistreatment for so long. I just kept hoping he'd change. God, Jenna. Is something wrong with me?"

"No. You're a victim, Anna."

A tear ran down her cheek. A victim. The word carried a pitiful ring.

"Listen, after you called me from the airport, I talked to a counselor at a battered woman's shelter."

Tears flowed, blurring her vision. She sniffled them back enough to quietly ask, "It's a call I probably should've made. What'd the counselor say?"

"That it isn't uncommon for abusers to turn on charm to lure you to them, then show their true colors once married or in a committed relationship. Every case is different. The abuse may start gradually or happen right away. And these men, they're always sorry afterward. Very sorry. Life returns to normal, and they act perfect. Until the next offense."

Anna stood and took a tissue from a box on the desk and wiped her nose. "You just described his pattern. How could I have been so blind?"

"Love is why," she said, her tone tender, filled with empathy. "He tells you he loves you, right?"

"Yes. Very much so." Her chest ached. His many messages of love came in abundance, feeling more like burdens as time passed. For if she'd left him, he would be hurt, and she couldn't hurt someone who loved her so much, trusted her… "I'm a fool."

"Don't be so hard on yourself, Anna. You're on your way out of this mess."

"Yes. But I ran off so I didn't have to face him. Now he's bothering my family." She needed to fix this before he showed up at her parents' house. "Maybe I should leave Germany."

"No! You should stay put. Something tells me the farther away you are right now, the better." A ping sounded in the background, then Jenna said, "Chuck sent a text. He's checked Patrick in at the airport Ramada Inn."

"Tell him he's the best brother-in-law in the world."

"Will do, honey," she said softly. "Hey, nobody knows where you are except me, right?"

"Just my neighbor's attorney, but I can't imagine he'd tell anyone."

"Why? Does he know about Patrick's problems?"

"No. Isaak's note to me was private, and Patrick wouldn't think to ask the lawyer. He has no idea Isaak left me money or even asked me to find this man for him. Plus, the inheritance will go into a new account I opened in my name only."

"What about the money for this trip?"

"The expenses for Germany are being paid through Isaak's estate by his lawyer."

Her sister stayed silent for a long moment.

"What's wrong?" Jenna tended to overthink everything, although it wasn't a bad thing right now.

"Did anybody see you leaving with your luggage?"

"No. Not a soul. Really, I think you're being paranoid."

Her sister sighed. "You're probably right."

"I'm more worried he'll fly out to Washington to see Mom and Dad."

"Chuck encouraged him to return to New York."

But the idea hung in the air, an anvil that might drop any second.

"It's late here. Guess I should try to get some sleep. I love you, Jenna. Thanks for being there for me."

"Love you, too."

They hung up. For a long minute she sat on the bed, debating if she should call her parents. She'd have to confess everything. And while she hoped they'd support her, the young teenage girl inside her had never let go of their lack of support when they brought a stranger into their home. A foster boy who'd brought his troubles with him that he passed on to Anna. And her parents had expected her to be understanding.

Resentment rose inside her, brewing for decades. She didn't want them to question her judgment. Suggest she work harder at giving Patrick support or a second chance. She'd given him more chances than she could count. So for now, she'd wait. Until she felt strong enough to fight back if they didn't trust her judgment.

She shut off the phone's roaming and returned it to the nightstand.

But her mind raced with a new problem. Patrick wasn't acting as she'd hoped, by seeing the reason in her decision to end their marriage. Instead, his anger appeared to be escalating, not calming down.

Chapter 13

"Josef?" The young redheaded nurse stood at the door holding a folder against her chest.

He rose from the chair, steadying himself with his cane. As he neared, she smiled sweetly. Before the crash, he'd have flirted with such a pretty woman. But in his condition, he figured she smiled out of pity.

"Sorry we're running so late," she said. "Dr. Weber had an emergency early in the day."

The hour delay had him one step from breathing fire, but he stuffed it deep down and nodded. "Not a problem." He hurried past her, despite the constant pulse in his leg from overdoing it this week. Between the sightseeing in Marburg, and a full day yesterday going to Wörrstadt, and Gau-Bickelheim to meet two more men, he'd pushed his leg's endurance. At the time, he hadn't minded. Now he paid the price.

She guided him to the office where he waited another twenty-five minutes, becoming increasingly furious as the clock ticked. His blood roiled beneath his skin with each passing second while the pain in his leg increased incrementally.

At long last, the doctor entered the examining room, appearing relaxed and happy since he hadn't spent half his morning waiting for someone. "Hello there, Josef. How have you been?"

"I'd be better if I could say goodbye to this cane once and for all."

Dr. Weber nodded as he bent his balding head to read Josef's chart. He grunted and glanced up. "So, you're not feeling any better?"

"*Nein*. Though I walked too much yesterday."

"Do the medications help at all?"

"Sometimes."

The doctor frowned. "Femoral shaft fractures like yours usually heal in four to six months. You are on the tail end. I had hoped by having you use the cane we would see some relief of your discomfort and faster healing."

The doctor performed an examination, moving Josef's leg in different directions, which only added to the dull ache he'd had upon entering. While the doctor re-examined an X-ray taken after the surgery, Josef tipped back his head, closed his eyes, and bit back his discomfort.

Dr. Weber placed a hand on Josef's shoulder. "I am going to recommend two things. There is a colleague of mine in Frankfurt I want you to see. I will send over your X-rays to her office to see if I have missed something about your physical condition." He walked to the window and looked out for a second, then turned around. "How are you otherwise, Josef?"

"You mean work? Because I hate working in the office."

"I know. You told me last time. No, I don't mean work. I meant personally. Accidents of the kind you went through can do more than physical damage."

Josef stiffened. "What are you trying to say?"

His voice softened. "A life was lost. Survivors often go through a variety of emotions. How are you handling things emotionally?"

"Just fine."

The doctor's expression didn't change. "Is there anybody at home you can talk to about what happened the day of the crash? Sometimes getting out the details can help."

"What details?" His voice rose and the dam of his restraint broke through. "I don't remember anything. NOTHING!" He clenched his fists and sucked in a breath, but his voice trembled as he continued. "I can't remember a damn thing. Possible driver's error, the accident report said. How can I not blame myself for that poor woman losing her life?"

The doctor frowned. "Yes. I am sure it is hard. And an understandable reaction." He turned to the counter, scribbled on a pad, and came over to Josef holding out a piece of paper. "This is another colleague of mine. I think you should go see him, too."

Josef read the note. *Henrik Gottlieb, Psychologist*. Josef cringed. Helga would be thrilled.

"It is not uncommon for physical pain to come from a deeper, more emotional place. You are carrying a large burden right now. My suggestion, deal with the emotional stress and you may find your physical healing is faster."

"You must be kidding—"

"Josef." The doctor frowned. "We will still look at the physical, too. The front desk can get phone numbers for both doctors. From my experience, the procedure done by the doctor in France should have made the injury less painful by now. To ignore any possible solution wouldn't be right, now would it?"

Josef shook his head, thanked the doctor, and left with the two referrals. At the front desk, he got the phone numbers. Half his day, wasted and in pain. He just wanted to be alone. Take his pain medication and go back to bed.

He limped to the tram stop, mulling over Dr. Weber's comments. Talking might help. When he'd confided things to Claudia and his sister, some of the pressure inside his head lifted. But talking to a psychologist? A stranger. It didn't feel right.

He dialed his brother's number. "Gabriel, it's me. I need some advice and you're just the man to give it to me. Want to meet up for lunch?"

They discussed a time and place. Josef shoved his phone into his back pocket, feeling a little better. His little brother always had a sensible outlook on things and could surely help Josef gain some perspective on what the doctor had said.

Within twenty minutes, he arrived back at his apartment. As he tossed off his jacket, he removed his cell phone from the pocket. He remembered turning down the phone volume while at the doctor's office. He pressed the button to turn it back up. That's when he spotted a message. From Anna.

Anna. He'd forgotten all about their appointment to meet today. He glanced at the time. Two hours ago. He pushed play.

"Josef. It's Anna. Um, well, we were supposed to meet today. Over an hour ago. I hope everything is okay. Guess we can reschedule."

Verdammt! He'd been so caught up, he forgot. He quickly dialed her number and it rang until finally going into a voice mail. He left a message and explained about the appointment, but he felt terrible. Lately, he'd been enjoying the time they'd been together and had even looked forward to today's trip.

He tried a second time, got the message again, and hung up. Maybe she wasn't near her phone. He dialed the main guesthouse number. Joachim checked her room and the grounds but couldn't find her.

Now he had another thing to feel crappy about. Well, he'd surely talk his brother's ear off today.

* * * *

"I never think of curry as a spice in German food." Anna speared another piece of pork sausage lathered in a curry-spiced tomato sauce, this chef's version of the dish better than the one she'd eaten at the wine festival.

Otto helped himself to more. "They say a woman named Herta Heuwer, who owned a food kiosk in West Berlin, created this back in '49. She supposedly acquired some English curry powder from soldiers stationed in the British sector of the occupied city."

"I had heard it was Hamburg." Ruth had on her sunglasses and had her head turned in the direction of the crowds in the square. "And not in '49, but in '47."

Anna braced herself for a healthy discussion by these two great academic minds about the food, but instead Otto laughed. "You might be right, my dear," he conceded as he popped in another bite.

Thank God she'd bumped into Ruth and Otto. After she'd been unable to reach Josef, they'd invited her to lunch. She worried about him. Up until now he'd been mostly punctual, but a message she received while on the tram ride into this part of town had said his appointment ran late. She'd buried her disappointment and hoped he was okay.

Ruth and Otto had suggested this café in Kirschgarten Square in the old city of Mainz. The lunch crowd bustled along the cobblestone pavement surrounded by half-timbered houses and the warm midday sun warmed the cooler morning air.

While they ate, Ruth and Otto shared places she should see in Mainz, like its stunning cathedral, and a museum dedicated to hometown boy Gutenberg, inventor of the printing press back in the 1400s. She considered herself lucky to land in such a pretty town with such interesting history.

Thirty minutes later, Ruth and Otto left to hear a lecture at the university. Anna ordered another cup of coffee and took in the view. She pushed aside her troubles in New York, always hovering close by, and people-watched, enjoying the way both young and old traversed the town square. Some in a hurry, others slow, like they had the day off.

Not too far away, a large tour group moved through the square. They all wore colorful, matching tie-dyed T-shirts, making them stand out against the rest of the crowd. She guessed they were retirees based on their appearances. A guide waved his hand for them to keep following as he spoke in English into a microphone about the square's history. As they passed, Anna smiled at the words *Woodstock Wanderers* on the back of their shirts. Their ages and shirt design suddenly made sense.

Several minutes later, when the umbrella no longer offered shade, she reached into her purse for her sunglasses.

Her hand grazed her cell phone. She pulled it out, flicked on the roaming in case her sister had tried to call again. After last night's call about Patrick's visit halfway across the country to find her, she held her breath.

The pings of incoming messages made her heart race, but she bravely faced them as they popped onto the screen. All were from Patrick.

Please, Anna. I'm worried about you.
Are you okay? Please call me.

I'll go for help, I promise.

I still love you. All I want is to know
you're safe, hold you in my arms. Come
on, babe. You know I love you.

He was worried? A brick dropped from the wall she'd built around her emotions on the day she'd filed for divorce. Just one brick. All it took to make her foundation shaky.

She didn't want him worried about her. No matter what he'd done, she hated to add to another person's grief.

She typed:

Please don't worry about my safety. I
am fine, but I need this time away.

For a very long minute she debated. She considered the outraged man who'd shown up at her sister's house. But was this really about her safety or more manipulations so she'd give in to him? She erased the message and turned off the phone. This was how he'd always gotten her. Playing straight to her heart. Not this time.

As she tucked the phone back into her purse, she removed her wallet to pay the bill. She unzipped the coin pocket and fished out a euro, but one finger looped around a band. Her wedding band. Hidden away with Ruth's encouragement and banished from the light of day since that evening.

She reluctantly removed the ring. The day Patrick had slipped this on her finger he'd stared longingly into her eyes. Oh, the power in those eyes, making her forget they were surrounded by family and friends while love inside her heart exploded with the joy of a fireworks finale.

The sounds of the nearby diners faded as she lowered the ring and secured it at the base of her finger. No fireworks this time. Only a reminder of what happened mere days after they'd returned from their honeymoon. The first time he lost control.

All over a jar of jelly she'd forgotten to add to her shopping list. He'd pinned her shoulders against the kitchen wall, demanding she go back out and buy some, refusing to release her as she cried out in pain. Not the worst thing he'd done to her, but the first step in both the mental and physical abuse he employed to tear down her self-esteem. One piece at a time, until she began to question herself.

A tear slid down her cheek. She yanked off the ring and stuffed it back in the purse compartment. One by one she ticked off the moments that had solidified her decision to file for divorce. Horrible memories that still made her belly tremble. The same moments that guided her to the lawyer's office. And now he'd been served. She inhaled deeply, expanded her lungs to their fullest, owning every bit of the pride she deserved.

The next step? Facing him. Even though her lawyer assured her she wouldn't have to talk to him if she chose not to, she *needed* to look him in the eyes. Bravely. Without fear. Otherwise, she'd spend the rest of her life looking over her shoulder, fearful he might appear.

A metamorphosis had started the day she walked out, though she wasn't quite there. But she'd faced Josef and his moods when they'd first met. And she'd been strong enough to not respond to the pleas of Patrick each time he called or texted. Every day, she grew a little stronger, a little more like the woman she used to be. Yet what happened just now showed how easily what she'd built could come crumbling down.

* * * *

Josef blinked as he stared outside. What had he just seen?

"You haven't been yourself since the accident," Gabriel said, tuning Josef back to their conversation.

"Yes, but a therapist? As if my pain is all in my head and this stranger will make it go away."

Again, Josef's gaze drifted out to the patio. He hadn't noticed Ruth, Otto, and Anna sitting out there until the older couple had stood to leave. Anna remained at the table alone, staring at her phone. Then she'd taken out a ring and slipped it on. As he watched her, she frowned and closed her eyes, so sad the pain seeped into his chest. The guilt of what he'd done to her this morning crawled back under his skin.

He slowly tuned back into his brother's words. "What?"

"I said, I am sure it isn't in your head, but…" Gabriel narrowed his eyes. "You aren't even listening. I thought you wanted to talk about this."

"I'm sorry. What did you say?"

Gabriel pursed his lips. "Maybe what the physician said, it couldn't hurt. Helga talked to me the other day."

He again glanced out the window. Was she crying?

"….and our mental and physical well-being is often tied together."

Josef snapped his attention back to his brother.

"The doctor's advice could be sound. Why not give it a try? But if not a professional, talk to Helga or me whenever you need to. It's never good to keep things bottled up. And maybe after a while, the idea of talking to a professional will feel more right."

"A good point. Maybe I just need to get comfortable talking more. I really have been trying. Thanks for listening."

Josef already felt better. Gabriel could be counted on for his honesty. He was as sensible as Josef was impulsive. Even in their attire, with Gabriel in his suit and Josef in khakis and a rugby shirt. And yet, the respect they had for each other bonded them.

Gabriel smiled and patted Josef's shoulder. "It is what brothers are for. I have to get back to the office." He stood and dug twenty euro from his wallet.

Josef held up his hand. "My treat. I'm going to stay and have another cup of coffee."

"Thanks. Next time, I pay. Hey, don't forget to let me know if you are bringing anyone to the wedding."

"Tell her I'm coming alone."

"I will. But if you change your mind, you have a little time before we notify the restaurant."

Gabriel walked out and passed by Anna's table. Josef's gaze drifted to her as she wiped her cheeks with her fingers. She had been crying. He looked away, giving her the private moment. But restlessness over what he'd done to her today made him get up, gather the check, and pay the bill.

Once outside, he approached her table. From here he could see her puffy eyes. He briefly considered she might not want company, but a gravitational pull propelled him forward.

When he stopped at the table, she looked up.

"Oh. Hi." She didn't smile the way she usually would. "I didn't expect to run into you here. Was everything okay this morning?"

"Yes. I—I…" Her somber expression ruffled something inside him, but he managed to say, "I was having lunch with my brother inside and saw you here. I came over to apologize for missing our appointment."

The tense muscles of her face softened. "Well, thanks. Don't worry about it."

"I really am sorry."

Her lips tightened, and she shook her head. "Trust me, I'm used to apologies, and yours sounded sincere." Her eyes watered, and she blinked the wetness away. "You're forgiven. You couldn't help what happened."

Used to apologies? What did that mean? "Mind if I have a seat?"

"Not at all. I'm finishing my coffee."

As she looked out at the square while sipping her coffee, he sat and rested his cane on the ground. "Why are you used to apologies?"

She looked at him, her dark eyes perfectly still, giving away not a single hint about what she might be thinking.

Uncomfortable, he averted his eyes to the table. They stopped at her folded hands. The ring that caused tears had been removed. He flicked his gaze back to her face.

She narrowed her eyes. "What were you just looking at?"

"Nothing." Though he expected she knew what he'd been looking at.

Her cheeks flushed pink. "Were you watching me from inside?"

She deserved his honesty. "Yes. I saw you put your ring on. Now I see it is off."

She blew out a soft sigh. "I was thinking about my husband—you know, the soon be to ex. The ring came out of hiding in a moment of weakness. He sent me a text, begging for forgiveness. But he's been sorry too many times in our marriage." She immediately put her hand on his. "Your apology and reason for giving it was fine. I'm just a little burnt from hearing it so often from my husband. That's all."

"For what does he want forgiveness?"

She leaned back in the chair and sighed heavily. "He—well, he'd overreact to things all the time and… Our marriage just wasn't happy." Her eyes watered. "It doesn't matter. Like I said, he'll be my ex soon."

He nodded. "I see. I promise if I am going to be late again to let you know. The news I got today wasn't great. Guess that is why I got lost in my own thoughts, forgot our appointment."

The tenseness on her face softened. "I'm sorry you got bad news. Want to talk about it?"

Compassion in her voice almost made him want to talk. Yet, he couldn't admit to her that a doctor just told him he was a head case. Besides, if he told her what had happened in the accident, she would never get in his car again. And he wanted her in his car. Those rides with her were helping him feel almost normal at times, at least behind the wheel.

"They are stumped why I'm not healing better," he said, kind of half-truthfully. "Not exactly what I wanted to hear."

"I'm sorry. Nothing is worse than not feeling like yourself. Believe me, I understand. I imagine you're anxious to return to your old job. It's hard not being able to do what we love."

"Yes. What do you love to do?"

She smiled, a tender smile that reached her eyes. "Write. Luckily, it's my job."

"What is it you write?"

"A syndicated column, for several major market newspapers in the States, called *Kindness Connects*."

As she talked about it, he pulled out his cigarettes, remembered their conversation about smoking two days ago and tucked them away.

"Anyway, writing the column has been very rewarding."

"And now *you* are helping someone."

She looked up and her brows rose. "Oh, you mean looking for Gunther?"

"Of course. Isaak is lucky to have you to do this for him."

"I never thought about it that way. I'm more focused on what Gunther did for Isaak. Did I mention that I'm writing about this trip for my column?"

"No."

"I'm pretty excited about the idea. I believe what happened years ago is a story worth sharing."

"I couldn't agree more." Something she'd said earlier still rang in his ears. "You mentioned that you don't feel like yourself sometimes. Do you mind if I ask what you mean?"

She furrowed her brows, such deep concentration it seemed as if the question suddenly meant everything to her. "My life for a couple of years has left me disconnected and confused. Feeling like I have no control…" Her voice drifted and eyes watered. "Probably because I can now see that my husband held all the power in our lives. But now I'm taking my power back."

"That must feel good." He understood that need. Gabriel's advice moments ago returned and Josef blurted out, "Control is what I am missing, too. Because of the accident." The weight of the truth lodged in his throat, but he swallowed it down. "I—I do not remember what happened that caused the car to crash."

"What do they think caused it?"

"I swerved, but they do not know why. They speculate to avoid something, but..." He stopped himself from telling her about Lily's death. He liked that she'd opened up to him and hadn't minded sharing some of his sorrows. But revealing he'd caused a death went a step too far. At least today, when so much more rested on his mind. "My hope is that if I remember, it will restore the loss of control I have felt since that day."

The words, spoken aloud to someone who carried her own form of pain, helped him make sense of the frustration eating away at him since he woke from the crash.

She didn't speak right away, only watched him with a thoughtful expression. "It's kind of ironic, isn't it?"

"What?"

"How you want to remember, but I wish to forget." Her eyes watered, and she looked down at her hand, the one that had held the ring.

He wanted to reach out, touch her pale cheek, make her feel better. Instead, he asked, "What do you want to forget?"

She looked his way, blinked away the wetness making her eyes glisten, and the corners of her mouth lifted. "Let's talk about something else. I've got an idea. I'm about to look around town. Otto and Ruth suggested I see the Gutenberg Museum, the Mainz cathedral, and the stained glass windows at St. Stephen's. Care to join me?"

In the short time he'd been talking to her, he'd forgotten all about the ache in his leg. "Sure. This is my hometown, you know. I'm happy to give you the deluxe tour."

She smiled, more brightly than before. "The deluxe tour? Guess it's my lucky day."

He returned her smile but knew he was the one who was having a lucky day.

Chapter 14

Josef walked unsteadily from his bedroom to the kitchen as the ache in his leg pulsed with furious reminders of his injury, denying him the sleep he craved. He dumped two ibuprofen from a bottle and opened the refrigerator door.

A container of yesterday's leftover pasta sat alone on the center shelf. He heated it up in the microwave and plunked down at the tall stool next to the peninsula with a fork, pushing the pills to the side.

As he ate, he gave in to thoughts about the rest of his day with Anna. Another reason he couldn't sleep. Her enthusiasm as they went sightseeing made the Mainz cathedral holier, the Gutenberg Museum more impressive, and the Marc Chagall stained glass at St. Stephen's glow with brighter blues.

Then dinner. Who'd suggested dinner? Right, it was him, when she'd asked him for recommendations on restaurants with authentic food of the region.

They'd gone to his favorite place in Mainz and devoured tender schnitzel with a bottle of dry local German wine. Surrounded by candlelight and rustic timber walls, they'd talked about themselves. An evening he'd never forget, so relaxing and filled with subtle intimacies.

Anna was a great listener and gave thoughtful responses to their topics of conversation. At times she offered wisdom he couldn't see on his own. So insightful, and yet delivered with a gentle hand. It didn't hurt the way she'd watch him with those mysterious dark eyes, and how her fingers twirled her loose curls, making him want to touch the strands to learn if they were as soft as they appeared. Her interest in his adventures made him feel ten feet tall, like he didn't walk with a damn cane. He'd discovered a whole other joy in her contagious laughter while he shared stories of the funnier things that had happened in his travels. At one point, it struck him how he hadn't seen her laughing that much since she'd arrived.

And he'd loved hearing about her life. The passion she had for her work came through when she discussed her early columns, finding an agent, and eventually syndicating in newspapers all over the country. He'd learned about Washington State and where she grew up on Whidbey Island.

Any time he neared the subject of her husband or her marriage, though, she gave a vague answer, then steered him away skillfully as a cattle rancher shifting the direction of his herd.

He ate the last bite of pasta, pushed the plate aside, and pulled his laptop closer. In the search bar he typed *Anna Abrams,* thought for a moment, then added *Kelly,* the name Joachim had said was originally given to him.

Several listings flashed on the screen with her name. He clicked on a link to the *Chicago Tribune.* Anna's photograph appeared on the top of the column. Same heart-shaped face, delicate as a porcelain doll's. Yet the newspaper headshot showed life in her eyes. A glow he hadn't seen until tonight at the restaurant.

A quote beneath the photo read *Never underestimate the power inside of you to change someone's day.* He considered those words. Not once had he moved about his day thinking about his actions in these terms.

After each story heading, there was a quote about kindness or compassion from someone famous like the Dali Lama or Oprah. Anna wrote brilliant opening lines that neatly tied into a message at the story's end.

Even as she spoke last night, one thing had been clear: Anna tried to search for the humanity in everyone she met.

Does she see anything in me?

The idea lingered, and he hoped the answer was yes.

Tomorrow they would visit another name on her list. He wished for her success, because he could see how much it meant to her.

And then a notion struck him smack dab in the forehead... Finding Gunther mattered to him. Her success would be his, too.

The story about Gunther's heroism felt personal to Josef, in ways he couldn't fully understand. Maybe because it mattered to Anna, to Gunther, and his family. But the search had taken a personal twist, leaving him curious and challenged. A new type of adventure.

He had become more than a mere driver. He was a party invested in the outcome.

So this all meant one thing: if tomorrow they did not find Gunther, he would do whatever he could to help her find the man. Beyond the responsibilities handed to him by Claudia. Beyond the scope of his job.

Josef picked up the ibuprofen and went to the sink. As he filled a glass with water and popped the medication, he looked forward to the prospect of getting up in the morning for a change.

* * * *

Anna quivered. Her knees. Her belly. Even her lips. "Pl-pl-please. Stop."

Pain scorched every inch of her skin as strong hands lifted her and slammed her into the refrigerator door.

Numbing pain. In her shoulder. Her neck. Her hip.

Her shaking knees couldn't hold her as she slid to the floor, her body still trembling as she landed. Not from the cool tiles, but from the dark figure looming over her...

Anna's eyes flashed open. Her body trembled and her heart pumped as if she'd run a race. She patted the mattress and found the duvet near her knees and pulled it to her chin. Shivering, she settled beneath the covers.

Morning light streamed through the French door's opaque curtains. She took a deep breath, wishing away remnants of the horrible nightmare. A rerun of an actual event about two months into their marriage. Patrick hadn't wanted her to fly back to Washington for a friend's wedding, but she'd desperately wanted to go and pressed him. That night had taught her one thing about her new life: her wants or needs no longer mattered.

How had she drifted off to sleep more content than she'd been in a long time after a wonderful evening, only to wake to the terror of such abuse? Patrick had pounded his sickness deep inside her soul, the way a chef tenderizes meat, breaking down the toughness. It might take more than leaving their marriage and a month away to forget his torture.

But didn't the awful memories always stay? Didn't the demands of others always supersede her desires? Hadn't she spent her first twenty years trying to please her parents? Dad's job as a social worker would lead to discussions around the dinner table about how lucky they were compared to most people. And then they'd taken in the fifteen-year-old foster boy with a troubled background. A boy who'd cornered Anna, put his hands around her throat…

She closed her eyes but could still hear the response of her parents.

Let's not report this, Anna. They'll send him to a juvenile home. He's a victim of circumstance.

After that, Anna made sure she was never alone with him.

But the message her parents had sent was loud and clear. *If someone less fortunate is hurting, your needs are secondary.*

Only recently had she started to see how, from Patrick's very first strike, her reaction to his violence had been rooted in the same logic. After an "incident"—what she called them in her mind—she'd remind herself of the mistreatment he'd endured growing up. Horrible beatings, followed by mental abuse that made her shudder the first time he'd discussed his father's irrational outbursts. All starting when his mother left both man and boy, never to return.

In their early months of marriage, she vowed she'd never leave Patrick the way his mother had done. Her parents had loved her, never raised a hand. But she *had been* mistreated, in an unsuspecting way. Her parents' message of altruism and forgiveness went a step too far. They loved her, of that she had no doubt. Still, it didn't erase years of a subtle form of neglect where others outside of the family often came first.

A voice carried in the quiet morning air outside the open French door. "Don't be late, my love."

She smiled. Florian. Karen must be leaving for work. Those two lovebirds didn't quit. Anna adored their overt displays of affection, reminding her love wasn't an illusion. It could be real.

In fact, here, she was surrounded by love, of all types.

A fresh, intense love between Florian and Karen.

The compatible, caring love she'd see between Regina and Joachim. Businesslike, but once in a while she'd catch an occasional peck on the cheek or a touch that spoke to their many years together.

And Ruth and Otto, who disagreed on many matters but were never hurtful or personal.

In every case, each couple showed respect for the person they loved.

Yesterday, while she and Josef had walked to the Gutenberg Museum, he'd offered an apology for all the times he hadn't been himself lately. A genuine apology. Not the pitiful, desperate kind Patrick always offered. Though she'd told him it hadn't been necessary, she appreciated he made the overture. But it reminded her of the respect she saw in the relationships around her.

Later, they'd had dinner. Maybe it was the candlelight, or the one-too-many glasses of crisp wine washing down their delicious meal. Or it could've been the way his eyes sparkled as he'd shared his tales of travel, giving her a glimpse into how much he loved seeing the world, not just the risk-taking adventures. But sitting close to him, with their knees touching beneath the table for two, rekindled feelings she'd lost from Patrick's abuse. A desire to be with a man again. Whenever he'd ask her questions, Josef would stare deeply into her eyes while listening. Every so often, his gaze would shift, drop to her lips, and linger a little too long. Each time, unexpected heat rushed through her.

Those hours spent with him made her happy. Fear-free. Craving intimacy. The way she wanted to feel all the time.

She arched her back, stretched her arms above her head, and tossed off the covers. On her way to the bathroom, she paused at the mirror over the dresser. Her eyes were sleepy and her hair a tangled mess. Still, she liked what she saw. A woman more at peace with herself, at least compared to the woman she'd left behind in Brooklyn.

What had Josef seen last night? A desperate woman escaping her problems or a woman who wanted to enjoy life again?

She turned sideways. The tank top she slept in exposed the remains of a bruise she wished would clear faster. She ran a hand lightly over the curve of her shoulder. No pain anymore. Just the shadow of the pain she'd endured that night. Soon it would vanish like the others. But she'd never forget how it felt. Never. Ever.

She turned and faced herself head on. With her hand, she traced the curve of her waist, pressed it flat against her abdomen, smoothed it to her breast. Slowly. Tenderly. The way she deserved to be touched by a man.

A man like Josef.

The thought seemed to come out of nowhere, but she couldn't deny it had been building. A little here. A little there. A lot more last evening.

He had problems and even shared some of them yesterday. Unlike Patrick, he didn't take them out on others. Just the opposite, in fact. Josef held them tightly, as if a strong wind might blow them away and leave him exposed. Be it from pride or privacy, she couldn't tell.

She entered bathroom and turned on the shower. Once inside, Anna tilted back her head and let the steamy water wake her, clearing the way for an excited buzz to ripple beneath her skin as she thought about today's trip to Müden. Another day with Josef. Time would only tell if last night's magic remained. But even if it didn't, she liked feeling this good.

Chapter 15

Anna's pulse raced while Josef spoke to the man at the door in their native tongue, his words fast and consonants strong. Their fourth try. Would he be the one?

She strained her ear, only catching an occasional word like Frankfurt or America, and focused on every smile, nod, and hand gesture for clues as to what they were saying. She didn't even know if his name was Gunther or a relative of the man she'd located in her search.

Maybe it was wishful thinking, but she saw a clear resemblance in this man's eyes to the photograph Isaak left her. This man stood with the door halfway open, blocking half his body on the side where the real Gunther had lost an arm. So she couldn't tell from that clue if this was him, or not.

She gave up on guessing what they discussed and admired the property. The address in Müden, on the outskirts of the small town, was set on a hillside. From the porch of the two-story house, the lawn peppered with several well-cared-for gardens, she enjoyed a view of the Moselle River and the sharp-peaked roofs of houses made with inlaid wood.

"Anna?"

She turned to Josef and he motioned her forward. "This is Siegfried, Gunther's brother."

The old man made eye contact and nodded.

She smiled. "Hello."

Before Josef could tell her more, Siegfried resumed speaking in German, his eyes getting a glassy sheen as he spoke. Josef listened with a frown and softened his tone when he replied.

He turned to her. "His brother has passed away."

"I'm so sorry," she said to Siegfried, and Josef translated.

Her research had been wrong. The records indicated this Gunther was alive, but she'd just learned a lesson in the accuracy of the databases she'd been using.

Siegfried's sadness made her feel horrible for coming here and reminding him of his brother, but she had to ask him one more thing. With a glance to Josef, she said, "Could his brother have been the man who helped Isaak?"

She handed the photo to Siegfried, who listened to Josef's question before scanning the image.

"*Nein.*" He shook his head, then rambled again in German.

No. When she'd set out, a part of her believed this search might be a challenge. Yet she'd hoped in a world of computerized databases and the internet, she'd find her man quickly. But she wasn't a private detective, or someone who understood the nuances of searching through mounds of historical data.

Josef listened to Siegfried's lengthy response. At times the older man's eyes welled with tears. This subject evoked so much emotion in those who'd suffered through the regime's terror. Anna felt horrible about bringing the topic to his day.

Josef finally turned her way. "The photograph isn't his brother. They did live in Frankfurt and knew many Jews, in both their neighborhood and local businesses. But Siegfried said none of them were able to help any of their friends who were in danger. He also wants you to know he admires the man who saved Isaak's life. He only wishes he could have done more in those days. The threats to anybody who worked against the Nazis were very real, making helping others a hard choice."

She glanced to the man, who watched her with a deep frown. She extended a hand. "*Danke schön.*"

"*Bitte.*" He stepped from the door, took her hands in both of his and gave a little squeeze that shot straight to her heart.

Anna stepped off the porch and waited on the walkway while Josef talked a minute more. She tried not to let her disappointment eat away at her. What if the data she used continued to be faulty?

He joined Anna and they walked toward the car. "You okay?" Josef asked quietly.

"Yeah. Thanks." She gave him a fast smile before looking away and getting lost again in her dismay. Maybe this was an insurmountable task. Or maybe Isaak would've been better off picking anybody but her to do this job.

"Josef, *halte durch.*"

Josef stopped and pivoted to the house, where Siegfried still stood at the door. "*Ja*?"

Anna waited while the older man said one last thing, then he waved goodbye and returned inside.

"Siegfried says he just remembered another Hinzmann family in Frankfurt who moved to either Wetzlar or Wiesbaden before the war ended. He cannot recall which."

"I vaguely recall eliminating choices from both of those towns in my research. When we get back, I'll double-check the records to see why."

"Good idea. Your records might even have another address for us to check." He pointed his cane into the distance, toward the town they'd driven through to get here. "But how about later? This is a pretty area to have lunch."

"Sure."

"Don't sound so unhappy." He smiled. "See? One door closed, another opened. Isn't that the expression?"

She chuckled. When had Josef become the most optimistic person in the room? She was glad to have him at her side. "Yup, it's something like that. I'll work on my attitude."

* * * *

Anna took the last bite of her sandwich. At first, lunch had distracted her from her worries about finding Gunther. As she considered how many men with that name showed up in her first search, though, a negative diatribe rambled in her subconscious. There was always a chance none of the men who had matching names were the Gunther she wanted. The hope she'd mustered up when they'd taken a table at the quaint café's outdoor patio withered like a short-lived bloom.

She'd been a fool to think she could find Gunther. If the month passed with no success, what would she do?

She glanced over to Josef. He'd finished his lunch a few minutes ago and stared in the direction of the river. She tried to change the subject weighing her down. "You're a world traveler. Is your country's bread good or all in my imagination?"

"Germans make delicious breads. Possibly the best. And so are our desserts."

She grinned. "Yeah, my waistline is well aware."

He laughed and stretched out his long legs. "Your waistline looks fine to me." The sun passed over the tree they sat beneath. He tilted his head toward the rays, shut his eyes, and lowered his sunglasses.

It didn't take long for the midday heat to make her sweat. Another day of unseasonably warm September weather, according to Josef. She used care pulling both arms from her lightweight sweater and drew the top edges against her collarbone, but left the buttons undone to stay cooler. A quick adjustment of the sleeve near her shoulder ensured her bruise remained covered.

"Are you awake?" she asked quietly.

Josef turned his head her way. "I am."

She motioned to a brick farm building, now turned gift shop and winery, not far from where they sat. "Do you mind if I make a quick stop in there when we're through?"

"Not at all. There is a medieval castle close by we could visit, too. *Burg Eltz*. It would be a shame to waste this beautiful afternoon."

She wanted to get back and do more research, possibly refuel the faith she was starting to lose in her ability to finish this for Isaak. Even take the time to jot down some notes to use in her column. Somehow today's setback seemed worth thinking about, because her column should reflect the challenges of her task.

But an afternoon seeing the sights wouldn't kill her and might even be good for her soul. She hadn't had a relaxing vacation since her honeymoon. "Sure. I guess we could."

"We do not have to. What is the matter?"

"Nothing."

"Nothing, huh?" He lifted his sunglasses to the top of his head and looked her in the eye. "You were too quiet at lunch."

"I'd hoped you wouldn't notice." As he grinned and shook his head, she confessed. "Since we learned today's stop wasn't a success, I've been wondering if Isaak picked the wrong person to find Gunther."

"He did not. You *are* the right one." He flipped back on his glasses and returned to his sun worship. "Look how far you have come. What you are doing is a difficult task. Besides, I will help you research more when we get back to Mainz. Two heads are always better than one." His lips curved into a smile and he looked her way. "Even one as smart as yours."

She smiled. Up until now, she'd believed Josef was simply doing a job for his employer. Knowing he cared enough to want to help her and have this search be a success made her feel happy and less alone in this pursuit. "Thank you. I would like that."

He nodded. "Besides, I think we are getting closer to finding Isaak's friend. A gut call, but I think I am right."

"I hope you're right."

They sat in companionable silence while she marveled in the faith he had in her, used it to dig deep and get her motivation back.

The waitress appeared and said something to Josef.

"*Zwei Pflaumenkuchen, bitte.*" He sat straighter in his chair and turned to Anna while flipping up his sunglasses. "I ordered you a piece of plumcake. Do you want coffee?" She nodded and he added, "*Zwei Kaffees auch.*"

Just as the waitress left, a bee flew in front of Anna's face, startling her. She swatted with both hands. Her sweater slipped, but the persistent bee buzzed near her face. She kept at it until the bee finally flew off. She reached down to her waist, grabbed the sweater, and yanked it over the bruise. As she did, she jerked her head up to look at Josef.

He stared at her shoulder. His gaze slowly drifted to her face.

"Damn bees." Buttoning the top button so the sweater stayed in place, she hoped her scorched cheeks didn't betray her shame.

Pity filled his face as he stared into her eyes, leaving a sting sharper than a bee's.

"Anna," he said quietly. "What really happened?"

Lie. Come on. You've done this before. Only for some reason, this time, the excuses she'd tossed like pennies in a fountain wouldn't pass her lips.

She turned her cheek, afraid to look at him. Afraid she'd see judgment. The way people judged a woman who didn't instantly leave a man who hit her.

Josef moved his chair closer and spoke in a soft voice. "Anna, did your husband do that to you?"

The walls closed in on her. Her chest tightened and belly trembled.

Josef caringly took her hand. Compassion radiated in his eyes, making her want to trust him.

"Y-yes. He did." She swallowed the hard lump in her throat. "He—he's done worse."

Joseph's jaw knotted and anger flashed in his eyes.

She lifted her chin, despite the trembling inside her gut. "Isaak asked me to visit Germany to find this man, but…" A lone tear rolled along her cheek, and she lifted her gaze to find sadness in Josef's expression. "Besides finding Gunther, he wanted me to take this trip for another reason. To get away from my husband."

Josef brushed away the tear. "Isaak sounds like a good friend," he said, his voice tender.

She nodded. "After I filed divorce papers, my lawyer advised me to serve them when I wouldn't be around. I'd never know what would set off Patrick's anger, but there was no doubt the divorce papers would. This trip came at the right time."

Josef flinched, a slight tug at his jaw. "Oh, Anna." The way he spoke her name sounded personal, as if he'd witnessed each strike Patrick ever gave her.

The waitress arrived at the table. As she set down their coffee and dessert, Josef released Anna's hand and sat back, but never took his gaze off her. The whites of his eyes glistened. She greedily drank in his sympathy. Not once after Patrick had hurt her had she been able to find true solace. Only lick her wounds until the next beating.

The waitress left and for a moment, neither spoke. Then Josef took her hand, carefully, as if she were made of glass. "I will listen if you want to talk about it."

A small gesture. But the kind of offer she needed. She told him everything, from learning about Patrick's childhood history of being abused right up to visiting the divorce lawyer.

Josef listened in silence, but every so often she'd catch an angry twitch when she mentioned details about Patrick's mistreatment of her. Yet, not once did he let go of her hand. Not once did he ask why she stayed.

Talking openly scrubbed away more of the humiliation eating away at her soul. Same as when she'd finally told her sister the truth. Proof that if others didn't blame her, it was high time she stopped blaming herself. Only the ability to do so felt just out of reach.

* * * *

Josef placed a hand on Anna's back and waited for her to pass through a doorway inside *Burg Eltz*. They stepped outside onto a concrete patio area resting between two tall turrets.

"What a view." She walked to the chest-high edge and stared out into the forest surrounding the castle.

He went to her side and pointed to a road visible between thick patches of trees. "We drove through that forest."

"Was that when we zigged and zagged on our way here?"

"It was."

Josef had driven the mountain road unhurriedly, carefully. Much like the path Anna steered him down at the end of their lunch. Where he peeked around the dangerous emotional corners of Anna's life. Her brave story pulled him in, cast her in a new light. The sadness of what she endured, though, left him grappling with emotions so raw he didn't know what to do with them. She'd stripped herself emotionally bare for him. Abused, but unwilling to give up. Respect he already had for her overflowed and seeped into the deepest crevices of his soul.

After all she'd been through, everyone received a smile from her, and she didn't dwell on her problems. Instead, she set out to help others with theirs. At one point, while she'd talked compassionately about her husband's past, Josef's reverence for her unfurled. She'd stayed with the man because he needed help. The ultimate in selfless concern.

Anybody could hate or be angry with injustice. It took a bigger person to show compassion.

Meanwhile, these past months, Josef had spent his days dwelling on his mistakes. Complaining, complaining, complaining.

Mein Gott! He could hardly stand himself.

Anna glanced at him and motioned over her shoulder to the others in their tour, who passed through the castle door with their guide. "Should we go?"

"Sure." He smiled to mask the disgust eating away at him.

"Hold on. Stand against the wall so I can take your picture."

He did as she asked while she lifted camera. "Say cheese?"

"*Käse*."

She laughed and took the photo. "I'm guessing that's German for cheese."

"You guessed correctly." He laughed along with her and his sour thoughts vanished.

The tour continued. They walked together, so close that a simple shift of her head would cast a trace of floral fragrance from her shiny hair. Each time their eyes met, his heart would jolt. When she wasn't looking, he'd skim the details of her face and memorize the perfect shape of her lips, the slight slope of her pert nose, or the curve of her slender neck. He half-listened to the castle tour. All his focus stayed on Anna. He wished he possessed one tenth of the compassion she outwardly offered to others. Especially when her personal circumstances could've easily stolen all her hope.

When the tour ended, Josef motioned to a concession stand near the exit. "I need coffee before we get back in the car. Want some?"

"Sure."

"Go ahead and grab a table." He handed her his cane. "Can you take this over?"

"Oh, let me get the coffee."

"Not necessary," he said quickly. "How do you want your coffee?"

"Milk and sugar."

As he waited in line, an overwhelming desire to return to the man he used to be swept over him. He hated the idea Anna felt a need to help him. Like he was elderly. For God's sake, he'd just turned forty-one.

He returned to the table and placed the coffees down, then carefully swung his bad leg over the bench seat. Anna stared out to the surrounding trees, the sun's gleam making her black hair glisten as if dotted with shards of onyx.

She turned to him and wrapped her hands around the cup. "Thanks. Imagine living here? This place is glorious. A far cry from Brooklyn."

He sipped his drink. "New York City has its own special flavor."

"Oh? You've been?"

"Many years ago, a vacation with friends. We visited New York for a week, then flew to Utah to do some hiking through your beautiful national parks." He shifted, bumped his cane and it fell off the table. "Damn this thing." He leaned over, grabbed the hooked top, and lay it on the bench beside him.

She sipped her coffee and watched him over the edge of her cup. "I have a confession to make. When I was in your apartment that day, I glanced at a newspaper article about the accident. A French paper. Is that where you got hurt?"

So, she was looking at the article that day. "Yes."

"I'm sorry. It was nosey. I only caught a glimpse."

"No. It is fine." Trust. She'd handed him hers during lunch. He owed her what he could give. "My sister says I am too… Oh, what is the word? Closed up? Withdrawn?"

She chuckled. "I'd say you are typical of most men. We have to pry things out of you."

"Helga, my sister, thinks this pain in my leg is really in my head."

"Hmmm. I can't imagine it's all in your head."

"No. Me either, but…" He met Anna's gaze. "As the article showed, I was not the only one hurt in the accident. A woman—Lily—she was with me. I met her the night before the crash. We, we hit it off. I had a week off tour. She suggested we drive to Nice to see some of her friends."

He stopped, unable to breathe, as if hands wrapped his neck and cut off air.

Anna slid her soft hand over his.

He managed to inhale and forced himself to speak the words he'd only spoken out loud to a few. "And she—she… She died in the accident."

Anna's eyes watered. "I'm so sorry."

He nodded, but his mouth went dry as he tried to respond. After taking a sip of his coffee, he said, "As I told you the day we saw Mainz, I cannot remember a thing from the crash."

"You did tell me. Still nothing?"

He shook his head. "My last memory is right before the accident, when everything was fine."

Anna watched him, blinking, waiting.

His heart beat wildly, like a marathon runner nearing the end of a long journey. "And no matter how hard I try, I cannot help but wonder what careless thing I might have done to have caused the car to crash. The police don't know either. They did not hold me accountable, but… I should have told you all this sooner. If you no longer wish my services after today, I will understand."

"Oh, Josef." She wrapped both her hands around his and her eyes watered. "You're my partner in finding Gunther, remember? Your driving is fine. You got us up that mountainside. I trust you." She paused and with gentleness in her voice added, "You need to start trusting yourself."

"Easier said than done."

"Don't I know it." She remained quiet for a moment, then added, "It took me a long time to step away from my husband after he'd done some pretty horrible things to me. I suppose I'd lost faith along the way, too."

"But you seem to have a handle on it now."

"Not really. Lately I've been wondering if I like to tend to others all the time to avoid my own issues."

He shook his head. "And my problems, that is all I think about."

"No you don't. You're helping me."

Anna's faith gave him a boost he hadn't expected to feel.

"Maybe we can learn a bit from each other." She tilted her head and her eyes softened with a weak smile. "What do you think?"

"I think it is a worth a try."

Chapter 16

Lucy and Ricky dragged Anna across the guesthouse patio with the strength of a mule team, their long noses pressed to the ground while Anna's hand wrapped tightly around their leashes. They led her through the propped-open dining room doors.

The room hummed with chatter from the breakfast crowd. Besides the house regulars sitting at their usual table, several weekend guests dined at some of the smaller tables.

The dogs headed straight to Max, each letting out high-pitched yips of excitement as they neared him.

He looked up from his breakfast and a smile bloomed beneath his mustache. "There are my babies!"

Anna released the leashes and the delighted pups scurried to him, their long, thin tails whipping back and forth.

Max dropped his fork, picked up the roll on his plate, and broke off several small pieces "Did you two have fun?" He paused as he gave them the handouts. "You did? Well, I will thank her." He smiled at Anna. "They said *danke*. They love it when you walk them."

"I have fun, too. Although we did have one little incident. Halfway through the walk, Miss Lucy decided to lie on her back on the sidewalk?"

"What?" Max's bushy white brows rose.

"She's quite a character. No matter how much I coaxed her to move, she wouldn't budge so pedestrians walked around her."

Frowning, he glanced down at the dog. "Lucy, *das ist nicht sehr nett*."

Lucy's ears went back.

Max glanced at Anna. "She apologizes."

Anna crouched down, ran her hand along the dog's back. "Aw, it's okay. It was actually kind of funny."

Max nodded. "She can be a funny dog." He took Anna's other hand and gave it a squeeze. "You are an angel. The medicine for my knee is helping. Soon I shall be able to walk the dogs myself."

"Glad you're getting better."

She took the seat next to him, across from Ruth and Otto, and fished her phone from the back pocket of her jeans. Jenna had sent a text ten minutes ago saying she might try to call on her way home from the hospital night shift. Anna's mind roiled with possible reasons her sister wanted to speak with her. Patrick wouldn't go to her house twice, would he?

Anna removed a roll from a cloth-lined basket. "Otto, could you please pass the hard-boiled eggs?"

"Of course." Otto handed her the bowl and she took one.

Ruth glanced up as she stirred her coffee. "Did you find your man yesterday, Anna?"

"No. We struck out again. But the person we located remembered another family with the same name in Frankfurt that moved to either Wetzlar or Wiesbaden after the war."

"That is good. So the trip was not a waste."

"Not at all. Afterward, Josef suggested we visit *Burg Eltz*."

"Ah, a lovely castle," Ruth said, then she sipped her coffee.

The group began to discuss castles on the Rhine. Anna spread sweet plum jam on the soft roll and listened, hoping to visit a few of the sights before leaving. As she was about to take her last bite, her phone rang. She glanced at the display. Patrick's name appeared, not her sister's. She pushed the button to send his call straight into voice mail.

Conversation continued around her. She sipped her coffee, ate, and tried to act like nothing was wrong even though her heart pattered quickly and her appetite shriveled. She felt positive today and didn't want think about Patrick. The phone rang again and this time went straight into voice mail. Two calls in a row. His sense of urgency couldn't mean anything good.

Ping! The message light flashed, ominous as a roadside hazard sign. She swiped up the phone and mumbled, "Excuse me."

Her heart racing, she hurried through the restaurant to a sitting area near the reception desk, far from the diners. She steadied her breath, sat in an oversized chair, and hit play. Patrick's calm voice greeted her. Eerily calm.

"Still avoiding me, Anna? I'm sure you think you're very clever with your disappearing act. Figured there was no possible way I could find you. And I've tried. Boy, have I tried. I'd just about given up, but then my luck turned. Do you remember Maria Rossi?"

Anna's heart raced. Maria Rossi? She didn't know anybody by that name.

"She's the realtor handling the sale of Isaak's home. Yesterday I ran into her after an open house at Isaak's. We had a long chat. Seems she loved meeting you and was enamored about running into the author of a column she loves to read. Oh, and she asked if you were having success in Germany. Surprised? So was I. It seems while handling the house sale she talked quite a bit with Isaak's lawyer's secretary, who didn't mind sharing with Maria about the delightful deed Isaak asked you to do for him. Ms. Rossi was curious if you'd found the man Isaak asked you to find.

So, now I know you are safe and won't worry about you. But I guess it's your turn to worry."

He hung up. Anna sat there, unable to move. Yes, now she remembered Maria. The pleasant and chatty real estate agent who caught her right before she'd left for the airport. Of course she'd have to deal with Isaak's lawyer, who would be handling the sale of Isaak's house. Or more likely Maria was working with the lawyer's assistant. The same woman who'd taken care of Anna's arrangements.

Her anger flared. Her private business. Discussed by others.

But why would the assistant or lawyer think her trip was a secret? They didn't know about Anna's marital problems. What Isaak said in his letter had been a private matter between the two of them. The assistant had only shared the joy of Anna doing something nice for an old neighbor with someone also involved in Isaak's estate. And Maria showed no malice by inquiring or talking to Patrick. Of course she'd have assumed Anna's husband would know about Anna's mission.

But would the assistant have given Maria details on the exact location where Anna stayed? That *would* cross a line. Anna would have to trust the assistant wouldn't go that far.

Patrick's call was only a desperate attempt to scare her enough to reach out to him.

Little did he know, she'd changed while away from her old life. No longer did the daily terror he'd pounded into her, either with his mind games or his fists, matter. She'd become more confident and less fearful. More like her old self. No, she wouldn't be tricked into calling him. And he certainly wasn't crazy enough to fly over and try to find her.

Or would he?

The calm in his voice had been the same calm that would precede his angry outbursts. A chill traveled her spine, but she shook it off and returned to finish her breakfast.

* * * *

Josef slipped on his leather jacket and gathered the papers on his desk. Anna would be pleased when she saw what he'd found late last night. There were strong odds the man he found in Wiesbaden was the Gunther she searched for. Oddly enough, located just across the river.

As he stuffed the papers into a leather satchel, he picked up his cell phone and dialed his brother's number. Gabriel answered on the first ring.

"*Guten Morgen*. Quick question," Josef said. "Is it too late to invite someone to the wedding?"

"Hold on. I'll ask Kirsten."

Yesterday, Josef almost invited Anna to join him at the wedding while they'd driven home. Only he'd clammed up. What if she said no? He'd have been forced to ride the rest of the way home feeling like a big loser. During the night, his courage had risen and he was determined to ask her today. As long as it wasn't too late.

"Kirsten plans on phoning in the final count tomorrow."

"Great. Then put me down for a yes. I am asking someone today. If she refuses, I will call."

"A woman, refuse you?"

"Oh, come on now…"

Gabriel laughed. "*Mutti* will be thrilled."

"Yes. But let it be a surprise."

He tossed the phone inside the satchel, located his cane in the kitchen, and hurried out to the car.

He pulled out of his complex, thinking about how to phrase this invite to Anna. As an extension of her German experience? Or because he simply liked having her at his side? The confidence that had procured him many dates over the years was another casualty of the accident. Yet, Anna seemed to enjoy being with him, as he did her. It still wasn't that easy. Every single time he got lost in her onyx eyes, or she'd smile at something he said, his heart pulsed a little faster. Around her, he felt settled. Content. A no answer would hurt.

He turned off the main road leading to the guesthouse, delightful thoughts about Anna dancing in his head. A motion in his periphery caught his attention, and something dashed in front of the car.

Josef slammed on the brakes, just in time to identify a cat scamper to the roadside and hide beneath a bush.

And that's when a memory flashed. Just a blink in his mind's eye, fuzzy around the edges but so real he could touch it. The scenic, curvy road. Lily at his side. A furry animal had darted out from the road's edge.

He pulled over and exhaled to calm his racing heart. Leaning over, he flipped open the glove compartment and reached for the pack of cigarettes. This time, he stopped himself, crumpled the pack, and shoved it in the pocket of his bomber jacket.

But as he sat there, he mulled over the gift of a brief recollection. Ironically bestowed to him on the first morning he woke and *wasn't* thinking about the accident. The drive here had been comfortable, without the usual fear guiding him behind the wheel.

Deep in his gut, he felt certain there had to be more to that day than him swerving to avoid a furry little creature. Maybe the rest would come back to him soon, sparked by this first step.

He pulled back out to the road. The moment seemed almost surreal, but it had happened. He couldn't wait to tell Anna the news.

At the guesthouse, he parked and rushed to the front entrance. Regina came down the hallway carrying a stack of towels. "*Hallo*, Josef. Anna just went outside for a walk along the river. If you hurry, you can catch her before she gets too far."

He raced through the restaurant as fast as his bad leg would allow, pausing only to toss the remaining cigarettes from his car into the trash. Once outside, he went straight to the sidewalk along the river. He glanced to the right but didn't see her. With a glance to the left, he spotted her wearing a bright red jacket that billowed behind her from a gust of wind. "Anna! Hold up."

He hurried to reach her, anxious to share his news with someone who mattered. As he neared, he noticed her tense expression.

When he was a few steps away, she finally smiled "Hi. I wasn't expecting you for another half hour. I left my laptop in my room, but I can grab it and we can start research now, if you want."

"No need. I think I've found the man you are looking for in Wiesbaden, just across the river. At least I'm almost certain it is him."

A passing breeze sent her hair flying and she brushed it from her eyes. "How'd you find him?"

Josef went through all the details of last night's search. "Once I got enough information, I located his Facebook page. The man I found is missing his right arm, just like the man in your photo."

"Then it must be him. Oh, Josef." She took his hands and smiled. "Thank you!"

"I am happy to have helped." Her hands in his gave him the courage to ask his question. "Listen, my brother is getting married next weekend. Would like to come along as my guest? You can see a German wedding while you are here, but mostly I would enjoy having you with me."

She squeezed his hands and he swore her cheeks turned pink. "Of course I would. I'm honored you'd ask me."

"Good." Relief washed through him. "So, shall we head over to Wiesbaden today?"

"Yes. I need a distraction."

"Is anything wrong?"

"Oh, my husband left me a message. There's not much to say. The calls just bother me." Her face brightened, though he believed she was trying too hard. "But you seem pretty upbeat. Besides the good news you just brought me, anything else going on?"

Josef walked at her side, sharing what happened with the cat moments earlier and how it had jarred a small remembrance of the accident. "But I get a sense there is more."

"That's fantastic. It's just a matter of time before you remember the rest."

"I hope so." But what she'd said about needing a distraction still bothered him. "Did something happen back at home with your divorce?"

She shook her head. "No. Not at all. It's still on track. I'm a worrier, that's all. Now, tell me about your brother and his wedding."

While he talked, he couldn't erase the image of how sad she'd looked when he arrived. Knowing her husband kept calling put him on edge, too.

Chapter 17

Josef pointed out landmarks in Wiesbaden as they headed for the northwestern corner of the town. Before now, Anna's view had only been from across the river, but close up the buildings had character and the busy streets were filled with Saturday shoppers.

Josef seemed different today. The tension often visible in his jaw when he drove had nearly gone and he touched the steering wheel lightly. It did her heart good to see him so happy when he'd arrived. All the more reason she not mention Patrick's message. Why dampen the positive mood of today's trip?

Soon, they entered a residential area with single-family houses, newer apartment buildings, trees, and parks. After a few turns, Josef slowed the car, craning his neck to see the building numbers.

"Here we are." He pulled against the curb in front of a tan stucco building with a clay-tiled roof.

Nerves tingled in her belly as she said a quick prayer. *Isaak, if you're up there watching, I think we found Gunther.*

She glanced over at Josef. "Do you mind doing the introductions and explaining why we are here? Like you have in the other places."

"I am happy to." His gaze skipped over her face. "You are nervous?"

"Kind of. I just want the man to be him so badly."

"Me, too."

They exited the car and approached the complex, tidy rows of townhouses, each with the same brown door. Walking along the path, she noted the little personal touches by various owners. Different window coverings, potted plants, or types of wreaths hanging off the door. At the last unit in the first row Josef stopped.

"Here it is." He motioned to a unit marked twenty-two that held an autumn floral wreath.

She drew in a breath and knocked. They waited. And waited. Nobody came.

Josef reached up and rapped with more force.

Footsteps pounded from inside. A few seconds later, the door flung open.

A slender woman, probably in her sixties, stood before them wearing jeans and a slightly wrinkled button-down shirt. A barrette held back her long dark hair, threaded with some gray. Several strands hung loosely near her temple. "*Hallo. Kann ich dir helfen?*"

Josef gave her a generous smile. "*Mein Name ist Josef Schmitt und das ist Anna Abrams.*"

Anna smiled. As soon as he started rambling in German, she watched the woman's every move. Her tilted head. A frown. A few nods. Josef finally finished with what sounded like his grand finale of statements.

The woman nodded. "*Ja. Der Name meines Vaters ist Gunther.*"

Josef turned to Anna. "Her father's name is Gunther."

"Oh, I speak some English." The woman glanced between them. "So you search for a man with his name?"

"Yes," said Anna. "I'm visiting Germany on behalf of a friend of mine from America, who asked me to find a man with your father's name." Anna gave her a brief explanation of why they were here.

"I see." She frowned. "My *Vater* rarely shares much about the war days, but I do remember him once telling a story about helping two boys left without parents. Perhaps he is the man you seek." She stepped aside. "Please come in. My name is Britta. Join me for some coffee. I just made a pot. *Vater* is resting but should wake soon."

They entered the foyer. Anna held her excitement close.

Britta led them down a hallway of blond wood floors that ended in a modern kitchen with skylights, granite counters, and a simple farm table near a sliding door.

"Please. Have a seat."

As she poured their coffee and arranged a plate of cookies, Anna removed the picture of the two men. She made eye contact with the photographed young Isaak, hoping his spirit watched this moment. Hoping it was their last stop.

Britta placed the mugs down and the cookies in the center of the table. "My father is not doing well lately, but at his age, we cannot complain about his health. It has been good until the past two years."

Anna reached for her mug and sipped the rich brew. "The Gunther Hinzmann I'm looking for once lived in Frankfurt, on…" Anna tried to remember the street name.

"*Staufenstraße,*" said Josef.

Britta's brows lifted. "Ah, yes. *Vater* lived there in his family's house until they moved to Wiesbaden to stay with relatives when the bombing in Frankfurt worsened."

"Did he serve in the *Wehrmacht*?" Josef asked.

"No, no." Britta leaned back in her seat. "He lost his arm in a factory accident at the age of um…" She glanced at Josef. "*Sechszehn*?"

"Sixteen."

"*Ja*, sixteen. The military would not take him. Though he did do work for the state labor department for some time."

Josef glanced at Anna. She remembered their conversation the first day she'd shown him the photo.

"I have a picture of my friend with the man we are trying to find." She pushed the black-and-white photo towards Britta.

The corners of Britta's mouth lifted into a faint smile. "Oh, yes. My dashing father in his younger days." She glanced up. "And this younger man, he is your friend in America who lived in Frankfurt, too?"

"He is…" A blend of bittersweet joy and relief flooded Anna's body. The joy of finding Gunther and sharing Isaak's thanks would come with the sad news of his death. "He was my friend. He recently lost a battle with cancer."

"Oh. I am sorry." Britta shook her head as she returned the picture to Anna. "Can you tell me what happened back then? My *vater* said that the boys' parents were victims of what happened on *Kristallnacht*. But he would not say more."

Anna bit back her discomfort and shared what she knew, every horrible detail.

Britta's eyes filled with tears. "Those poor boys." Her shoulders dropped and tone went flat. "Hitler. A madman, bringing grief to so many. The elders in my family hated that party. Refused to join. All but one aunt on my *Mutter's* side." Her lips pursed.

Josef frowned, carrying the same dejected expression on his face as Britta. "Let us hope such power never infiltrates our government again."

Anna tried to imagine living in a place where the leader inspired bigotry and anti-Semitism, and took away people's rights. She couldn't. But many Germans had never expected Hitler to become so powerful, yet he had.

Britta patted Anna's hand and stood. "Let me see if *mein Vater* has woken up. Maybe I can get him to sit up in his chair. His mind is still sharp; only his body is failing him. He does not speak English, but Josef and I can translate. I will call down to you if he is ready."

As she walked away, Anna stood and went over to the set of sliding doors leading out to a back patio. The weight of the moment pressed to her chest. Happiness. Justice. Sadness. All part of the story that brought them to this point.

Josef's chair scraped on the floor and he appeared at her side. As he stared out the window, he took her hand, as if doing so were the most natural thing in the world for him to do. "I am excited to meet Gunther. I confess, a little nervous."

"Me, too." She looked up, wandered in the blue-green hue of his eyes. The familiar scent of his after-shave coiled around her, while the warmth of his hand leveled her anxiousness. "I'm glad you're here with me."

His eyes softened. For a moment they stood, neither moving. He smiled, so gently his lips barely curved.

She placed a palm against the soft grain of his cheek. "And I have you to thank for us finding Gunther today."

"We worked as a team," he said quietly. He placed his hand on her shoulder and stroked her neck with this thumb.

"Anna, Josef?" Britta yelled from the second level. "You may come up."

They stood for a moment, one she wished wasn't about to end. Josef drew in a deep breath. "Let us go."

* * * *

Anna sat on the edge of the bed watching Britta, who squatted by her father's wheelchair. In one hand, she held Isaak's letter, reading it to him in German—as Isaak had written it. Britta's slender fingers wrapped tightly around her father's unsteady hand as his square chin trembled and tears leaked from the edges of his eyes, making Anna's do the same. Decades had changed the man in the photograph. His dark hair had turned silver. Thin age spots dotted his temples, and his bulbous nose had widened, now filling his face.

Meeting Gunther, the brass ring of her journey, left her with a mixed bag of emotions. Delivering this letter brought to life Isaak's words from beyond the grave. A quiet honor to all those who'd risked their lives during the war. People she'd only read about, but their stories would forever reside in her heart. It left her with hope that if someone in her own lineage had faced the same brutalities, they were able to find saviors, too.

Heaviness pressed its weight to her shoulders. She'd give anything to have Isaak here at this moment. Gunther's raw emotion filled the small bedroom, touching them all. Emotions no doubt stirred by reminders of the war and the fears he'd lived with on a daily basis. Yet, every so often, he'd smile at something his daughter read, hopefully taking joy in the story of Isaak's survival.

Anna glanced at Josef, who leaned against the bedroom door with his arms crossed, watching Gunther. In Josef's glistening eyes, Anna saw compassion and sadness.

His gaze drifted to her, searched her face. A second later he stepped over and sat next to her on the bed's edge.

Leaning close, he whispered in her ear, "I will translate the letter for you when she is through."

His hand slipped into hers, his touch instant comfort to her soul. She might never have fulfilled this mission without him at her side. She rested her head on his shoulder and he leaned in. She'd stood alone with her problems for so long that she'd almost forgotten how good support could feel.

Britta finished and reached out to her father, hugging him as he sobbed.

Anna's eyes blurred, and she turned to Josef, just in time to catch a tear rolling down his cheek. He gave her a sad smile and put an arm around her.

For a long moment, they all sat in silence with their tears and thoughts. Perhaps all that could exist at a time like this.

After a minute, Anna looked at the elderly man. "Gunther?" He sat staring at his lap and slowly lifted his head. "Valor like yours inspires people. It inspires me, though I'm not sure I possess your bravery."

Britta translated. Gunther reached out for Anna, so she moved to his side and took his hand. He responded, his voice sounding very sad.

His daughter nodded. "My father says the risk was the same if you did nothing, so he did what he could."

Isaak's note to Anna had said something similar about risk. She imagined that the young man and teenage boy had spoken about what they were doing, possibly agreeing on the sentiment about taking chances during such a dangerous time.

Britta added, "He only wishes he could have helped more people."

Anna squeezed the man's hand. A true hero, even if he wouldn't embrace the title.

Gunther talked to Britta. She leaned back, listened. A moment later, she looked at Anna. "My father kept in touch over the years with the Lambert family in Belgium. They helped him by taking in Isaak and his brother to get him out of Germany. When Belgium was invaded, the family managed to get Isaak to England, but then lost track of him after that. He wonders if you might be able to visit them. Share this letter?"

"Well, I suppose I—"

Gunther started to speak so she waited. How on earth would she find a family in Belgium? She glanced at Josef, who listened to Gunther.

"Ah, I see." Britta got seated in a chair next to the dresser. "My father has their address. They own a farmhouse outside of Bruges, still in the family. Up until about ten years ago he kept in touch with them. The children of his friends now run the farm. The kids used to spend time with the two boys, while they were in hiding. I am sure they would love to see this letter and meet you."

"I can try. I am not sure how far—"

Josef said something to Gunther then turned to Anna. "We will go. I want to take you."

She nodded, because the depth in his eyes proved to her that he didn't mind doing it at all.

For the next half hour, Gunther asked questions about Isaak's life in New York. Anna answered as best she could, with both Josef and Britta switching back and forth between English and German. Gunther shared stories about his friendship with a spunky boy named Isaak, who lived on his street. Anna laughed, because although she only knew Isaak as an older man, she told Gunther that he still had spunk until the very end.

By the time they finished, Anna believed she had found a friend in Gunther, a sweet and intelligent man who had a heart of gold. As she hugged him goodbye, she felt the frail bones beneath his sweater. Would she ever see him again? She hoped so.

Once downstairs, they exchanged email addresses. Britta took Anna's hands. "My father shared stories with you I have never heard. I am glad he finally did. I think it is good for him to talk about such things." She drew her close. "Thank you for making this trip."

She hugged Britta tight. "I will let you know how our visit to Bruges goes."

They returned to Josef's car and started a quiet ride back through the busy city of Weisbaden.

As they entered the city proper, Josef glanced Anna's way. "So we will decide on a day to drive to Bruges? We may need to stay overnight, unless you want to drive the distance in one day. It is about five hours each way."

"Is Bruges nice?"

"It is spectacular. Canals, cobbled streets, medieval buildings. You would love it."

"Then how about we stay for a night? I'll pay, since this is still part of Isaak's reason for sending me here."

He stopped at a traffic light. "Would you like to do some sightseeing along the way?"

"I would, so maybe we could take our time. Unless you have to get back."

"No. You are my client until you are done with me."

He gave her a playful wink, but she didn't smile. He was more than her driver.

"What is wrong?"

"I—I guess I consider you more than the guy hired to drive me around. We've been through a lot."

He reached for her hand. "Of course I do, Anna. It was, oh what is the word? An expression. Today, what happened was more than just my job."

She smiled, squeezed his hand. "Okay. I'm glad."

The light changed, and their hands parted. They drove in silence, her heart wrapped around emotions from today's visit plus mounting feelings for Josef. A bonus she hadn't expected to find on this trip, and one she wasn't sure how to handle.

A sign they passed listed a Holocaust memorial not far away.

She thought about the lost links to her family's Judaism. "Dr. Walker mentioned the Holocaust memorial here."

"Want to stop?"

"If you don't mind."

"Not at all." Josef took a few turns, pulled over, and parked along the street. "We can walk from here."

As they walked past shops and restaurants, Josef glanced her way. "This synagogue was built around 1860, but destroyed in 1938."

"Destroyed before the war started?"

His Adam's apple slid down his throat and it took him a moment to answer. "It was destroyed on *Kristallnacht*. One of many synagogues destroyed."

Hate had no boundaries that night. Places of worship. Businesses. Private homes. Innocent civilian causalities, like Isaak's parents. Grief bottled in her throat and, as if Josef sensed it, he took her hand.

They rounded a corner onto a wide, brick-paved street lined with pretty buildings and restaurants. He motioned to an area where three tall, stone-gray walls connected at each edge had been arranged on a sidewalk.

"These walls represent the synagogue's shadow," he said in a quiet, respectful tone. A dark gray engraved metal plate ran along the lower portion of each wall.

They moved closer. The engravings held names, next to them dates, and a place.

"This honors the Jews from Wiesbaden who died during this time in our history." He pointed to a name. "It shows the birthdate and when the individual died…" He motioned to the word Auschwitz. "…and where they died."

Josef kept a tight grip on her hand, as if he worried the weight of this memorial might pull her into its undertow, drown her in sadness. With each step, with each name, the pain of death stuck in Anna's throat, left a gaping hole in her heart. They silently and slowly walked past each walled section, honoring the memories of those who had suffered.

These victims had a powerful and hateful force enter their lives, one nations had been defenseless to stop. It made her problems pale. Hate had invaded her life, too, but she had choices that these people hadn't.

When they finished, Josef guided her across the street, where they sat at a bench and stared at the memorial. A dark cloud hung over their heads, filled with the sadness of so many lives lost. Too many. Anna's eyes watered, then tears spilled in mourning for every one of those names and the victims she might never know about.

Josef cried, too. He wrapped her in his arms, and they sat together that way for some time.

Chapter 18

"Who will pay for this trip?"

Claudia spoke in her direct, don't-mess-with-me tone, but it never intimidated Josef as it did some of the other staff at Wanderlust Excursions. He shifted the phone to his other ear while he poured a cup of coffee and before he could answer, she resumed talking.

"Our agreement was for you to take this client to places in this country. You can say no. I know the driving—"

"The driving is fine. I am adjusting. Besides, the estate of the man who sent her to Germany will pay for our travel. Second, I don't want to say no. I want to—"

"Oh my God! What is that husband of mine doing? Hold on."

He added some sugar to the coffee and stirred, tired and raw from the emotion of what happened in Wiesbaden this afternoon. His world had been flipped upside down, exactly what the doctor ordered.

"I'm sorry." Claudia returned. "Where were we?"

"I was telling you that I want to go to Belgium. If I were to be honest, I have grown to...well, to care about this story. Meeting Gunther touched me very deeply." Josef's chest tightened each time he thought about the elderly man's face, filled with agony as he shared some of his sadder stories. "And Gunther wants Anna to meet the family in Belgium who helped Isaak, eventually getting him to England. We took a copy of the letter Isaak wrote to deliver to them." He drew in a deep breath and didn't care if he sounded ridiculous. "This is a journey I feel I *must* complete. For me as much as our client."

Claudia went strangely silent for a moment, then softly said, "Well, why didn't you say so. Of course you should go."

"And, I've been thinking. Don't pay me for the trip to Belgium. Anna has already insisted upon paying you for more of my time. Take the money. Donate it to one of the many memorial funds for Holocaust victims. I don't care which one."

"I can see this has touched you. How about I donate some of the money my company made, too?"

"It would be the right thing to do."

"So, what are the next steps?"

"I dropped Anna off at the guesthouse an hour ago. I'm going back there in a while for dinner so we can plan the days we will be in Belgium."

"I see." She got quiet again. "Days? Are you comfortable going away that long with this woman?"

"What are you digging at?"

"Just wondering if there is something more going on."

Her tone teased, but he wasn't about to confess to Claudia emotions for Anna he hardly had his own head wrapped around. "We have become friends."

She chuckled. "I see. Well, be safe while traveling."

"We will. *Gute Nacht.*" He hung up.

He sipped his mug of coffee on the way to the bedroom, where he pulled on tan khakis, a clean white oxford shirt, and belt. While patting on a little cologne, it struck him how the weight of the day's events left a heavy imprint inside his chest. So many times he'd heard the stories of his country's history and visited Holocaust memorials, always leaving him somber afterwards. As they should.

Today's visit, though, pulled him to a deeper level of sadness and understanding. Gunther and Isaak's story would forever be part of his life, reminding him that in a world blackened by the deeds of the devil, a ray of sunshine could still be found in the hearts of humankind.

Strong forces lately guided his life, leading him places like the Holocaust memorial. They opened his eyes to the fact he'd been blind these past six months. His problems were as insignificant as a grain of sand on a beach compared to the horror those people went through.

He could still feel Anna's slender frame in his arms, the wetness of her tears as she cried. All while he silently released the demons owning him since the minute he woke at the French hospital. The pity he'd clung to. The blame he believed he'd owned. All slowly evaporating because of this journey taken with her.

He went to the mirror and ran a quick comb through his hair. He paused at his reflection. The angry edges on his face since the accident were gone.

Instead, he saw life in his eyes. A happy glow he used to see all the time. Or did they glow because he was about to see a woman who made him feel alive again? Made him yearn for a deeper relationship. The type of closeness he used to keep at a distance. Anna's magic made him open up to her. Or maybe he had changed.

In either case, he would grab this time with her and embrace every second.

* * * *

Anna furiously typed on her keyboard, hoping to get down some rough notes on everything that happened at Gunther's house. A powerful day. Exhausting and exhilarating.

They'd found Gunther. She still almost couldn't believe it. And Josef had been at her side the whole way. Sharing in her excitement, lifting her when she'd faced disappointments. Even offering deep insights about what it all meant.

She reread a line she'd thought of during their car ride home this afternoon. *Each person added a link to Isaak's chain of hope.*

Yes, the phrase described perfectly the multiple links needed for one man to survive. Finding many people who hadn't lost faith in mankind and were willing to take a risk to make good things happen. A point she would surely highlight for her readers.

She glanced at the time, saved her work, and stood. At her wardrobe closet, she retrieved an oversized sweater and slipped it on with black leggings, smiling as she thought about her column.

A chain of hope.

Because of Isaak, a new link to the chain had been added. Decades later, when he'd handed her a lifeline to leave Patrick. A move leading her to this house full of strangers. Each of them a link in her chain, making her examine her world and relationships.

Dr. Walker encouraged her exploration of never-discussed family history.

Ruth and Otto's oddly tender bickering proved that disagreement could be found in the folds of love in a non-abusive way.

Regina and Joachim hired Josef for her. Without him, she might still be trying to find Gunther. And on a personal note, Josef had proven that there were still caring and honest men in the world.

She softly touched her cheek, the way Josef had earlier, right before hugging her goodbye. He'd talked so excitedly about what they could see in Belgium. She couldn't wait to see the country or spend time with him.

On paper, she remained married, a technicality to her heart's desire to get to know Josef better. A relationship that might be nothing more than two people becoming close friends. Or was there more going on with him than she wanted to admit? And if so, did she face an ethical dilemma if she saw Josef as more than a friend?

Logic. Truth. Her own needs. What mattered the most? She wished she could roll the dice and get an answer. But one thing remained certain….

Somewhere between bruises, the love she once gave to Patrick had been shattered, left in too many pieces to ever repair. Maybe Patrick never fully understood how to care for someone, but his problems no longer mattered to her. She'd tried so hard to fix him and nearly went down with the ship. Now, it was up to him to get professional help.

She deserved better. To be supported, treated the way Josef treated her today. With genuine caring and support.

Once finished brushing her teeth, she grabbed a hand towel and wiped her mouth while staring into the beveled mirror. Gone was the empty stare that greeted her these past two years. Tonight, her face radiated happiness.

She straightened her shoulders, jutted out her chin. A brave warrior stared back at her, no longer afraid of the big bad wolf. A brave woman whose heart tingled each time she looked at the man who stuck to her side on this new journey of self-discovery.

This task would've been different without Josef. Accomplishing it might have been possible, but he brought sensitivity to the table, gave everything he touched more meaning. He'd even shared his own painful memories with her, in a way that drew them closer.

In contrast, during her marriage, Patrick handed her only his pain.

Moments dashed through her mind like flash cards. The way she'd edit every sentence for fear of setting him off. The times her careful words didn't matter, and how he'd slap, punch, and kick her further down a dark hole. All stemming from unhappiness *he* didn't know how to channel.

A sense of urgency barreled toward her, insisting she make sure Patrick understood she no longer loved him. Each time he called, it showed he still had hope for their marriage.

There wasn't any, though. It wasn't only because she'd met a man who showed her how it felt to be treated properly. It was because she stopped loving Patrick long before filing those divorce papers.

She needed to tell him again. Now. Not later. She didn't want him trying to come to Germany hoping to work things out. It wouldn't happen. And though she'd said it in her note and in her actions, Patrick wasn't listening. She'd give it one more shot. That way she could pursue this new feeling of being alive knowing she'd been as direct as possible. Then it wouldn't feel wrong to get closer to Josef, if that was where things took them.

It was early afternoon in New York. Before she lost courage, she removed the phone from her purse and started to dial his cell phone but stopped. He might not answer for her. Instead, she punched in the main switchboard at his office. The receptionist answered.

Anna said, "May I have extension 3405?"

As his phone rang, Anna's heartbeat raged like a warrior facing a battle. *You can do this!* She closed her eyes, willed herself to be strong.

"Patrick Kelly here."

"It's Anna."

After a silent beat—filling the space like an eternity—he said, "Oh, you couldn't talk to me before, but now that I know where to find you, you finally call."

"I needed time at first and didn't want to talk to you."

"What a bullshit move, Anna. Serving me those papers at work. I have never been so humiliated in my life."

Two words dangled on the end of her tongue. *I'm sorry.* But she wasn't. "My lawyer advised I serve the papers in a public place."

His voice boomed, sending a chill up her spine. "I don't care what—" The slam of his office door carried over the phone lines. "I don't care what your lawyer told you. You embarrassed me!"

Her stomach quivered. She'd never spoken back to him. But did it make a difference? He used to strike her unprovoked. "I never meant to humiliate you," she said. "But if you want to talk about humiliation, let's talk about how you degraded me for two solid years."

"How can you say that? I loved you. I didn't—"

"Yes, Patrick." Her hands trembled, and a ball of nerves vibrated inside her belly. "You degraded me. Hurt me, both physically and mentally."

He went silent. She took a deep breath to steady her shaking body.

"But you promised you'd never leave me." The voice of a fearful child. A man whose mother left him behind and alone with an abusive father.

A plea causing her tough stance to soften. *No. Don't let him take you there.*

"I would've stayed if you'd gotten help, but you wouldn't. So many times I asked you to, but you'd ignore me once I'd forgiven you. I never wanted our lives to turn out this way."

"No, Anna?" His voice rose, rapid and fierce. "All I know is you promised me you'd never leave. You're a liar."

"No. What you've been doing to me is wrong. It's abuse! I am done living in fear of you."

"I'll get help."

She snorted. "No, you won't. You've said that so many times, I've lost count."

Silence. Deadly silence. If she were standing in front of him, she'd be bracing herself for his strike.

But she wasn't.

"Patrick, you need help. Not for us, but for yourself. There is no us. I no longer love you. Do you understand?"

"Big talk since you're so far away. What makes you think I can't find you?"

"Stop with the threats. What are you going to do, fly to Germany and hunt me down? For what? To hurt me again. *That* is why I left you!" She inhaled deeply, conjured up what little kindness remained for him in her heart, and softly said, "Patrick, we don't hurt the people we love."

"No, we don't, Anna. And those divorce papers hurt me."

Click. The line went dead.

She sat on the edge of the bed and threw the phone down at her side. The injustice of his remark stung. After all she'd been through, he viewed himself as the victim?

A part of her wanted to call back, scream at him every bottled-up comment stored away over the last two years. But she didn't. Because she'd faced him, spoke up, and jumped a hurdle in the battle to regain her life. A plus in her column.

But it bothered her how Patrick lived in an alternate reality, because with that mindset, there was nothing predictable about his behavior.

Chapter 19

Ricky Martin's techno beat softly vibrated through the car and woke Anna. From her reclined position in the passenger seat, she saw houses, not the rolling Belgian fields and grazing cows she'd fallen asleep to.

She rolled her head toward Josef, whose gaze focused on the road, his brows furrowed as if he was in deep thought. "Where are we?"

He glanced over. "Just outside of Dinant."

She pulled the lever to straighten her seat back and stretched her stiff neck. "Was I asleep long?"

"Almost an hour."

Two days ago, they'd set their plans in motion for the trip to Belgium. Now they were on their way, starting with a leisurely drive through the beautiful country, where Josef had selected places to stop. Then, on to the medieval city of Bruges for their two-night stay. The plans had put her in a fantastic mood.

Then yesterday, while she'd worked from the guesthouse on her column, Patrick's texts began rolling in. Text after text, demanding to know when she planned on coming home. After he'd played the victim card before ending their last call, it became clear he would never give up. It left her more concerned about his mental health, but certain there was nothing more she could do to help him.

"Here we are."

Josef pulled into a town set on the banks of a narrow river and parallel parked on a street. Connected buildings held charming storefronts and restaurants, with some taller concrete structures on the other side of the road that were more businesslike. The place didn't look like much from a sightseeing perspective, but two long tour buses parked in a lot indicated otherwise.

Anna slipped on her jacket and got out just as Josef came around to her side. He smiled, but it lacked enthusiasm.

"Everything okay?" she asked.

"My leg is just a little sore."

"We don't have to do this."

"I want to."

She took him at his word and they started down the busy sidewalks. Voices of Americans and Australians could be heard everywhere, perhaps visitors off those buses.

"Lots of tourists here." She walked slowly to keep pace with him. "I'm surprised. The town is so…ordinary."

"In a minute, you shall see why they all come."

They peered in storefront windows and ogled the beautifully crafted knickknacks and bakery delights decorated fancifully as works of art.

At the end of the street, they neared a bridge. She squinted, certain her eyes were playing tricks on her. "Are those huge saxophones?"

He grinned, suddenly relaxed as a pair of worn blue jeans. "This is what they come to see. Dinant is the birthplace of Adolphe Sax, inventor of the saxophone."

She hurried to the corner, where a sign read Charles de Gaulle Bridge. Human-sized replicas of the wind instrument lined both sides of the bridge. Spaced evenly, with about twenty feet between each one, the enormous saxophones had been painted with bright yellows, bold blues, and intense reds in a myriad of designs.

"Was Charles de Gaulle born here, too?"

"No. He was shot on this bridge in World War I. Come on." He offered her his arm.

She slipped her hand onto it as they crossed, pausing to admire the unusual artwork.

"The patterns painted on these instruments come from the countries that make up an international saxophone organization." He pointed to colorful flags angled upward along the bridge railing. "Also each country's flag."

At the end, they turned to head back. Halfway across, Josef took her arm and gently guided her to the railing. "Look at the town from this angle."

From this spot, Anna caught the charm of Dinant. Connected row houses ran along the river, the facades plain, but painted in vibrant colors. And the real majesty of the view came from the cliffs towering over the village, a dramatic backdrop that dwarfed the buildings and made this a truly unique setting.

"See the building at the top of the cliff?" Josef pointed, and she nodded. "That is the Citadel of Dinant, a fortress built in the 1800s. There is a trolley that goes up there. Shall we go after lunch?"

"Yes, most definitely."

He leaned on the railing overlooking the narrow river and a dock where several ships were stationed. She joined him, standing close enough that their elbows touched.

After a minute, he tapped her elbow with his. "You seem quiet today."

"Me? I was worried about you."

"I guess I am thinking about you." He studied her for a moment. "How I will miss you when you leave."

His response caught her off guard, but she was glad he brought it up. "I'll miss you, too."

"You have helped me change my life, you know?"

"Me? I can't imagine how I did that."

He stared back out to the water. "You took me along on an adventure. A different kind of exploit. It put my troubles in perspective, made me think about someone besides myself for a change." He slowly turned to her. "That is what I learned from you. To think about others."

"But you do, Josef."

He shook his head. "I am not searching for compliments. I know the man I have been and…and the man I shall try to be from now on."

Anna took his hand, larger and rougher, yet always a gentle touch. "No matter how you see yourself, nobody else sees you that way." She could see everyone loved being with him. She did, too.

A river breeze blew a strand of hair in front of her eyes and he reached out, brushed it aside. A small gesture, but the type that made her feel noticed, cared about. The kind he seemed to do without thinking or expecting anything in return. Their gazes locked and the voices of tourists around them faded.

His hand rested on her shoulder. "How is it you always see the good in people?"

Josef saw her in a light she didn't deserve. She shrugged. "I'm not perfect. Sure, I try to see the good, but maybe that's flawed. Sometimes it's easier to deal with other people's problems instead of my own."

A family with two young girls stopped at a saxophone not far from them and she went silent. The father instructed the girls to stand together as he adjusted his camera. One of the young brunettes wore a big smile; the other looked miserable.

She whispered in Josef's ear, "Those little girls remind me of me and my sister. Jenna and I are complete opposites."

"Same with me and Gabriel."

She smiled while watching the family continue down the bridge, but her mood sobered. Jenna had seen straight through Patrick's abuse. Her gaze flicked to Josef. "Jenna never would've stayed with a man like Patrick. Maybe seeing the best in people isn't a great quality."

He tucked his finger under her chin and lifted it so she'd look in his eyes. "No. Do not change who you are. Something about you has helped me seek the best in myself. That is a gift, not a flaw."

Another gust swept across the bridge, causing the flags to flutter in protest. Anna's hair flew across her face. Josef pushed it away, cupped her cheeks with strong hands that held her tenderly. She was aware of every part of him. The nearness of his broad shoulders. The shallowness of each breath. The slow caress of his thumb against her lower lip. His lips parted, just before he leaned in and gently pressed them to hers. Once. Twice. She slipped her hands inside his open jacket, drew him close. Kissed him with a hunger he'd awakened in her.

Slowly, they leaned apart, but his gaze remained on her face. He quietly said, "Promise me you won't change."

She'd never dreamed she'd want another man to touch her again. Not this soon. And she'd vowed not to change any part of herself to keep a man happy. But Josef's only request had been for her to have compassion for others. So maybe it wasn't such a bad trait. "I promise."

He tilted his mouth in a smile. "Hungry? There's a place in town that has great croque monsieur."

"Sounds perfect."

* * * *

Josef rolled onto his side. If the clock on the Queen Anne nightstand was right, he'd been napping for a half hour. The long drive to Bruges had tired him out, at least compared to what he could do before the accident.

He threw off the simple cotton bedspread and stood, giving his back a long stretch. There was just enough time to take a shower and meet Anna downstairs for dinner.

He went to the window and opened the heavy curtains. A small boat glided along the canal as the setting sun burned with an orange glow. They'd been lucky to get two canal view rooms on such short notice. It helped he knew the guy who ran this place. Being in the travel business had its perks.

As he scanned the shimmering water, his gaze stopped at Anna, sitting on the canal wall taking a picture of an approaching tour boat. She'd changed into a long, loose sweater dress, dark leggings, and short boots. A colorful scarf wrapped her neck.

A force inside of his chest churned. Need. For her. He could still feel her sweet lips, the eager way she'd pressed against his frame, responded to their kiss. Where this relationship would go he didn't know, or if stepping into it was right or wrong with her marital situation. For now, he would enjoy the simple pleasure of their time together.

He snorted a laugh over his idea to be nice to her as an effort to redeem himself for his role in the accident. An utterly ridiculous notion, though desperation had driven him to it. He *did* feel better lately. Only because he'd started to forgive himself.

He showered, quickly dressed in clean jeans, a collared shirt, and loafers. He grabbed his jacket and headed downstairs.

Anna wasn't in the lobby, so he went out the main doors. He glanced to his right and spotted her heading back to the hotel along the quiet canal street. Next to her walked a tall man with strong facial features and thick, dark hair. She tossed back her head and laughed at something he said.

A wave of jealousy drove like a nail straight through Josef's chest, catching him by surprise.

Her gaze fell on Josef, and her smile widened. She waved and yelled, "I didn't keep you waiting, did I?"

"No. I just got down."

The man smiled and said something to Anna, waved to Josef, then crossed the street and hurried away.

She walked quickly until she reached Josef. "That guy was just telling me that the Smurfs were created by a Belgian man."

Josef nodded, relieved to know it had been such a casual conversation. "You mean the blue cartoon elves?"

"Yeah. Who knew?" She looped her arms around his neck while her floral scent wrapped around him. "What are the plans for tonight?"

"Dinner and a stroll?" He drew her into a hug, nestled his face next to hers and wandered in the softness of her skin. He kissed her hair, her cheek, and moved to her lips, already waiting and willing.

She tipped her head back and watched him with heat in her eyes. "Sounds perfect."

"There's a place that makes the best mussels, an area specialty. But they have other dishes, too."

He slipped his hand in hers. They ventured along the sidewalk next to the canal as a few swans paddled quickly toward the bridge.

"There are so many swans here."

"Bruges is known for them. I have heard many versions of why, but it goes back to politics in the 1400s, taxes, and a curse on the city. Now they have become a symbol of the town."

As they turned the corner and crossed over the bridge, Anna stopped and turned to look in the direction they'd just come from. "Hold on. I want to take a picture of our hotel."

He waited behind her and studied the snug, narrow buildings with pointed roofs and exteriors painted in white, tan, bright colors or brick.

She snapped a few pictures then he put his hands on her hips, kissed the back of her head. "I told you Bruges is beautiful."

She turned in his arms. "I never doubted you for a minute."

"Let's take a picture of us both. Can I use your phone?"

She handed it to him. Josef held it out and positioned them in the frame. "Now smile like this is a moment you never want to forget."

He watched her in the frame. A slight pause and then she smiled. The instant he snapped, she turned and looked at him.

He lowered the phone. "What?"

"I don't need a picture. I won't ever forget this moment," she said quietly.

He leaned down, placed a gentle kiss upon her lips, but found the words he wanted to say stuck in his throat because he'd never forget it, either.

* * * *

Josef took Anna's arm and guided her toward a brightly lit storefront. "Here is another local treat you should not miss."

She peered into the window of a waffle shop. Waffles with fruit, drizzled with chocolate, and doused with fresh whipped topping. Her aching stomach groaned. "Are you trying to get me fat? I'm stuffed from dinner."

He laughed. "By tomorrow you will be begging for one of these."

She grinned. "I hate to admit it, but you're probably right."

They continued their walk. Shop windows glowed now that it was dark, drawing attention to masterpieces of uniquely designed chocolates, more drool-worthy desserts, and delicate lace fabrics.

They entered an open, cobblestoned square. People crisscrossed the big public arena while a horse-drawn carriage passed by, the horse hooves clopping on the ancient pavement. A huge medieval building with flags stationed at various corners and a tall tower jutting from its center occupied one corner. Spotlights on the ground beamed to the tower top.

Anna took it all in. "It's as if time stood still one day hundreds of years ago."

"That is because nobody ever developed here. It was once a rich city, but so poor by the 1800s that nobody invested in it. So it stands as we see it today." Josef motioned to a bench. "Shall we sit?"

They settled on a bench seat, shoulders touching, hands locked. Josef pointed to the big building she'd noticed when they arrived. "The tower is called the belfry. In the morning we can climb up. It's got over three hundred and sixty steps."

"Good thing you didn't suggest climbing tonight." She patted her full stomach. "And we should do it *before* we eat the waffles."

He laughed, a happy sound. He'd seemed more relaxed since they arrived. She felt that way, too.

At a statue in the square's center, travelers took photos of the area while a group of teenagers goofed around.

Anna stood, walked closer and took a few photos. Josef smiled at her as she returned to his side and put an arm around her shoulders.

As they people-watched, a man nearby started to speak loudly and harshly. She glanced over her shoulder. The speaker was a man who stood in front of a woman sitting on a nearby bench. She kept her head down and remained quiet through his rant. Anna guessed he spoke Dutch, the language used in the Flanders region of Belgium, but his anger needed no translation.

She turned away and tried to block him out, but his tone made Anna's stomach tighten. She tensed, absorbing every bit of the poor woman's shame.

Another sensation crept over her, one that stole the developing intimacy she felt for Josef. A little voice whispering reminders of what the sex in her marriage had become. Pretend. No longer done because she cared, but because she was afraid.

She never said no, for fear of setting off his anger. Patrick had never forced himself on her, but as things got worse, she'd had no doubt he would. So she was always willing. Ready to pretend. Kissing him like an actress playing a role. Moaning in the right places. Inside her head, though, she'd wanted to scream when he'd hover over her, press inside her, find satisfaction in this act of love, while his cruelty lingered in her thoughts. His tenderness and harshness had become one to her mind and ruined the sexual being she once was.

What would happen with another man? Josef made her want to learn the answer, but finding out came with the risk of learning it was worse than she thought.

The man's voice rose. Anna dared to glance back again. The woman lifted her head, but before she could say anything, he yelled, roughly grabbed her arm, and they left.

"Anna."

She turned to Josef, who watched her carefully. "You have left him," he said quietly. "That cannot happen to you anymore."

She sank into his hold, a place that felt warm and safe. But what she'd witnessed tore open a wound that had barely scarred. Would she spend the rest of her life terrified each time a man raised his voice?

The quiet air suddenly filled with the sound of magical chimes.

"The belfry plays," said Josef.

Such beautiful music brought life to the historic setting. Anna erased the man's tirade from her mind. The images of forcing herself to be with Patrick. She wanted to be fully here, enjoying this moment.

Josef rubbed her shoulder, sending warmth to her core as his touch replaced the bad memories. She turned to him, taking in his strong chin, masculine Nordic nose, trimmed beard. "Thank you."

He glanced over, raised his brows. "For what?"

She stared into his kind eyes. Warm and passionate eyes. The strong Belgian beer they'd had with dinner floated inside her head, loosened her tongue. "For helping me feel safe with a man again. I wasn't sure it would ever be possible."

He slipped his hand to the back of her head, his fingers working their way through her hair, caressing her nape.

She pressed her lips to his. They were soft and waiting for her. Josef drew her closer, kissing her deeply. Passionately.

As the clop of horse hooves on the pavement neared, he tilted back his head. "How about a carriage ride on this beautiful at night?"

She nodded. He took her hand and they walked over where a couple had just exited one of the coaches. As they got settled with a blanket over their laps and headed out for the road, Josef drew her close and kissed her again.

Chapter 20

Josef pulled alongside a Mercedes sedan and parked. “GPS says this is the place.”

Anna stared out the passenger window, nervously twisting the strap of the purse. His gaze drifted to her lips, shaded in a cherry red that popped out against her white blouse. A bold color, but it spoke to the increased confidence he saw in her lately.

Last night after their carriage ride, he’d returned to Anna’s hotel room. Over a lifetime, he’d been with many women, only a few serious. With Anna, though, it seemed prudent to push aside his usual fools-rush-in attitude. She was in the middle of changing her life. Or perhaps it was his own emotional state he worried about. He finally felt good, but what about when she returned to America? And though last night’s passion made leaving hard, he sensed her ambivalence, too, so left before they ended up in her bed with regrets.

He shut off the car and took her hand, so small it fit easily into his. “Nervous? You said Eloïse seemed very nice in your emails.”

She barely smiled. “I’m sure they are all nice. I was just thinking about Isaak, how he would feel knowing I’m here. At a place where he hid for so long. Probably terrified he’d be caught, although I’m sure this wonderful family did the best they could for them given the circumstances.” Her eyes watered. “He was safe from his enemies, but still imprisoned.”

Josef touched her cheek. “Yes. That is true about his time in hiding. I still believe Isaak would be grateful for your visit.”

She blinked away the wetness. “I hope so.” She drew in a deep breath. “Let’s go.”

They walked through a gate leading to a compound of rustic, white brick buildings. A cobblestone path took them between two fields, where grazing sheep welcomed them with their soft bleats on one side, and cows quietly ate on the other.

Anna reached for Josef's hand, latching on comfortably, as if they'd been doing it for ages. Not two days. Yet it felt right to him, also.

The closest building was the main house. Dull peach shutters and blue trim popped out against the white brick facade.

A loud bark sounded and seconds later a Bernese mountain dog barreled toward them. The furry dog swarmed around their legs as the house front door opened.

A slender woman with short gray hair stepped out and approached them. "Welcome. You must be Anna and Josef. I am Eloïse." She spoke English with a strong Dutch accent.

She shook their hands and smiled warmly. "I am so happy to meet you."

Anna seemed to relax, the tense lines fading from her face. "Me, too. Thank you for having us over."

The dog barked and Eloïse laughed. "Forgive me. This is Samson."

Anna ran her hand along his thick fur. "He's gorgeous."

"And he is very spoiled. Well, I should start by thanking you for bringing us the news about Isaak. How is Gunther?"

"His daughter says his age is catching up with him."

Eloïse frowned. "I am sorry to hear that. It was my parents who brought Isaak into our home. I was a young girl of five when he arrived but have many memories of his time here. My brothers, who used to play with him, are here and so is an uncle, who remembers the time Isaak spent with us. We are all very eager to hear about his life."

"He would be so happy to know I'm here. Your farm is lovely."

"Oh, thank you. My husband and I have run it for many years, since my parents got too old to do the work. We are getting ready to turn it over to another generation. Let me show you around."

They followed her from building to building. She introduced them to one of her brothers, who'd come out of the main house carrying a basket to get some fresh eggs. Josef liked it here. Everything was earthy, back to basics. Why was he always looking for excitement in his life, when sometimes the simplest pleasures could bring him so much more?

As they entered the horse stables, he glanced at Anna and winked. Her smile made his heart leap, and that's when reality hit him… Maybe the adventure he'd been missing his whole life was being with a woman who caused that kind of reaction.

* * * *

The eighteenth-century farmhouse was as warm and welcoming as the family who owned the property. Anna lowered her fork to her plate, unable to eat another bite of the delicious meal, though others around the long table still dug into theirs.

A large, brick fireplace sparked with life and three candelabras on the table brightened the dining room's brick interior. Overhead, rustic dark beams spanned the ceiling, and detailed oil paintings hung off the cracked walls.

Her gaze trailed to the people joining them. Eloïse's brothers, Tristan and Laurent. Their spouses and children were all here, and even a few close cousins. All of them had been interested in learning about Isaak's life in America, and also hers living in New York City.

She leaned back to listen while Tristan talked about the farm operation to Josef. He slipped his arm around the back of Anna's chair and she settled into it.

Last night, swept up in the romance of the old canal town and their horse carriage ride, she'd invited him into her room. Gentle kisses spun into passion. She'd never wanted a man more. Yet the voice that had cornered her while they sat in the town square returned. Stirring up all the doubt again. She wanted to conquer this feeling, so she didn't return home with regrets about what she wished she'd done with Josef.

Eloïse returned carrying a pie. Her niece walked behind her with another. She lowered them to the table and got seated across from Anna. "May I see Isaak's note?"

Anna took the copy of Isaak's letter from her purse and passed it across the table. "This is a copy for you to keep. I'm sure Isaak would've written you a letter of his own if he ever dreamed I'd make it this far."

"This means so much to us." Eloïse's voice softened and her eyes glistened in the candlelight. "I only wish my parents could have been here for this visit." She forced a cheery smile. "Now everyone, eat up. That pie is straight out of the oven."

Anna nibbled away at the sweet dessert and listened to the conversations around her while Eloïse silently read the note. Before sitting down to dinner, several family members had shared their stories of the war. They discussed some French family members who had suffered greatly during the Nazi occupation of that country. Jewish neighbors taken from their homes, sent off on trains. Anybody thought to be doing anything against the Nazis, even minor infractions, could have lost their lives. More sorrow. The heaviness accumulating in Anna's heart since the start of this journey swelled with a new layer.

She'd also learned the family had documents forged for Isaak by the resistance, explaining how he got out of Belgium after the invasion and reached London, ultimately leaving for America.

Josef finished his pie and returned his arm to the back of her chair. She turned and found him watching her, a soft smile set on his lips that spoke volumes without words.

Eloïse stood and clinked her glass with a spoon. "I would like to read aloud the letter Anna has delivered to us. Josef has been kind enough to translate the German into English for me."

The room went silent. Eloïse's reading carried strong emotion, at times her voice quivering, causing many eyes around the table to tear up. Even the youngsters listened with an attentive ear. They had heard the stories about the war, handed down from generation to generation.

A half hour later, they left. Hugs were shared and email addresses exchanged with promises to see each other again.

On the drive back to the hotel, Josef remained quiet but rested his hand on her knee. Anna tipped her head against the headrest and closed her eyes, lost in thought about the wonderful gathering of new friends. Thinking about the rest of their night, too, and how it had ended last evening.

After Josef parked, she climbed out of the car and took an unsteady step. Her head wandered in the haze of too much wine. Josef came up from behind and swooped his arm around her waist, keeping her upright.

He chuckled. "Do not tell me you are drunk."

She liked him this close and kissed his cheek. "Okay. I won't tell you."

He softly laughed. They walked along the canal toward the hotel while the water glistened from the moon's touch. Once inside and through the lobby, Josef guided her to the elevator and hit the up button.

"We will take the lift. In your condition, I am sure you cannot walk to the third floor."

"Yes I can."

The door opened. He guided her inside and tapped the button. The second the doors clamped shut, he wrapped a strong arm around her waist and drew her close. His voice thick and husky, he said, "Lucky for you I am not a man who takes advantage of drunk women."

"Even if she wants you to?" Anna slipped her hands through his hair and brought her lips to his.

He kissed her deeply then pulled back, his eyes softening, skipping over her face. "Yes, even a beautiful temptress who has been teasing me all night with her ruby lips."

"So, this temptress teases you?" She undid top two button of his shirt then walked her fingers through the matted cinnamon hairs on his chest. "Good God, she sounds desperate."

He gave her a devilish smile as heat flared in his eyes. He slipped his hands around her backside, drew her against him then kissed her again.

The doors dinged, then opened. He pulled back, took her hand, and they stepped out.

At her door, she searched her purse for the key while he stood behind her, his warm breath on her neck, his hands moving slowly along her hips. Making her body burn, quake for more. She wanted to rid herself of the past, and maybe this was the only way to do it.

When she found the key, she turned into his waiting arms. "Don't go. Stay with me."

His gaze skipped over her face and heat burned in his eyes. "Are you certain?"

She placed her hands on his cheeks. "What I want, while we are still together, is to be with you."

He stared into her eyes, for one, two, three seconds and finally nodded. "It is all I needed to know."

* * * *

A sliver of dawn light peeked through the crack in the curtains. Anna lay curled at Josef's side, facing him. Her chest rose and fell with slumber. He wanted to touch her smooth porcelain skin, thread his fingers through her soft hair. Instead, his gaze moved to the remnants of the bruise on her exposed shoulder. How hard had she been hit for the bruise to remain all these weeks later?

Rage sizzled inside his veins. How could anybody do this to her? To anyone, for that matter. Two years of such treatment could make the strongest of people cynical and angry. Not her. Anna still smiled and proved she was made of tough stuff.

Anna's eyes fluttered open and she smiled at him. "What time is it?"

"Just after six."

She groaned and pressed her warm hands to his chest. "We don't have to get up, right?"

"No. Go back to sleep." Josef rested his arm on the curve of her waist and shut his eyes.

He listened to her breathing, his arm rising and falling with each breath. Though he wanted to make love to her again, he let her rest. Soon his thoughts got fuzzy, one step from slumber. She shifted, moved close. Her soft lips grazed his chest, his shoulder, nipped the side of his neck, then she slid on top of him, pressing her flesh against his so they melted into one. He hungrily kissed her mouth, placing his palms on her back and following her sensuous curves while getting lost in the dim scent of her perfume. Her hands moved, touching him all over, making his skin burn and forcing utterances of pleasure to escape from his lips. All while he explored the places that made her whimper in satisfaction, a sound that sent his blood coursing through his veins.

Later, she fell back to sleep in his arms, but all he could think about was the day she returned home. To a place where she would have to face a man who abused her, and he wouldn't be there to keep her safe.

Chapter 21

Though the sun shined brightly, Anna still shivered from a breeze as the riverboat passed by a hillside with a rustic house next to several fields of grapes.

Josef put his arm around her shoulders. "Cold? We can go down below."

"I'm happy right here, with this beautiful view."

He pressed his lips to her temple. "It is beautiful," he said softly.

"It was nice of Claudia to give you another day off after we got back from Belgium."

"She's tough but fair." He slowly rubbed her arm, making her warm. "My family looks forward to meeting you at the wedding."

"I can't wait to meet them, too. What are they like?"

Josef talked about his sister and her kids, his mother, and brother with ease. His laughter during several anecdotes revealed they were a family he loved and enjoyed spending time with. This past week, he'd been so relaxed, happy. She wanted to tell him Patrick had learned she'd gone to Germany, but no time ever felt right.

He pointed out a building set on a long strip of land in the river. "Look. That white building is Pfalzgrafenstein Castle." The boxy structure, sitting on the island, had a black roofline dotted with quite a few small towers including a large pentagonal-shaped one. "It was built as a toll-collecting station."

"Recently?"

He laughed and his eyes crinkled. "No. In the 1300s. Are you messing with me?"

"Yes." She warmed from his smile, but her prior thoughts broke the magic. If even a teeny chance existed for them to have a long-distance relationship, she couldn't simply avoid topics because they bothered him.

"Remember the day we went to Wiesbaden?" she said casually.

"I will never forget it. Why?"

"Before you picked me up to leave, Patrick left me a message that was upsetting."

"Yes. I could sense something was wrong. And…?"

"He knows I'm in Germany." Josef's hand, still in hers, tensed, but she continued to explain about his conversation with the real estate agent, leading him to the lawyer's office. "I doubt the lawyer's assistant handed over specifics, like where I am staying."

"Did you call the lawyer's office and ask them what happened?"

"Yes. The assistant was away for a few days. The lawyer apologized and doubted she would give out specific details without asking him first."

Josef stared straight ahead as they passed the ruins of another castle, silent, his jaw taut as a stretched rubber band. Finally, he said, "Have you spoken to your husband since coming here?"

"Just once, and he texted me quite a few times after he hung up on me."

"He hung up on you?"

She nodded. "Sadly, he sees himself as the victim in my divorce filing."

The tops of his ears turned scarlet and he grunted a sound of irritation. "Germany is a big country. If he did not get an address, he should not be able to find you."

"Exactly what I figured. I just wanted you to know."

The tightness in his jaw softened as he studied her face. "I am glad you told me."

Josef stared at the rolling hills on the horizon, but she sensed deeper things churned inside his head.

He finally said, "Where will you go when you return to New York?"

"Not Brooklyn. I've booked a hotel in midtown Manhattan for several nights. I'll contact my lawyer to make sure things are on track and if he can arrange for me to get into my place to move my personal things without Patrick being present."

He nodded, relief showing on his face. "That would be smart."

"Since Patrick knows I've left the country, I worry he'll try to contact my parents. They don't know about the divorce or that I'm here. Last night I tried to reach them. I should've called sooner. They weren't home, and I left a message. With any luck, they'll get back to me soon."

He only nodded, continued to look at the view. Silent. Serious. Her life was a lot for even her to absorb.

After a few minutes, Josef tugged on the end of her scarf.

She glanced up.

"I am sorry if I seem tense when his name comes up. I worry, that is all."

"I know."

He smiled. "You okay?"

"I am."

"Good. Just remember, I am always here for you." He kissed her gently, reminding her that being honest worked in functional relationships.

* * * *

Bzzzzzz. Bzzzzz.

Anna's eyes flashed open and she sprang upright in the bed, her head clouded by the fog of sleep as she tried to locate the source of the insistent buzz. Her eyes fell on the dresser, where her phone glowed and vibrated. She must've left it on by mistake when she checked messages earlier. She flew from the bed, snatched it up. Her heart grated against her ribcage as she read the display and sighed with relief.

She cleared her throat. "Hello?"

"Anna, honey," chirped her mother. "We just got back from an overnight at Aunt Linda's house and got your message."

"Hey, Anna," her father said, talking loudly as he always did when they used the phone's speaker. "We haven't spoken in a while."

"We haven't." She rubbed her eyes to wake up. "I was just checking in."

"How's the weather down south?" he said.

"Down south? Right. Well, um…yeah. Listen, first, sorry I've been off the grid."

"Not a problem," said her father. "So did you stop in Charleston, like we suggested?"

"Not really. Well, you see…" How did she start something like this? "I hope you're both sitting."

"What's wrong?" her mother squeaked.

"Nothing, Mom. I'm okay, but I don't know how to say this, so I'm just going to blurt it out. I'm not traveling along the east coast. I'm in Germany."

Silence. She could picture her father's dark brows raised and her mother's understanding, sweet face turning into a frown.

Finally her father said, "Germany? Is this a business trip of Patrick's?"

Before she could answer, her mother cut in. "You know, Anna, since you married, you keep to yourself more, but leaving the country is something we'd like to know about. What if something happened to you?"

"Yes. I'm sorry. But there was a reason I didn't tell you." She paused to sort out her words, came up with nothing, and opted against coddling the blow. "I've filed for divorce."

Her mother gasped. "Divorce?"

She shared the details of her marriage, from the very first time Patrick's anger surged until the last incident, all over the stupid necklace. She told them about his father, and the abuse Patrick suffered in the years after his mother left. Her parents were oddly silent, but she marched forward with her story. They might say she made the wrong choice, but she wanted them armed with the whole picture.

"Patrick made me promise I'd never leave him. Once I agreed, I felt like I had no choice. He wasn't going to make leaving easy for me. I suppose both fear and pity kept me there longer than I should've stayed. It took hearing other abuse victims talk about it for me to see my own life. And I tried to help him. More than he deserved." Her throat swelled and vision blurred behind tears. "He'd be sorry, nicer for weeks, then hurt me again. No matter how much I begged him to get help, he didn't. So I filed for divorce."

"Oh, my…" Her mother's voice cracked.

Anna drew in a breath and continued. "My lawyer suggested leaving town when the papers were served. This trip to Germany, to take care of something for my neighbor, came at the right time. The papers were served to him two days after I left."

"Why wouldn't you tell us about this, Anna?" her mother asked, sadness evident in her voice.

"I always knew something wasn't right with him," her father growled. "Yes, why on earth didn't you tell us?"

"Because Patrick needed help. He was a victim of circumstance and I couldn't shame him by telling you. Isn't that what you always taught me?"

"Well, yes," replied her mother. "But not at the expense of your own safety."

"Mom, really? When you and Dad brought Tommy into our house, you told me to give him a chance even after he tried to hurt me. Remember? You said he'd been a victim of having bad parents."

Her father's voice sounded solemn. "Sweetheart, Tommy's father sexually abused him, and his mother's drinking problem left the kid with no support. A deck stacked against a pretty good kid, given the right guidance. We wanted to help him get in with an aunt from another state, not add another mark on his record." He sighed. "But we never wanted him to hurt you."

"I realize that. And yet, he did." Her parents showed such concern for Tommy that her candor even now didn't feel right. "Sorry to be blunt. I understood both back then and now how you wanted to give him a break, so maybe he could have a better life."

Dad's voice suddenly sounded frail. "Oh, Anna. You always try to understand. I'm so sorry we screwed that up. We didn't want him to succeed at your expense."

Anna sat on the edge of the bed, stunned but unwilling to keep her voice buried as she'd done for most of her life. "Well, in a way, he did. He still bothered me, even after I told you. But I didn't want to see him suffer any more than he had either."

"Sweetheart," said her mother. "We're so truly sorry. I guess we didn't really think our actions through. Chet, we made a big mistake."

"Yes," her father mumbled. "We didn't mean for you to suffer."

The regret in their voices sounded sincere. Anna wanted to let go of whatever they'd done. Being with Patrick had shown her why clinging to the past rarely brought good. Even with that logic, a little piece of her couldn't fully let go. Still, she considered all the times they'd been there for her, and holding on to the one time they hadn't seemed unfair.

"Anna, can you forgive us?" her mother said quietly, her voice filled with shame. "You know we love you."

"I know, Mom. I'm not mad at you. Just need to sort out my feelings. I love you guys, too."

They loved her. Erasing age-old feelings wasn't easy. Maybe if they'd protected her long ago, she might have possessed the backbone to stand up to Patrick sooner. Maybe not.

Or was she stronger because of what they'd done?

Anna wasn't even sure it mattered. They supported her now.

For a few minutes, they talked about what she'd been through. She heard relief in their voices as she fully explained about serving the divorce papers.

"Why did your neighbor send you to Germany?" asked her father.

She told them about Isaak, their friendship, the inheritance, and his final request.

"I can't believe you're in Europe," said her mother. "How is it?"

"Beautiful. Sad at times. Fulfilling Isaak's wish has been satisfying. And I've made some wonderful friends. I like the Germans." She laughed. "They remind me a little of New Yorkers. They take a no-nonsense approach to life, but are incredibly welcoming, too."

She told them about some of the towns she'd visited, the trip to Belgium, as well as the assistance of her guide, Josef.

"And, Dad? While I've been here, I've been thinking about your grandfather. You've only told me a little about him."

"A little is all I know. My dad told me his father came to this country as a baby. Only in his adulthood, after being raised Catholic and not knowing much about their original country, did he learn about what his parents had left behind in Poland to live safely in the US. You know, Uncle Stanley did an ancestry test about six months ago and started to build a family tree. How about I give him a call and see what he's learned?"

"I'd love that."

"So wait," said her mother. "If you're over there, isn't the time much later?"

"It's around one a.m."

"Well, my goodness. You should get back to sleep."

"I'm glad we talked."

Her mother's voice softened. "And, Anna, we are sorry you felt abandoned by us."

"Yes," her father chimed in. "Sweetheart, it was never our intent. In my line of work, I sometimes lose sight of my personal priorities. We dropped the ball."

"It's okay, you guys. I always knew you loved me."

"It wasn't okay," her mother said softly. "And we are here for you now."

A minute later, she hung up and returned to the bed. Dark silhouettes danced on the walls, lurking like the past. But as she drifted back to sleep, they faded away.

Chapter 22

Josef's mind whirled as he struggled to open his eyes. Images floated in his conscious, some sharp as a knifepoint, others fuzzy and just out of his reach. But there was definitely a cat in his dream about the accident. A fact he'd confirmed while driving to pick up Anna the other day.

He stumbled out of bed, made a pot of coffee, and sat outside on his patio while the crisp morning air woke him further. As he sipped the rich brew and stared out into a small patch of woods behind his apartment, the dream's details slowly came into focus.

The tabby stalking his sleep only materialized for an instant before transforming into Lily. Goosebumps prickled up his arms remembering the moment, her presence real as a ghost. He closed his eyes, straining every ounce of brainpower to claim more details.

Focus. Focus!

And just like that, a bag appeared. A white one with writing and… and an image. He took slow breaths, drowned out the sounds of cars on the nearby road, and concentrated on the image. Potato chips? He almost laughed, but the rest of the information flooded his mind, vividly showing the lettering. *Bret's Chèvre & Piment.*

Yes! He'd seen this before. In the car. With Lily. Elated at the discovery, he forced himself to still, search for more. There must be more. With each slow breath, he pictured the chip bag, over and over and over until his body drifted, drifted, drifted…

"I am starving," Lily announced.

"What did you pack?" He glanced from the driver's seat to the fun-loving woman at his side.

She unhooked her seatbelt and lustily batted her eyes as she turned to reach into the back seat. "All kinds of decadent treats."

He stirred, desiring her again. Those alluring dark eyes. The sexy French accent. The very things drawing him to her at the bar the night before.

While she searched through a canvas bag, he stole a glimpse of her slender body stretched out before him, the dip in her waist, the roundness of her bottom. Then she swung around and held a bag of chips. "Bein. Goat cheese and hot pepper. My favorite. You will try some?"

Josef's eyes flashed open and the moment before impact suddenly appeared, clear as a cloudless sky.

The chips. They'd nibbled on them for a few minutes, then she'd tossed the bag aside, tucked her leg beneath her bottom, and turned in her seat. "I want to read your palm."

Of course. She'd moved with ease, unencumbered by the belt as she'd reached for his hand.

He squeezed his eyes shut, searched for the flash of the moment…yes! That was when the cat darted in front of the car. He'd swerved. A blind curve. The grill of an oncoming car. He jerked the vehicle back to their lane. Too far. The car bumped on the grass. He couldn't steer. A tree jumped out.

BOOM!

He shivered, opened his eyes. Yes, the tree in the newspaper article, attached to the front end of Lily's car.

He'd avoided one head-on collision but steered them into another. If Lily had had her seatbelt back on, though, the outcome might have been totally different.

The weight of blame for over-steering remained on his shoulders, but if only she'd re-buckled the seatbelt… A near-constant pressure in his head lifted. Day after day, trying to remember what had happened. His heart still ached for Lily's loss. Maybe he should've reminded her about the seatbelt, but he hadn't.

Sinbad stepped onto Josef's patio and mewed a greeting. Josef swooped up the cat, placed him on his lap, and scratched his neck. Sinbad purred. Mrs. Freudenberger was either going out of her mind looking for the pet, or the cat had slipped out and she hadn't realized it yet.

"You know, I dreamt about a cat."

Sinbad looked up at Josef and mewed.

He laughed. Years ago he'd read that dreaming about cats meant you were reflecting delusions you had about yourself. Delusions that gave you a false sense of control. That something you believed deep down wasn't true.

Perhaps it was true. This crash had forced him to question everything he knew about himself.

The old Josef was a delusion, a boy mimicking his father. Believing that being bold, brave, and noncommittal to others gave him some control over his life.

The accident crushed the man he used to be, changed his life. These months had been occupied with a rebuilding of himself from the ground up. Physically and mentally. If he hadn't been hurt, he wouldn't have been driving Anna around. Without Anna, he wouldn't have taken Isaak's journey. Steps that made him gain focus on his own problems.

These past weeks were a gift. How lucky he'd been to spend them with her. Because of her mission, he woke each day a changed man. He'd seen things in his country through new eyes.

When she left, he would miss her. And even though she'd leave, he had no regrets about getting too close to someone so special. Memories of their journey together could never be stolen from him.

* * * *

"Josef asked if we would drive you to his brother's *Polterabend*." A breeze ruffled Regina's short blond hair, and then it fell back in place as quickly as it lifted.

Anna stopped to peek in the gift shop window in downtown Mainz, thinking about buying some chocolates to give to her parents. "His what?"

Regina laughed. "Pol-ter-ah-bend. A German wedding tradition. He told me he invited you."

"He mentioned a gathering the night before the wedding. I asked if it was similar to our custom of a rehearsal dinner, and he said yes."

"I see. He did not share the details, eh?" Regina grinned.

This shopping trip for a dress she could wear to the wedding was the first time Anna had seen Regina take a break from her work at the guesthouse. She and Joachim worked very hard.

"No." They continued to walk through the modern shopping area, quite different than the old city located a few blocks over. She glanced at Regina. "So what is this *Polterabend* all about?"

"Guests must break porcelain at the affair as a sign of good luck to the newlywed couple."

"You get to break things?" She laughed. "Doesn't sound like any custom we have in the US."

"It is a fun and casual night." Regina motioned ahead to a large department store. "Here is where will we shop. Peek & Cloppensburg."

Anna slowed at one of the display windows, her gaze resting on a beautiful pair of royal blue pumps with a slender heel. "Maybe I can find a dress to match those shoes."

A reflection in the store window of the brick courtyard behind her made her still. A man watched her. He wore a cap, and his jacket collar hid part of his face. But those eyebrows. Dark, distinctive. Like Patrick's. Her heart raced. Before she could turn around to look, Regina touched her arm.

"Let us go in." She pulled open the glass door.

Anna followed, but before entering, she spun around. The man was gone. She shook her head. Patrick would be thrilled to know he caused all this paranoia.

She forced a smile at Regina and headed inside.

For over an hour they shopped in the modern, well-stocked department store. Anna found a beautiful blue-patterned dress that hugged her curves, dipped into a V-neck, and had trumpeted sleeves. A perfect match for the shoes she wanted to buy. She even purchased a pair of black suede boots, if for no other reason than she loved them.

Afterward they stopped for coffee and cake at a little café, and, once done, went the tram stop.

As they waited on a bench for their ride, Regina said, "I think Josef has grown very fond of you."

"I've grown fond of him, too."

"We have known Josef and his family for a long time. Around you, he is the most relaxed we have ever seen him." Regina raised her pale brows. "So? Has he charmed you the way he does the rest of us?"

Knowing others saw in them what Anna felt confirmed so many of her feelings. "Yes, he has."

Regina's broad smile reached her rich blue eyes. "*Sehr gut.* That makes me happy." A tram approached and she stood. "This is ours."

Once boarded on the crowded car, Anna got separated from Regina and stood further down holding onto a metal bar. As the tram pulled away, she stared blindly at the busy sidewalk, thick with pedestrians. Her gaze brushed past a man. She backtracked. Same dark brows, cap hiding his hair, and flipped up collar hiding the lower half of his face. She squinted. Could it be—

Someone tapped her arm. As she glanced down, a man in a suit rose from his seat and motioned to it. "*Bitte?*"

"*Danke.*" She smiled and took the seat, quickly craning her neck to see outside the window. The Patrick look-alike had vanished again.

She had to be losing her mind. Surely he wouldn't hop a plane and come all this way. Or was he just that insane?

* * * *

Josef hurried up the front walkway of the guesthouse and entered the small reception area. Anna was on her way down the stairs dressed in a suede skirt that wrapped tight around her slender frame, black tights, and black-heeled boots.

She smiled and hit the last step. "You're right on time."

He slipped an arm around her waist and gave her a kiss. "Because I missed you today. Ready to leave for dinner?"

"Yup. Where to?"

"There's an Italian restaurant not far from my apartment. My friend is the chef there. Then later, we can go back to my place for the night. Is that too presumptuous on my part?"

"I'd be disappointed if you didn't want me there."

He helped her with her coat and kissed her again. "*Gut.* Then we are of the same mind." He winked, took her hand, and they headed outside. "Let's catch the tram."

As they crossed the street, he said, "I have news. I had a breakthrough in my memory this morning." He shared with her the dream, the cat, and how it led to his realization about Lily's seatbelt. "It doesn't change the sadness I feel over her death, but some of the blame I carried has gone."

She stopped and drew him into a hug, whispered in his ear, "That is fantastic news, Josef."

He talked more about the return of his memory, and he couldn't remember when he'd felt so good. As they approached the tram stop, their ride neared and they boarded. The minute they got seated, Anna turned to look out the window. Her brows furrowed as she squinted at the pedestrian-filled streets.

"Looking for something?"

She turned around. "I'm probably being neurotic, but twice today, while Regina and I shopped, I saw a face in a crowd that I swear was Patrick's."

"So you think he might here?"

"He flew to Texas, to my sister's. Germany might not be out of the question."

"But the lawyer believed his assistant didn't provide Patrick with the details, right?

"Yes. But he wasn't certain."

Josef worried. What if Patrick was a persuasive man, who'd manipulated or lied to get her actual location?

"I called Patrick's office when I got back from shopping today. He didn't answer, but his voice mail didn't say he was away."

"So that should reassure you."

She shrugged. "I suppose. I'm probably being paranoid."

He placed a hand over hers. "No, you aren't. As long as I am by your side, I will not let that man lay a finger on you."

"Thank you." She smiled, a half-hearted one. "So we're eating Italian food in Germany, huh?"

He chuckled. "Do you think we only eat *weiner schnitzel* and drink beer?"

"Yup. And wear lederhosen, too." Her mouth curved into a simple smile, and she watched him with a dash of merriment in her eyes.

"Ah, I guess you will think it is corny if I wear my lederhosen to the wedding then."

The smiled vanished. "Oh, I'm sorry. Were you going to—"

He laughed and she narrowed her eyes, quickly followed by a smile. "Okay, wise guy. You got me."

He enjoyed seeing her relaxed, but it lasted only seconds. She turned and stared out the window, her smile vanishing as her worried gaze combed the city streets.

Chapter 23

"Anna's reason for coming to Germany is a remarkable story." Joachim stepped to the side and encouraged Anna into his group of friends as he addressed them. "Do you remember a man named Isaak who I met in America when we visited Regina's brother?"

While Joachim spoke about Anna's search for Gunther, she scanned the backyard where Gabriel and Kirsten would celebrate their *Polterabend* for any sign of Josef. He needed to help get tonight's event organized, the reason she'd come with her guesthouse hosts, who were close friends with Josef's family. She didn't mind. Kirsten's parents were delightful and almost everyone she'd met at the casual gathering spoke a little English.

For a split second, she thought she spotted him beneath one of the tents near a long table holding food platters, an arrangement of autumn flowers, and a multilayered chocolate cake. But it wasn't him.

Guests began to clap. She turned just as Josef entered through a gate leading to the backyard with a couple at his side. The man's long face, strong chin, and blue-green eyes were like Josef's. They stood close in height, but the newcomer had a bulkier build—not Josef's lean frame—and dark brown hair with a clean-shaven face. Not a glimmer of auburn coloring or facial hair, like Josef. A curvy blonde held the man's hand.

Regina touched Anna's arm. "That is the bride and groom, Gabriel and Kirsten."

The couple beamed. Why wouldn't they? The event held such promise, brimming with the excitement of a lifetime together. A feeling Anna had experienced not that long ago herself, though it seemed as if a hundred years had passed since that day.

People gathered around the new arrivals, offering hugs and congratulations. Josef talked and laughed with many of them. Just watching him smile made happiness swell inside her heart. She selfishly wanted him to herself right now, but he belonged at his brother's side.

Josef stopped talking, lifted his sunglasses to the top of his head. He panned the yard. She waved and his eyes lit up. After saying something to his brother, Josef came over to her.

He shook Joachim's hand and gave Regina a peck on both cheeks. "Thank you for bringing Anna."

Slipping his arm around Anna's waist, he gave her a kiss. "I am glad you made it." His gaze fluttered over the open neckline of her peasant top and continued to her ankle-tight blue jeans and flats. He met her eyes. "You look pretty. Come." He took her hand. "Meet my family."

Heads turned as they walked through the crowd. No doubt everyone knew Josef, and they were curious about her.

"Gabriel, Kirsten," he said as they neared the engaged couple. "This is Anna."

"I am so happy to finally meet you." Gabriel embraced her and then so did his bride. Gabriel tossed an arm around his brother. "The woman who has brought a smile back to my brother's face."

Josef groaned. "Now come on. I did not invite her so you could embarrass me." He flicked a glance her way and she smiled.

A shorter woman, with chin-length graying hair and eyes the same blue-green as Josef's, spoke in German and the others laughed.

Josef smiled tenderly at the woman. "Anna, this is my mother. I just got a little reprimand for not introducing her first. She says she is very happy to meet you."

Anna took his mother's hand. "*Danke*. I'm very happy to meet you, Mrs. Schmitt."

Josef's gaze softened and stayed on hers, and for a moment they were the only two people in the world. All she could see, all she wanted to see, was the promise in his eyes. Be it from the love in the air due to the wedding or something between them, she couldn't be sure.

Three young boys burst into their small circle, talking excitedly.

A woman with full curves and a pretty face hurried toward the kids. Her shiny auburn hair swayed as she shook her head and wagged a reprimanding finger at the children in between words.

Anna didn't need a translator to know a motherly rebuke, though the kids barely seemed to hear a word she said.

A tall man strolled over and stood behind the woman, relaxed with a smile on his kind face. He firmly said something and the boys quieted down.

Josef waved his hand to the group. "Anna, these are my nephews, and this my sister, Helga, and her husband, Christian."

Anna shook their hands. Before she could say anything more to the boys, they ran off after other children who'd just arrived.

"Anna, I am happy to meet you." Helga's brown eyes were warm, welcoming. "How do you like Germany?"

While they talked, Josef whispered, "Be right back."

His family proved to be friendly, all of them working hard to speak in English and make her comfortable. Josef soon reappeared and made an announcement. The guests started leaving the backyard.

"Come." Helga touched Anna's forearm. "We are about to begin."

The group of fifty or so gathered in the driveway, forming a semicircle with the bride and groom in front. People shouted out things to them that had everyone laughing. Josef and a couple of other guys pulled several large plastic bins filled with plates and cups from the garage and spread them out amongst the group.

Anna stood next to a waist-high brick wall running along the edge of the driveway to observe and enjoy the air of excitement. Josef appeared at her side and hoisted himself up onto wall to sit. "Now the fun starts."

Gabriel gave a shrill whistle, and everyone quieted. "*Scherben bringen glück...*"

Josef guided her in front of him, wrapping her in his arms and kissing the back of her head. His warm breath landed close to her ear. "Gabriel said shards of the pottery bring luck, but his luck came when Kirsten agreed to become his wife."

Josef continued to quietly translate. She liked being in his arms, nestled in the space between his legs. One by one, each guest approached a bin, took out one or two pieces of the dinnerware and smashed them on the driveway. Anna flinched at the sound, but the louder the crash and bigger the pile, the more enthusiastic the crowd became.

Josef's youngest nephew selected two plates and heaved them onto the mess like a champ. She glanced over her shoulder to Josef. "What happens after we break all those?"

"The bride and groom clean them up. Together."

"That doesn't sound fun."

He chuckled. "It is not supposed to be fun. The purpose is to make the couple aware that they will have to work as a team through difficult conditions during their marriage."

The words settled like acid in her stomach.

Every day since she'd made the decision to leave Patrick, she'd felt confident about the choice. But every so often a little voice would whisper in her ear. *Did you do enough to save your marriage?* She rationalized she had, but the moral of this event allowed the doubt to tiptoe back inside her head.

Josef surprised her when he turned her in his arms, putting them face-to-face. "Listen to me. I know what you are thinking."

"What? How—"

His voice softened. "You are tense. From everything you have told me, you worked very hard to keep your marriage together." He tilted her chin up with his finger. "You deserved better than that man gave you."

Certainty glimmered in Josef's eyes. How did she find such a man? He filled her heart, made her whole, pushed aside her self-doubt. "Thank you. I just needed a reminder."

"You are welcome." He slid off the wall and took her hand. "Now come on. It is almost your turn to smash something. Are you ready?"

"No. But if I must..."

"You must." He grinned.

The person next to them gleefully smashed two saucers.

"You go now." Josef motioned to the bin.

Anna went up, self-conscious with an audience. She selected a large dinner plate and walked close to the broken pile.

"Go, Anna," Joachim yelled.

"Give it a good smash!" Regina said.

Anna lifted the plate over her head. Josef's words fed her confidence. She had worked hard to help Patrick and deserved better. Damn him! A Herculean power she didn't know she possessed unfurled inside her. She heaved the plate to the ground, jumping backward as the porcelain shattered loudly. The crowd cheered.

A wave of confidence washed over her. She *was* strong. So strong that if any man ever tried to hit her again, she would have the strength to fight back.

Josef smashed a plate after her, then he returned to her side at the edge of the crowd.

After the last plates were broken, two of Josef's nephews rushed to the bride and groom with brooms.

The youngest of his nephews came running over to Josef, clearly upset and talking wildly. Josef listened, then kneeled down to the boy's level while he answered him.

He glanced up at Anna. "Tobias here is upset because his brothers got to deliver the brooms." Josef pointed to Anna and said to his nephew. "*Das ist Anna. Kannst du hallo sagen?*"

The young boy studied her for a moment, then said, "*Hallo*, Anna."

"Hello, Tobias."

He studied her carefully, then asked Josef a question. Josef chuckled, hesitated, then responded. The boy threw his arms around Josef. "*Danke Onkel Josef.*"

He ran off to watch the cleanup with his brothers and some of the other children.

"What was that all about?" she asked.

"Oh." He rose to full height and shrugged. "Tobias wanted to know if he could bring us our brooms when we have our *Polterabend.*"

Anna laughed, mostly to hide the awkwardness of the question. "What did you tell him?"

He took her hand. "I told him that if I was ever lucky enough to find a bride like you, that I would definitely let him deliver our brooms."

She squeezed his hand, kissed him gently on the lips, but wasn't sure what else to say.

Without a doubt, she felt the same way about him. Life back home beckoned, though, and needed to be sorted out before she could even entertain such a notion.

* * * *

The lamppost outside Josef's apartment cast a light into his bedroom, the shade only partially closed. He curled his body around Anna and she snuggled in. A perfect fit. He listened to her even breaths, shutting his eyes and lying still so he didn't disturb her sleep. They'd had a late night at his brother's party.

How lucky he was to have such a loving family and good friends. He'd been away so much over the past fifteen years, only using this Mainz apartment for short stops between tours. After six months in town, though, he felt closer to these people and this community than ever before.

Whatever forces kept him here, this was exactly where he needed to be to heal. The soreness in his leg had subsided to a dull ache every so often and a general sense of contentment soothed the angry beast that had taken over his soul.

So many times tonight he'd found himself simply watching Anna interact. His family adored her. They'd told him more than once. He smiled recalling how she'd enchanted Tobias when he'd dragged her into a game of *Topfschlagen* with a small group of his friends. Anna quickly caught on to the rules of helping the blindfolded person who was "it" by shouting cold or hot as they searched for a hidden candy. Josef loved hearing her yell *kalt* and *heiß*, learning some German from the kids quite fast.

And when the sun rose soon, they would attend the wedding.

He mentally counted the days until she would leave. Not enough time. He'd cherish what time remained. It was all he could do.

Silly, really. He hardly knew her. Yet they'd connected. The kind of connection you don't find every day.

Tonight, his sister had asked him if he planned to go visit Anna after she returned home. He told her he didn't know. Sure, he had asked himself the same question in recent days. But he hesitated to bring it up. Her life was in transition. He didn't want to pressure her.

She stirred and rolled onto her back. He opened his eyes and found her watching him.

"I keep waking up for some reason," she said in a tired voice.

"Me, too." He reached out, took her hand, and tucked it close to his chest. "Did you enjoy yourself tonight?"

"It was the best time I've had in ages. I can't remember when I laughed so much."

"My family loved meeting you."

"Well, I loved meeting them." She yawned, rubbed her eyes. "They made me feel so welcome. Everyone was so friendly. And funny, too."

"Funny? Germans are not known for their humor."

"Why would you say that?"

"It is a common fact." He shifted his pillow and propped his head more comfortably onto it. "For example, what's the world's shortest book?"

She shrugged. "I don't know."

"A German joke book."

Her sleepy laughter filled the dimly lit room. "Okay, well, maybe—"

"And you know what Mark Twain said about the topic?"

"No."

"He said, 'German jokes are no laughing matter.'"

She chuckled. "Okay, okay. You win. Not funny. But fun. Will you accept that Germans are fun?"

"Ah, now that is true. We know how to party." He gathered her close. "I was thinking about something."

"I hope it's something good?" Her hand slipped along his chest and her lids softened, stealing his train of thought.

But he'd gathered the courage to ask and ignored the distraction. "When you return to America, would it be possible for me to visit you sometime?"

She cupped his face in her warm hands. "Yes. Please *do.* I was hoping you'd want to but wasn't sure how to ask."

Relief flooded through him. He wasn't sure what he'd have done if she had said no. He took her in his arms, closed his eyes, and relaxed in the comfort of knowing her feelings for him were as strong.

Chapter 24

From the dark wood pew where she sat with Josef, Anna studied the intense blues and vibrant reds in the stained-glass windows at the front of the church. One caught her eye, an image of Mary and Joseph holding up the baby Jesus.

Josef unbuttoned his suit jacket and their shoulders bumped. He gave her a wink and she smiled back.

But her attention drifted back to the image of Jesus. Most Sunday school lessons were long forgotten, but lessons about God's grace had stayed with her. The kind of grace she'd chosen to show Patrick when he'd been at his worst. These days the idea of redemption occupied her mind. She wanted to stop feeling stupid over allowing Patrick's mistreatment and begin to trust herself again. But it wasn't so easy.

Josef placed his hand on her thigh, tugging her away from a problem that she couldn't seem to solve. The warmth of his palm reached her skin through the thin fabric of her new dress. She slid her hand over his. When she returned home, she'd miss his touch.

The Wiesbaden church where Gabriel and Kirsten would marry was an architectural masterpiece. The altar sat below a domed ceiling, its height so tall it appeared to reach the heavens. Behind it, detailed stained-glass windows lined the curved wall, each telling a biblical tale. Two chairs were placed in front of the altar, both covered with satin covers and secured by a large white bow in the back, waiting for the bride and groom.

Josef moved his thumb in a slow caress. She looked over and caught him watching her.

"You look very pretty," he said quietly.

She smoothed the lapel of his charcoal jacket. "And you should wear a suit more often."

"Thank you." His eyelids hooded, and his gaze trailed from her face to the *V* dip at her cleavage. He leaned over and whispered in her ear, "I look forward to helping you out of your dress tonight."

Heat swept to her belly, but the spell broke when his mother turned around in her pew and asked him a question. He leaned forward and answered her quietly, leaving Anna to miss his touch.

The idea of going home had become increasingly difficult. Every day, every hour, she and Josef grew closer. His family and friends had welcomed her as if she was one of their own, and she liked that feeling. Much like her life in Washington State, where her job in Seattle kept her close enough to Whidbey Island to visit her loved ones whenever she wanted. Before Patrick had dragged her clear across the country and made sure he kept her isolated from people who cared about her.

What a fool she'd been! He'd accepted the job transfer from Seattle to the east coast without even asking her. A small part of her thought the move could be an adventure. New York City sounded romantic, exciting. But he insisted they live in Brooklyn, far from the buzz of Manhattan. Whenever she dared to step out and try to meet new people, he showed his displeasure. It was as if he wanted her waiting at home, for him. Only him.

She dropped her chin to her chest. Yup, she'd been a fool. A stupid fool.

Josef leaned back and took Anna's hand, making her stuff the humiliation deep inside of her.

"My brother and Kirsten have arrived," he said.

She nodded, put on a happy face. A clergyman approached the altar, his black gown billowing behind him. When he faced the filled pews, an organ piped in the wedding march. The guests stood and turned to the back.

Gabriel and Kirsten moved slowly down the aisle. Earlier, Josef had explained that in Germany most couples marry in a civil ceremony before the religious service. Nobody gives away the bride. Rather they enter their new life together to have their union bonded in the eyes of God.

Kirsten's golden-blond hair had been swept up and secured with a pearl-beaded headband. She wore an ankle-length, white lace gown. Simple elegance. Both bride and groom's expressions glowed as they took their seats up front. The mix of music and memories made Anna's throat thicken. Drew her back to the same moment in her life…

A mild late spring day—almost sunny by Whidbey Island standards. She and Patrick had joined in matrimony surrounded by fifty of their closest friends and family. The event held all the hope of a lifetime. Little did she know their bond would soon tear apart at the seams. And her mercy served as the adhesive holding their marriage together as the months passed.

Her gaze drifted to the stained-glass window again. Redemption. Salvation. Grace. Offering forgiveness to others came easily to Anna. Forgiveness extended to her parents when they stood by a foster child, not her. Forgiveness extended to Patrick too many times to count. Yet why couldn't she pardon herself?

She considered Josef, a man who'd blamed himself for a lost life in the car accident. She'd seen him start to move on and wanted to be strong, like him. Maybe it wasn't about forgetting her past, but accepting what she'd gone through.

Salvation. God's grace. The words taunted her. Wouldn't a caring God grant such a thing to a woman who so easily extended the same to others?

The compassion she reserved for others seeped into her heart. All she desired was a small dose of self-forgiveness, an elixir to cure the shame of being so weak in her marriage. She closed her eyes, bowed her head. *You tried to help the man you loved. That was why you stayed. There's nothing wrong with that. So let it go. Let. It. Go. The pain. The shame. Everything you ever did for love, do now for yourself.*

A force washed over her. She mentally pushed away ghosts that haunted her dreams. *I have changed,* she repeated over and over until they evaporated. And it took a moment, but a gentle ripple of pride expanded in her chest. Pride that cleansed her spirit of self-imposed blame, and eroded an ache inhabiting her for too long.

She quietly released the breath, opened her eyes. From now on, she had permission to put the past where it belonged.

* * * *

Strobe lights pulsed above the dance floor and the crowd bopped to a dance medley spanning the decades from Elton John to Black Eyed Peas, who had a feeling it was going to be a good night. So did Anna.

Two dances ago, she'd kicked off her heels and continued in her stocking feet. Josef managed to keep up, a slower, more careful version, but for a guy with a leg injury, he'd performed some decent moves.

Both the lights and music slowed. Norah Jones's silky-smooth tone crooned about coming away with her. Josef placed his hand on the small of her back and moved her slowly along the dance floor.

His breath fell next to her ear. "Tired yet?"

"Don't worry. I can keep up. How's your leg?"

"Starting to hurt. I will sit soon." He brushed his lips to hers and tucked her close.

She rested her head on his shoulder, her mind lost in thoughts about the fun day. Good food, dancing, and many raised glasses while the crowd yelled *Prost*. Josef and Helga had put together a slideshow about Gabriel, from diapers to now and Kirsten's sisters had done the same for her. Throughout the reception, people stood and spoke warm words about the wedded couple. There were even games and a skit performed by Kirsten's cousin. The whole celebration was thoughtful, an intensely personal way to celebrate the joining of two people.

Josef hummed to the music. The song's lyrics played to every wish she had right now. To stay in this other world, where she remained safe, sound, and pretty darn content.

Joachim glided by with Regina and slowed down. "Oh, hello, you two. Josef, this has been a fun wedding. Gabriel looks like a happy man. I know your father would have loved his bride."

Josef patted Joachim's shoulder. "Thank you. I think he would, too."

Regina touched Anna's arm. "I forgot to tell you. After Josef picked you up to go to the church, someone called the guesthouse for you."

"Did they leave a name?"

"I asked, but he didn't say and hung up rather quickly. Sounded American."

He? Her limbs suddenly felt shaky and her gut like a rock had settled in it. "Did the call come from overseas?"

"You know, I am not sure. We get calls both internationally and within the country, I hardly take notice." She shrugged. "I suppose he will try again."

Joachim led Regina away, but Anna stopped dancing. Josef watched her, the worry in his eyes equaling the terror seizing her body.

He took her hand. "Come on." As he neared their table and grabbed his cane, he said, "Let's get a drink."

She slipped on her shoes and took her purse from her chair.

They walked toward the bar. She should've asked Regina if the hotel phone had caller ID. Even if she said yes, Anna would have to wait and check later. If she went now, Josef would insist on coming with her. She didn't want to take him away from this special family affair.

Josef ordered two glasses of wine and handed her one. "There is a quiet spot nearby where we can sit."

As they walked, he glanced at her. "You are worried it is your husband?"

"Who else would call?"

"You mentioned Dr. Walker might put you in touch with an expert to trace your family history."

"Then why wouldn't he have said so?"

Josef shrugged, frowned. They entered a lounge with leather seating, a stone fireplace, and large windows looking outside to a dimly lit patio with tables. He motioned to one of the sofas.

She sat and sipped her wine, but her mind whirled with worry. It was Saturday afternoon in New York. Patrick could be anywhere, but he could always be reached. Maybe she should call.

"Anna, even if he found out the guesthouse address, flying over here seems like a dramatic move. This could be another attempt to frighten you."

"Yeah, well, he's doing a good job."

Josef's jaw tightened.

"See. Even you look worried."

"Only because I am concerned about you. Do you really think he would fly here to find you?"

"Yes and no. I sense his desperation. But just how far he'll go is anybody's guess."

He lowered his glass to the coffee table, taking hers and doing the same. As he gathered her hands, he let out a sigh. "I cannot bear the thought of you returning home and having to face him alone."

"I won't be alone. After our last conversation, I only plan to see him with the lawyers present."

"Yes, but…" Josef shook his head. "I do not worry any less."

"His behavior has me worried, too. I'd hoped he would calm down after the initial shock of the divorce hit. If anything, he seems angrier. I'll get a restraining order, if need be."

"I wish I could be at your side to kick his ass if he tries anything."

She smiled. "I appreciate the offer, but I have to learn to face him on my own. It's the only way I can move forward. Know what I mean?"

"Yes. I know. I do not have to like it though." He stood, wincing as he reached for his cane. "I'm going to the men's room. Be right back."

She watched him walk away. Regina's message pounded away at her thoughts. She took her phone from the purse and turned it on to roam, but the service in here was terrible.

She went to the large windows near the patio. When that didn't work, she headed for a door leading out to the unoccupied patio, propped it open with her hip, and waited. One service bar. She stepped out. A few feet away from the building, she got a full signal.

Her eyes adjusted to the dark as she dialed Patrick's cell number. The furious thud of her heart echoed in her ears as she paced. One ring. She'd flat out ask if he called. Two rings. *Come on! Answer!*

On the third ring, strong arms wrapped her, swiftly lifted her off the ground, sent her flying. Pain shot through her back as she hit the concrete building. Stunned, breathless, head spinning, she tried to focus. Her knees gave way and she headed for the ground, but two hands grabbed her shoulders and slammed her to the wall.

A spotlight on the building's corner cast a slice of light her way. She blinked. Patrick stared back; bulging eyes glared, a vehement blast that made her shrink inside herself.

His strong hands dug into her flesh. "Did you get my message?" he asked through gritted teeth.

His coal-black eyes flared as if a demon had crawled inside his skin and taken over. She struggled to free herself, but he pressed harder.

Terror wound so tightly around her heart she could barely breathe. "How did you find out where I—"

He pulled her forward then slammed her hard against the wall again, knocking the wind from her lungs. "Shut up! You're going to pay for what you did. Why would you embarrass me at work?"

Anna quivered. Pain pulsed in her head, torso, and shoulders.

"Answer me," he screamed.

She struggled for air and finally drew in breath. "I told you. My lawyer advised me to do it."

Patrick let go. He lifted his hand. She braced herself. The stinging slap to her cheek made the back of her head slam into the wall. Tears welled in her eyes as old instincts kicked in. *Play it quiet as a possum faking dead. Soon he'll be done.*

As she stilled, the force of throwing those dishes last night rushed back to her. The power in her muscles and the sound of the shattering glass. Quiet and submissive was the old Anna. The new woman possessing her body could move mountains…or at least try.

He again pinned her by the shoulders, leaving her arms dangling at her side. In one swift movement, she drew in a deep breath, clenched her fists, and slammed them hard as she could against his chest and pushed.

He stumbled back several steps and his dark brows rose. When he steadied himself, he tilted his head and studied her like a bull just before the charge. "Oh, you like to fight back now? Is that what you and your new boyfriend do?"

"Go to hell!" she screamed while stepping away from him. Raising her voice at him gave her a surge of confidence. "You're sick, Patrick. I told you on the phone. I don't love you anymore."

His eyes narrowed, like a snake about to ambush his prey. He stepped toward her before she could move and grabbed her hair. "You've turned into a real—"

Josef slammed into Patrick's side, knocking him down and forcing him to release her hair. The two men landed on the ground and Josef's cane skidded along the patio. Josef hovered over Patrick, punching him multiple times in the face.

Patrick moaned, but Josef kept at him. "Hurts, doesn't it?" he growled.

As Josef raised his fist, Patrick let out a primal yell, slammed his knee into Josef's groin, and gave him a shove. Josef curled in a ball, doubled over, nursing his pain as Patrick scrambled to his feet.

Blood dripped from Patrick's nose as he stepped backward but kept his fists positioned to strike.

Josef moaned, but slowly rolled onto his knees and staggered to his feet. As he took steps toward Patrick, Anna saw fear in Patrick's eyes.

"If you want to fight, asshole, then fight me. Or are you afraid to face a man?"

Patrick stopped. "I'm not afraid of you."

Anna watched, horrified and defenseless as he charged Josef. The two men swung at each other, sometimes catching a good punch, other times blocked. Josef limped, but held his own.

"Stop!" Anna screamed. "Leave us alone, Patrick."

He glanced her way, smirked. "Oh, don't you worry. You're next."

Before he could look away, Josef charged with his shoulder forward. The impact sent Patrick down, but he scrambled back to his feet almost immediately. His dark eyes glowed with rage as he lunged at Josef, pushing him to the ground close to the stairs. Josef howled in pain and grabbed his bad leg.

Patrick stepped toward Josef, watching him with a sickening gleam of satisfaction as Josef clutched his leg and moaned.

You're next.

Patrick's words rang in her ears. She had a split second. Taking a step forward, she swiped Josef's cane off the ground. She wound it like a baseball bat over her shoulder then swung with all her might, landing a blow on Patrick's chest.

"Arrrgh!" His hands flew up as he wobbled. He lowered his hands, glanced sideways at her, the muscles of his throat and jaw throbbing with anger.

She swung again, this time aiming for the back of his knees. Patrick's hand flew behind his body and he grabbed the cane and jerked it from her hands. "Damn you, Anna!"

Anna's gaze caught movement on the ground. Josef's outstretched arm reached for Patrick's ankle.

As Patrick surged toward her, Josef grabbed his ankle. Patrick glanced down. That's when Anna charged forward, not caring what part of him she hit. All she wanted was for him to stop.

Her shoulder slammed into Patrick's solid frame, sending a shockwave through her body.

He stumbled backward, then teetered at the top of the staircase.

Anna reached out, but too late. Gravity pulled him down. Patrick wailed with the first thud, his agonizing cry filling the night air. A bang sounded each time his body hit a step. Down, down, down, down, until he plopped like a limp rag doll at the bottom.

Chapter 25

People wandered everywhere. Police. Paramedics. Wedding guests. Voices speaking gibberish that echoed incoherently inside Anna's head. She tried to lift her arms to cover her ears, but her trembling body prevented her from moving. Instead she squeezed her eyes tight, shut out the flashing lights of emergency vehicles, and drew the warm blanket someone had handed her tightly around her shoulders.

"Anna."

She opened her eyes and lifted her chin as Regina came over and rubbed Anna's back. "You poor thing. Can I get you something?"

Anna's teeth chattered as she moved her lips to speak, but she managed to mumble, "No th-thanks."

Josef appeared at Regina's side. She hugged him, and they spoke in hushed tones.

After she left, Josef crouched down near Anna and looked up into her face. "The medics say he is badly hurt but alive."

Relief flooded Anna's body. If she'd pushed a man to his death, she wasn't sure how she'd live with herself. Even a man as mean as Patrick. His cry of anguish before he lost consciousness pounded inside her skull, only silenced by the thud each time he hit a step.

I did that. I hurt someone.

Her heart tightened. Remorse sprouted like a weed in the center of her chest. The stairs. She'd seen them, but self-defense had become her own preservation. She'd just wanted him to stop hurting them. Not send him hurtling down a flight of stairs. A tear trickled down her cheek, followed by another and another, yet nothing washed away the guilt of having almost killed a man.

Josef sat on the bench and held her. She cried into his chest and he let her without saying a word. In his arms, she was warm and safe. Soon her teeth stopped chattering and tears dried up.

She lifted her head. "What happens now?"

"They will take him to a hospital. He will be under police watch. I told them everything I saw and what happened after I came out. They want to talk to you."

"Am I in trouble?"

He stroked her face. That's when she saw the bruise on his temple, the blood on his collar. Pain he'd taken for her safety.

"Of course not. The police know he was trying to harm you. Both of us." His jaw tightened. "I have never wanted to physically hurt a man before, but when I saw him strike you…" He looked down, shut his eyes. "I wish I could have helped you more."

She slipped her hands from beneath the blanket and cupped his face. His eyes opened. "If you hadn't come out, I'd probably be going to the hospital right now. Or the morgue."

His eyes glistened. "I don't want to think about that outcome."

"I'm sorry my problems followed me here. This ruined your brother's wedding."

"You have no reason to be sorry. They are not upset, only concerned."

A police officer came over, intimidating in his dark slacks, crisp shirt, and a windbreaker that read *Polizei*. He glanced between them while speaking in German. Josef replied, then motioned to Anna, saying in English, "This is Anna Abrams. She is an American who is…" He paused and his brows furrowed. "Who is married to the man who attacked her."

The officer nodded and began asking her questions in passable English. She told him everything, from the abuse at home, to the divorce papers she'd served him three weeks ago after entering Germany.

Several times when she mentioned some of the harsher details, Josef winced. Yes, it was uncomfortable to hear. But this moment made clear how the silence of being battered was what had given her abuser power.

Josef remained at her side listening, his hand in hers. She held on tightly, the touch of his hand the only thing that allowed her to keep going.

* * * *

Josef was thankful for two things. That he'd come out when he had, and that the son-of-a-bitch was under police watch.

He listened as Anna talked to the officer, who took copious notes. Her hair was disheveled and her cheek bright red from where she'd been hit.

His gut wrenched as images bombarded him. A man screaming at Anna, pressing her against the wall. He'd lifted his hand, struck her face. Josef flinched, the blow one he could still feel. Rage had sent him flying out the door. Even now, fury pulsed like hot acid through his veins. Stories she'd shared about her abuse paled next to seeing it live. He blew out a breath, wishing for the negative energy to subside. Anna needed his support, not more anger.

She continued to speak in a soft voice, seeming unaware of his angst. Each word she said expanded the sadness in his chest. Her pain was his. But a new pain had evolved, this one unexpected.

This is Anna Abrams. She is an American who is married to the man who attacked her.

His words to the officer had been a harsh reminder that Anna was, by law, still married. A fact he'd always known, but he'd given himself permission to care deeply about her because she'd said her heart belonged to no one.

The officer closed his pad. "Thank you, Mrs. Kelly."

Josef flinched. Of course her ID showed her married name even though she'd been very clear she be called Anna Abrams with all she met.

The officer glanced between them. "Security will be placed at Mr. Kelly's hospital door, though he cannot move far on his own. The medics say he has a broken leg and arm. He is lucky to be alive."

"Is he under arrest?" she asked.

"He is under watch, but it is up to you and Mr. Schmitt if you want to press charges."

She turned to Josef. "I don't know. I don't want him in jail. I just want him to leave me alone and not make the divorce difficult."

Josef wanted to lock him up forever. He looked at the officer. "We do not have to decide right now, do we?"

"*Nein.* You should speak to the prosecuting attorneys if you want to understand the legalities. Either way, we will notify the US Consulate to have a representative speak to him about his rights. You may want to speak to them, too."

Anna nodded and extended a hand from under her blanket. "Thank you, Officer."

He shook her hand and left.

Josef put his arm around her. They sat quietly for a minute.

She mumbled, "I can't imagine what your family and my new friends think of me."

"They understand he victimized you." He tipped up her chin so she'd look him in the eyes. "And they see your courage."

"Right now, it feels like a hollow victory." She slipped the blanket off her shoulders. "I should say I'm sorry to Gabriel and Kirsten. Then I think I'll call a cab and go back to the guesthouse."

"I am not leaving your side."

"It's a special family day. I can't ask you to leave, but I'm very sore right now."

"Then come back to my place. I will run you a hot bath. I just want to be there for you. Besides, the wedding probably would have ended soon anyway."

She glanced around the patio. "Well, I would feel better with you."

"*Gut*." Relief showered him. He wouldn't sleep a wink if she were anyplace else.

He took her hand and they went back inside. Heads turned as they passed through the room. He drew her close, hoping to steal any discomfort she felt about the attention. What happened exposed a very personal side of her life and had to be uncomfortable.

She stopped walking and looked at him. "I've been thinking about how I hid this for so long. If I want to beat this thing with Patrick, then it's time I learned to speak up about what went on. Not feel ashamed."

He squeezed her hand. "I am proud of you, Anna."

Together they said their goodbyes. Josef's friends and family all shared their sorrow for Anna's attack. Outside, he helped her get into his car. He started the engine and leaned over and tenderly kissed her, hoping to show her everything that had built up in his heart for her. Then without a word, he buckled up and took them home.

* * * *

Anna sat on the edge of Josef's bed feeling somewhat rested. A hot bath when they'd returned last night had helped her relax and fall asleep in Josef's hold.

But now the scent of coffee beckoned. She slowly stretched her arms above her head, easing into her aching muscles. When she'd left for Germany, she'd hoped to never again have to wake up with the remnants of Patrick's abuse. This, she vowed, would be the last.

She stood, a little wobbly at first, then made her way to the bathroom. When through, she wandered to the kitchen dressed in the large T-shirt

Josef had handed her to sleep in; a red jersey with the words *Deutschland Fussball Bund* surrounding a soccer ball.

She stopped near the peninsula. Josef stood at the sink dressed in baggy sweatpants and a fitted T-shirt while vigorously scrubbing at a plate. In an eating area near sliding doors, a small round table held an assortment of breakfast foods, like hard-boiled eggs, cucumber slices, cherry tomatoes, rolls, and cut-up sausage.

"Good morning," she said.

He glanced over his shoulder and smiled. "Oh good. You are up. Hungry?"

"I am."

She went up behind him at the sink, pressed against his back, and slipped her hands around his torso while he scrubbed a plate. "Just how I like my men, barefoot and making me breakfast."

"Oh, you do, huh?" He chuckled, and the vibration of his laugh rumbled through her.

She moved to his side. "You're going to rub the pattern right off that plate."

"Payback for not cleaning it yesterday morning." He lowered the plate into the sink, wiped his hands on a towel, and turned to her, placing his hands on her shoulders. "How do you feel?"

"Sore." She shrugged. "Sad to say, but there have been times he's left me in worse shape than this."

She felt his muscles tense then he drew her close, hugged her. She inhaled the laundry-fresh scent off his T-shirt, enjoying every second in his arms. "Can we eat?" she mumbled against his chest.

He let go. "Everything is ready. Will you grab that sugar and milk?"

She did while he filled two mugs with coffee. At the table, they plated food, quiet in their thoughts.

"It is supposed to be a rainy day," Josef said, glancing out the sliding doors.

"Then you'll just have to keep me entertained inside." She made certain her voice carried hints of innuendo and found herself disappointed when he didn't respond. "Is anything wrong?"

He seemed preoccupied, waiting a few seconds before finally meeting her gaze. "Anna, I was reminded so many times last night that you are still legally married."

"Only until we finalize the divorce."

"But as we—got close…" He shook his head. "I do not want to be the one who complicates your life."

She slid her hand over his. "While committed to my marriage, I never, ever considered being with another man, even though I stopped loving Patrick a long time ago. But my marriage has been over for some time."

He nodded. “And I understand this. But Patrick could use our relationship against you.”

“Then let him try. What he did to us last night will be a black mark on his record, too. On top of everything else he’s already done to me.”

Josef stared into her eyes for a long moment, then nodded and gave her a relaxed smile. “Then I am by your side all the way. Now eat up.” He motioned to her plate. “We need to keep you healthy and strong for the battle ahead.”

Chapter 26

"We are here." Josef turned the car into the main entrance of the Catholic hospital in Mainz, where purple banners with the institution's name lined the driveway.

Anna studied the beige concrete building. With rows of wide windows along the plain facade it looked like every hospital she'd ever seen in the States. The only difference: her former abuser lay in one of the beds, believing he would soon be speaking to a representative from the consulate. He had no idea Anna would be joining them.

Nobody knew she'd visited here once before. The day after Patrick's brutal attack, she'd taken a cab to the hospital, fully prepared to face him. Prove to him she was strong. Even when he'd tried to drag her back into his nightmare, she was not the woman he married, who passively allowed his mistreatment.

When she'd walked into his room, she'd found him lying in the bed sleeping. Tubes and wires connected to his body. Weak. Vulnerable. How she'd felt their entire marriage. Although she'd expected to bask in the triumph of being the one still standing, she couldn't do it. Anger because he'd stolen two years of her life would never vanish, but gloating wouldn't make her superior. So she left without waking him, hoping with their secret out in the open, Patrick would finally get the help he needed.

Josef parked along the curb, shut off the car, and took her hand. "I can come up with you, if you want."

"I should face this alone." She smiled. "But thank you."

He frowned and quietly said, "Understood."

Her lip service to being brave didn't diminish the size of the pit in her belly. Over the past five days, she'd been in touch with Tom Clark, from the American Consulate in Frankfurt. He'd given her phone updates on Patrick's healing progress, plus advice on the legalities of what he'd done. There were some serious matters at hand. But Tom had offered an idea that ensured Patrick left her and Josef alone, both in Germany and back in the States. She and Josef had agreed with Tom's proposal. Now, all they had to do was get Patrick on board.

"I will be right out here. Waiting." His eyes filled with worry. "If you need me sooner, call. I will come right up."

"I will. But I'm sure I'll be back down here before you know it, and then we'll leave for our two nights in Berlin."

He let go of her hands and tenderly ran his fingers along her throat, her jaw, her lower lip. Every spot he touched left an imprint on her skin and had her burning for more. His lips covered hers, claimed them with a deep kiss.

He whispered, "Now remember, that is how I feel about you."

She took his hand, pressed it to the spot where her heart raced beneath her skin. "And remember. This is how I feel about you."

His gaze softened. She got out, blew him a kiss, and hurried off to get this meeting started. As the elevator rose, she touched her lips, still tender with Josef's message.

All the way up, the beehive in her belly buzzed with nervous energy, but she walked tall as she stepped off and turned to the waiting area where Tom said they should meet.

Amidst the visitors, a man with thinning, graying hair dressed in a dark suit stood out. He read a newspaper but glanced up as she approached.

"Tom?"

"Yes. Are you Anna?"

"I am."

He stood and dropped his paper on the chair. They shook hands, and he withdrew a card from his jacket pocket. "I'm glad to finally meet in person. Here's my card, so I don't forget to give it to you."

Next to his name, it read *Senior Foreign Service Agent*, giving her some comfort in knowing he'd been doing this job for a while.

"Before we go in, have you and Mr. Schmitt considered my idea?" He glanced at the other people sitting nearby and motioned to a bench seat near a window. They went over and sat down.

He continued. "I ask because, ideally, we don't like to see American citizens in jails abroad. But in a case like this, we feel you deserve some protection, too. We're hoping your husband will see the light with this offer."

"Well, he has yet to see any light but his own."

"Yes." He hesitated. Speaking in a neutral and calm voice, one befitting his position as a diplomat of the US, he said, "The consulate staff has found him difficult at times."

"He's in for a rude awakening. If he refuses to take this offer, he'll have to lay in his own bed of problems."

"And Mr. Schmitt feels the same way?"

"Yes, Josef does. He's outside. After we speak with Patrick, why don't I get him and the three of us can talk?"

"Good idea."

"Do you mind if I have a few minutes alone with Patrick, before we see you together?"

"Not at all." He bent over and picked up his attaché, then gave her a close-lipped smile. "Are you ready to see your husband?"

This was her moment. To reclaim the stake in herself Patrick had destroyed in a blitzkrieg of mental and physical destruction. She stood. "Lead the way."

They walked down the hallway. At the door, a security guard who'd been assigned to keep watch nodded for them to enter.

As she started to go in, Tom said, "I'll wait right here in case you need me."

"Thank you." She hoped she didn't need him until she got out everything she wanted to say.

She entered the quiet room to find the curtain partially drawn. She stepped forward to the opening. Patrick rested beneath the crisp white sheets, his eyes closed and head tipped back, the tubes and wires from a week ago gone. Blue and dark purple bruises peppered his face. She remembered how hard Josef had hit him. His arms lay limply at his side. More cuts, these no doubt from the fall.

Pity roused during the first visit didn't show up today. Instead, seeing his bruises revived memories of every mark he'd ever left on her body. The great efforts she'd undertake to hide them from others, thereby protecting the man who inflicted him.

She took a deep breath. "Hello, Patrick."

His eyes slowly opened, and he lifted his head. "Anna."

"How are you feeling today?" She held her chin high, made sure she sounded strong, sure of herself.

"Fine." He scowled. "Nice you came to visit."

"You attacked me and my friend. Assaulted us. You're lucky I'm here at all."

"Your friend." Red rushed his cheeks. "From what I've seen, he's more than a friend."

She moved to the end of the bed. "What's wrong with you? I couldn't believe you showed up at my sister's house, but then to fly all the way here? How did you know I was staying at the guesthouse?"

"Easy," he said a bit too smugly. "While talking with Maria, I learned the name of the lawyer Isaak used. I popped into his office one day when he'd stepped out for lunch. His secretary was persuaded to give the address to your husband once I told her I'd misplaced the information and was supposed to be meeting you in Germany."

Even the most reasonable people weren't immune when he pulled out the charm. "And you've been following me for a couple of days, haven't you?"

"All over town. Seeing what you've been doing, waiting for the right moment." A dark flash crossed over his face. "I have to say, Anna, I never figured you'd cheat on me."

"I didn't come here to be with another man. It just happened." She moved to his bedside, to prove he no longer frightened her. "You seem to have a misguided view of your role in our marriage falling apart. When you beat me, that violated our marriage vows, too."

He snorted, but instead of a quick comeback, he looked at his hands as they twisted the edge of the sheet.

She walked over to the window, pushed aside the curtain, and stared out into the city. "Do you understand why I filed for divorce?"

"I thought you loved me, Anna. You promised me you'd never leave."

She swung around. "Answer my question."

His head jerked back.

"Answer me! Do you understand why you were served those divorce papers? Why I had to do it the way I did?"

"Look, we both know I have some problems. You can't blame me. My father—"

"No! At some point, you need to stop blaming others and start taking responsibility. God only knows what other women you've hurt along the way."

His face reddened. "You've turned into a real bitch."

"Call it what you want. I'm finally standing up for my rights. You lured me in, then took advantage of me. I tried so hard…" Anger swelled in her throat. "So damn hard to help you. For the first year, all I wanted was for you to get better. More than anything. My love for you was stronger than the love I had for myself."

She stormed over to the bed, her rage fueled by memories of every time he hit her. "And I let you beat me up, all because I believed we could work on your problems. Heal you. And then…then I could heal, too. Luckily, I saw the truth."

"The truth?" He laughed, a condescending chortle. "The truth is you only cared about yourself. Look at you now."

"And you've proven me right once again. You'll never change. You'll never admit you were wrong. I made the right call by divorcing you."

"You're a cheater, Anna. I never cheated on you."

She snorted a laugh. "I'd thank you, but you seem to take no ownership for what you *did* do to me."

He shifted uncomfortably, the first sign that, perhaps, he *did* see what he'd done.

"I came to Germany for Isaak, not myself. Josef helped me navigate that search. He's shown me how I deserve to be treated. And you know what? I will never feel bad for opening myself up to that feeling."

Patrick's face reddened, and his jaw tightened.

"Now you'd better pay close attention to what I'm about to tell you. Mr. Clark is out there, but I'll give you a preview of what we're going to discuss. Your choices for getting out of this situation are limited. The authorities here want us to press charges. You attacked a German citizen. And you attacked an American. The American consulate has advised me I have rights, too."

His eyes widened.

"But we are willing to make a deal with you, so you can get out of Germany and return to the States."

"A deal?"

"Yup. Three simple things."

Fury burned in his eyes. He turned away from her, stared at the window.

"First, you must promise to get help for your anger problem, so you never hurt another woman again." He flinched, but she continued. "Second, you will agree to proceed with the divorce in a quick and problem-free manner."

He pressed his lips tight and turned to stare at her through narrowed eyes. "And the last?"

"The German authorities have asked you sign an agreement saying you will stay away from Josef and me. My lawyer will get a restraining order, too. A violation of any of these terms will mean the charges here can still be made against you."

"Yeah? How will the Germans know?"

"The authorities in the US will tell them if I notify them." She stayed quiet, giving him a minute to mull over the conditions. "Just say the word and Mr. Clark will come in and go through the fine print."

"What happens if I say no?"

"Then Josef and I are prepared to press charges." She gave him a no-biggie shrug, just to scare him a little. "And if you lose your case under their system of justice, you will probably spend time in a German prison."

Patrick crossed his arms over his chest, his mouth turned down in defeat. After a long minute, he mumbled, "Send him in."

* * * *

"Close your eyes." Josef said to Anna as they entered the guesthouse's small lobby. "I have a surprise for you."

She looked at him. "Surprise?"

"Yes. Now close your eyes."

She gave him a funny look, then shut her eyes.

He guided her down the hallway while she laughed and made a few wisecracks about making sure she didn't trip. After two glorious days seeing the sights in Berlin, he still couldn't get enough of Anna. She'd be leaving tomorrow, a notion that flowed in and out of his head like the tide, making it impossible to ever get away from the idea.

He turned her into the dining room.

The guests had arrived, standing quietly, and watching her entrance with smiles on their faces. Ruth and Otto. Regina and Joachim. Dr. Walker stood beside Max, who sat in a chair with his two dogs waiting at his feet. Florian stood by a table filled with food, a large spoon in his hand as if their entrance had caught him in the middle of cooking. Even Josef's sister came, with her family and his mother. Gabriel and Kirsten were on their honeymoon, but they'd left a note with Josef to give Anna.

Josef looked beyond the usual suspects and his heart caught in his throat. Britta stood behind Gunther's wheelchair, a big smile on her face. Someone had decorated with streamers dangling from the ceiling, loose helium balloons, and a big sign reading *We will miss you, Anna.*

Josef got close then made her stop. "Okay. I'm going to count to three, then you can open your eyes. "One." He hurried over to be with the others. "Two. Three."

Anna's eyes flashed open.

"Surprise," everyone yelled.

Her jaw dropped, and her cheeks flushed. "Oh my." She turned her head, panning the guests. "You didn't have to do—oh, Gunther." She walked closer. "I can't believe it." She turned to Josef and tears glistened in her eyes. "Did you arrange this?"

"A group effort. Joachim made me swear not to ruin the surprise or he threatened to no longer let me drink in the biergarten."

Everyone laughed. Anna made her way around to the guests, talking and hugging them.

Josef went over to Joachim, who handed him a beer.

"I can't believe we pulled this off on such short notice." Joachim poured himself a beer from the tap.

Anna stood across the room, her cheeks glowing as she talked to the guests. Josef's heart nearly exploded with joy to see her so happy. "She deserves this," he said to Joachim. "She never deserved what that bastard of a husband did to her."

Joachim frowned and nodded. "How did things go at the hospital?"

"Exactly as we'd hoped. Her husband agreed to the terms. Let's hope he abides by them."

"And what is in the stars for you and beautiful Anna?"

"Next I will take a trip to America to visit her."

His heart twisted, though, both in the pleasure of their feelings for each other and the pain of her leaving. The plans they made to see each other soon were sincere, but life always had a way of taking over.

Chapter 27

"Where ya headed?" asked the cab driver.

"Brooklyn." She gave him the address and got into the backseat.

She settled into the seat, so tired she didn't care about the diesel scent filling the air or the long lines of honking cars trying to leave JFK. It was a long trans-Atlantic flight and a wait to get through customs.

She tipped back her head, closed her eyes, and found comfort in Josef's tender goodbye kiss. She'd never forget how he'd held her tight and whispered, "I will miss you, Anna. We will be together again when you are settled."

According to her lawyer, it would be another four or five days before the hospital released Patrick. Time she'd use to return to their Brooklyn brownstone and pack.

She must've drifted off to sleep, because it felt like no time had passed when the cab turned onto her street as the sun lowered to the horizon. She sent off a quick text to Josef that she'd arrived home safely, paid the driver, and took her luggage up the steps to her front door.

So many times she'd bounced up these steps and found Isaak peeking out his curtains, waving for her to come inside so he could talk. The bittersweet moment made her pause at his door. She wished she could go in there now and share every detail of the journey he'd asked her to take.

She rested a hand on his door and said, "Thank you, Isaak. You may have saved my life." And despite what more logical minds might think, she chose to believe he heard her.

She slipped in the key and turned the knob. An eerie silence greeted her, but she entered and flipped on the hallway light. Home. A place she no longer belonged. Where bad memories haunted her.

Leaving her bag by the door, she turned on lights as she walked toward the kitchen. She slipped off her backpack and put it on the table as she scanned the room.

The note she'd written had been torn into shreds. Next to it, the chain of the necklace had been ripped into two pieces. Broken. Just like their life together.

Dirty dishes, take-out containers, and open food everywhere. She sighed, turned her back on the mess, and took her luggage upstairs.

Her dresser lamp lay in the corner with the ceramic base shattered, the shade crushed. Most of her drawers were left open, articles of clothing either hanging half out or on the floor. The same with her closet.

She went to the bathroom and removed a dustpan and brush from beneath the sink.

As she swept up the ceramic base, she remembered the potent message behind Kirsten and Gabriel's *Polterabend*. Maybe she cleaned alone right now, not with a partner. But she faced the mess her life had become. In a strange way, she suspected this solo cleanup ritual might bring her a little bit of good luck down the line.

Once through, she opened her luggage and took out only the necessities, then got another piece of luggage. She switched on the bedroom TV for company and started to pack the rest of her clothes. Tomorrow she'd get some storage boxes, pack her belongings, and ship them her parents' house.

About a half hour later, as her eyelids threatened to close, she shut off the TV and cleared off the bed. Her phone pinged downstairs. She yawned and went downstairs to see who it was.

Want to Skype?

Josef. She smiled.

Give me ten minutes.

She quickly picked up the mess on the peninsula top and removed her computer from the backpack. While it started, she threw together a peanut butter and jelly sandwich then sat in front of the computer and ate it before dialing his number and waiting. Her heart warmed when his faced appeared on the screen, a pillow tucked behind his head and his bed's headboard visible.

He smiled. "Bet you didn't think you'd hear from me so soon."

"No. But I'm glad. Why are you up so late? It's two in the morning there."

"I woke, saw your text, and could not stop thinking of you."

She told him the condition she'd found the place. "I feel like at any minute he might walk through the door."

"You can rest assured he will not. I hope you do not mind, but I swung by the consulate after dropping you at the airport. Mr. Clark confirmed Patrick remains in the hospital and under watch. He planned to personally escort him onto the plane and contact you when they release him."

"Good. I'm relieved you double-checked. Now I can pack up my belongings and ship them to my parents' house more comfortably. Oh, on the plane I did some research on rentals in the town where my parents live. And I've already sent emails asking for appointments to see them."

"Good." He frowned. "Claudia told me to give her a heads up as soon as I plan to visit. I will miss you until then."

"I'll miss you, too." She put on a cheery smile. "But you know what?"

He grinned. "What?"

"I wouldn't change a thing about having met you."

"Nor would I, sweet Anna. Nor would I."

* * * *

A cold breeze chilled Anna's skin and sent her open jacket flapping behind her as the ferry hit the choppy waters where Puget Sound met Possession Sound. Getting closer to the place she'd been raised. Here, the sun played hide-and-seek a good part of the year, and the rich waters surrounding the islands cradled the land in its hands.

She leaned on the railing, stuck her face out to the faded sunshine. Ahead lay Whidbey Island and the ferry stop in Clinton.

She couldn't wait to drive the length of the island, reacquaint herself with the places that charmed visitors. The historic fishing village in Langley, South Whidbey State Park, Coupville's waterfront and historic museum, Deception Pass State Park. All places she'd take Josef to see once they worked out a time when he could visit.

She pulled out her phone and took a picture of the view ahead. Houses along the coast were dwarfed by large, dark pines and lush greenery beginning to turn red, gold, and sienna. She sent the picture to Josef, one of several she'd sent during her travels, and wrote, *Almost home.*

He responded quickly, like he always did.

I am enjoying your virtual tour. Soon
I will see everything in person.

They'd talked possibly about Christmas, two and half months away. It would give her time to get settled in her own place. He suggested next year she would visit Germany at Christmas to shop the markets with him. Next year. An invite proving everything they'd shared these past weeks had been real.

Once the ferry docked, she took 525 North. She made a quick stop at the grocery store not far from her parents' house to pick up a few items. On Anna's way into the store, she passed a mother who stood with a young girl next to a box sitting on the ground.

"'Scuse me," said the little girl. "Do you want a kitten?"

Anna paused, glanced into the box. Four teeny white-and-peach-colored kittens sat on top of a blanket, three of them playfully pawing each other, one fast asleep in the corner. "Aw, they're adorable." Anna squatted down for a closer look. "How old are they?"

The mother said, "Ten weeks old. We already have three cats, or I'd keep them myself."

The sleeping kitten lifted its peach head. An all-peach cat, except for white paws and a ring of white around its neck, like a mane. Anna stuck her hand out. The little creature shakily stood, stretched, and came over to Anna and rubbed soft fur against her finger.

"They're free," said the mother.

"That one's my favorite." The little girl crouched next to Anna. "We call him Mr. Socks."

Once she got her own apartment, she could use some company during those long workdays alone. And she'd make sure she found a place that allowed pets. Many did.

"You know what? I'll take Mr. Socks."

They held the cat for her while she ran into the store. Besides the items she needed, she visited the pet aisle for food and litter. When she came out, they had Mr. Socks in a box with a towel, ready to be transported. For a brief moment she worried what her parents would say, but her goal was to be out of there as quickly as possible. Hopefully, they wouldn't mind.

In fifteen minutes, she'd arrive at her parents' contemporary ranch. Mr. Socks mewed a few times, but quickly went back to sleep. She hoped he remained this easily content once they got there.

Things were falling into place. At the end of this week, her dad had arranged for Uncle Stanley and Aunt Lenore to come to dinner. According to Dad, her uncle had uncovered a great deal about their family history in his research. She couldn't wait to hear about it.

The trip to Germany left her with a burning desire to learn everything she could about the people in Poland who were her ancestors. What had made them change their faith? Realistically, she might never know.

Either way, she had been learning about the Jewish faith, reading the books Dr. Walker recommended, and taking away what she could. Faith had helped her get this far. Faith in herself, and in many other people who'd helped her along the way. And if that wasn't God's hand at work, then she didn't know what was.

Chapter 28

Two and a half months later...

"Here we are."

Josef opened his eyes at the sound of Anna's voice, taking a moment to clear the fog in his head. The last thing he remembered was exiting the ferry, getting into the car, and telling Anna he might shut his eyes for a moment.

He shifted upright in his seat as she drove them uphill through a condominium complex. No snow, unlike Germany. Yet doors holding holiday wreaths decorated with red ribbons, and colorful lights peeking through the branches of towering evergreens hinted to the holiday season.

"How long have I been sleeping?"

"Close to an hour." She shifted her dark eyes his way and smiled. "You've been traveling for well over half a day, so I'm sure you're exhausted."

"I could not sleep on the plane. Every time I drifted off, the man next to me bumped my elbow or the baby a few seats back wailed." He slipped his hand to the back of her neck. "But maybe a cup of coffee will help me wake up."

"Best coffee you'll get in the US is found around here. I'll make a strong brew." She turned into a parking spot, shut off the car, and turned to him. "I don't want you falling asleep too soon."

"Oh, you do not have to worry about that." He leaned over the console, kissed her, slowly and deeply. "I have missed you far too much."

She smiled. "Good. I thought a night alone would be good, even though my dad is dying to meet you."

He chuckled. "Ah, yes. My new Facebook friend. He seems like a nice man."

"He is." She frowned a little. "I'm glad he likes you. Turns out he was always a little uncomfortable with Patrick."

Josef nodded, massaging her nape, finding it easy to be around her again. "And Patrick, is he abiding by the agreement?"

"Yes. We only communicate through the lawyers. The divorce will be finalized in March." She reached beneath her steering wheel and lifted a lever that popped the car trunk. "Let's go inside, where it's warmer." As they got out and went to the back of the car, she added, "Mr. Socks is anxious to meet you."

He pulled his luggage and backpack from the trunk. "And me, him. I still cannot believe you got me to Skype with a cat."

She laughed and took the backpack from him, and they crossed the parking lot and headed for one of the modern-styled buildings. "Oh, come on. You seemed to enjoy it." They walked up a flight of stairs to a second story unit and she glanced back at him. "Or have you forgotten the two times you asked to see him?"

He laughed. "I'm turning into Max."

She chuckled as she reached a door holding a wreath that smelled of sweet pine. As she inserted the key, she glanced over her shoulder, grinned. "*Mein Haus ist Ihr Haus*."

"*Danke.* You speak German now?"

"Not really. I just practiced that a whole bunch of times. Did I say it right?"

He slipped his arms around her waist, kissed the back of her head. "Perfectly. I will teach you more if you want."

She pushed open the door. "*Ja, bitte*." She entered the foyer, flipped on a light, and leaned his backpack against the wall. "After all, I have a good reason since learning my great-great-grandfather was born in Hanover, Germany."

About a month ago, Anna had called him excitedly with the news that a Jacob Abraham from Germany was a link in her family tree. Jacob later moved to Poland, married, and had a son, Micha. In 1922, just before immigration to the US tightened, Jacob took his son and wife to America, but they traveled under a different surname—Abrams—and a different faith as Protestants.

He debated telling Anna about his latest venture at the travel company. He'd planned for it to be a surprise, tied into a gift he wanted to give her Christmas morning.

The cat came running in from the other room. "Here's my boy." Anna leaned over and swooped him up, nuzzled her cheek against his fur. "Josef, meet Mr. Socks, or Socks for those of us close to him."

He put out his hands and Anna passed him over. The cat purred happily. "Nice to meet you, Socks."

"Come see the view that made me fall in love with this place."

He followed her into a spacious living room with gleaming hardwood floors partially covered by colorful area rugs, a stone fireplace, comfortable furniture. A small Christmas tree stood in one corner, filling the room with the scent of pine and the glow of its bright lights.

They stopped at a set of sliding doors and he put the cat down. He slipped an arm around Anna's waist and stared out into a spectacular view of rich blue water in the foreground and snow-capped mountains in the background. "I can see why you fell for the place."

"You're looking at Oak Harbor Bay. In the distance are the Cascade Mountains. You'll see them better tomorrow since it's starting to get dark."

"Spectacular. It is beautiful here."

He drew her into a hug, her smile fading as she looked up into his eyes. He slipped his fingers through her hair, kissed her harder this time. She pushed his coat off his shoulders, let it drop to the floor, and shimmied out of hers. All while he got lost in her tender lips and the feel of her hands sliding along his torso.

Tilting back her head, she smiled. "Coffee or bed?"

"You have to ask?"

He let her lead him to the bedroom, where he pulled her close and covered her mouth with his. Shoes were kicked off. Pants and shirts randomly tossed. Soon they stretched out alongside each other. Every kiss, every touch, coming from deep inside his heart.

The sky darkened while they were lost in each other. Later, they lay together, the glow of the Christmas tree in the next room tumbling into the doorway. Being together again felt good, and reinforced all the feelings that surfaced while he wasn't with her.

A little while later, he unpacked and they both put on comfortable clothes to stay in for the night.

As he entered the living room, Anna approached him, carrying two fluted glasses and placed them on a table next to a cream-colored, comfortable-looking sofa stationed near the fireplace. "Take a seat."

She walked to the tree, squatted down, and picked up a gift that she set on her lap after getting seated.

The cat hopped on the couch and curled in Josef's lap.

She laughed. "He likes you already." She picked up the gift wrapped in shiny gold paper. "I was going to save this until Christmas morning, but I can't wait."

He handed over Socks and tore off the wrapping to find a box. Excitement twinkled in Anna's eyes. He took off the lid and found three thin picture frames inside. He lifted the one on top.

Mounted against a beveled mat was a document on linen paper. *Kindness Connects, by Anna Abrams*. He glanced up. "Your column."

"Yes. It'll be published soon."

The top corner showed a date. January 2. A week and a half from now. A closer look showed the content wasn't the actual newsprint but a neatly typed version. His gaze dropped to the first line.

Over seventy years ago, a man saved my neighbor's life. Little did I know that this single act would someday save my life too...

Her journey. He looked up to her glistening eyes and she smiled. He took her hand and continued to read.

The column told about her reasons for going to Germany, both her personal reason and what she hoped to accomplish for Isaak. And she wrote about meeting Josef. Her first impression of him made him laugh. No, he hadn't put his best foot forward. But in her words, she began to see how Josef was suffering, too.

She wrote about the towns they'd visited, the disappointment of not finding Gunther right away, but how her trusted guide took those moments to show her the beauty of Germany in places like Marburg and *Burg Eltz*. All steps that she recognized as part of the bigger picture of her journey. Perhaps even a necessary part as she got close to a stranger…him.

Words grabbed his heart as she wrote about every bittersweet moment with Gunther, followed by a stop at the Holocaust Memorial in Wiesbaden. A moment she described as drawing her heart to the man who brought her there.

Josef has become part of my chain of hope.

His eyes watered and looked up, met her glistening gaze. "Oh, Anna. I am so touched. I cannot think of a better gift."

"There are two more columns in there."

He picked up the next frame. A second article in the series, scheduled for a week later, highlighted their trip to Belgium to meet the family who housed Isaak for close to two years. The third article talked about her personal journey. Her marital problems, and how she'd been abused but remained silent. She even divulged how she planned to work on a book about the plight of abused women and the importance of never feeling it was too late to change your life.

He lowered the frame, reached out and stroked her cheek. "My God, Anna. The columns are perfect. I'm so proud of you. And honored to have been part of your journey."

She smiled. "Your opinion means everything. There's one more column for me to write tied into this trip, but I'm not ready. It's the story of my ancestors, mainly about leaving behind their faith. I believe it's a story people should hear, to make them think about what prejudice can force some people to give up."

He reached for her hand as a tear slid down her cheek. "Isaak gave me two gifts. He helped me escape a horrible marriage. But this journey also made me take an interest in my family's past. I hope what I wrote reflects those sentiments."

He laid the box on the table and took her hands. "Every single word was perfectly said. I—I just do not know what to say. This is a gift I will treasure." He leaned forward and brushed his lips to hers. "You have filled my heart, dear Anna."

She smiled. "As you do mine."

He stood. "Stay right there. Now I will get one of my gifts to you."

* * * *

Josef disappeared into the bedroom. Anna grabbed a tissue from a box on the end table and dabbed at her wet eyes. Writing those columns had drained her emotionally, but the time to reflect gave her enormous perspective on everything gained during those four weeks away.

He returned to his seat, holding an envelope. "I have been thinking about you, too. About your ancestry research. Many people out there seek the same, especially from this country."

"Well, we are a nation of immigrants."

He nodded. "So with a little help, I have uncovered some information on your relatives."

"You did? Why didn't you tell me earlier?"

"Because I wanted to surprise you."

"And that little help… Any chance that's how the Facebook friendship you have with my dad evolved?"

He laughed. "Let's say this helped it along. Seems we both watch soccer, too."

Her heart warmed knowing these two special people in her life had connected.

"Your father supplied me with the information you and your uncle found. I searched on my side of the ocean by making some trips to record offices in Poland."

He removed a sheet of paper from the envelope. "So far, I have located some of your great-great-grandmother's family who remained in Łódź, Poland. Here is an extended family tree. Your dad sent me what your uncle put together."

She searched the boxes of the expanded tree, with branches and names showing people in both Germany and Poland. Several boxes of family in both countries showed they'd died between 1938 and 1945.

She looked up at Josef, a pain in her heart as she quietly asked, "These relatives who died during the war and pre-war years, was it because they were Jewish?"

"Yes. It appears so. I tracked down where they died, made copies of the records. Many were at the camps. I am sorry." His mouth turned down. "As I say this, I can see this is not such a happy gift."

"No, no! This is exactly what I needed to know. Even if it's sad."

The pained expression on his face brightened. "But there are these people who survived. And look." His finger moved across several boxes. "There is family there today."

She studied each name, saying them aloud, taking a minute to make connections for layers of aunts and uncles, second and third cousins. Almost more than she could grasp at this moment. Many were taken too early. At least some had survived.

She lowered the paper. "Josef. This is a wonderful gift.

"There is more." He removed a long letter-sized envelope. "Here."

She opened the unsealed flap and pulled out a folded paper. Lufthansa Airlines? Her gaze flowed down the document. A flight to Warsaw, Poland in early April. She skimmed back up. Passenger name: Anna Abrams. "You got me a ticket to go to Poland?"

He nodded. "I plan to meet you there. I will drive. A few weeks ago I made some contact with your family and they would like to meet you. Many live near Warsaw. I thought we could go to Łódź, too. It is not far from Warsaw."

She read it again, as the impact slowly sank in. Josef had handed her a ticket to her family's past.

She put the ticket aside and hugged Josef, tears flowing for what was both lost and found. When she finally had a handle on her emotions, she looked up to him. "I'm stunned. This is the best gift in the world."

"If you can take a little extra time off, or somehow work while we travel, I am hoping we can drive together back to Germany. Maybe by then we will have uncovered more about your family in Hannover, Germany. Then your return flight is out of Frankfurt. My family would like to see you again, too."

"I would love to. And this won't interfere with your work?"

"That is my other news. Claudia got very excited to learn about my research for you. She thinks I might be just the person to set up a new division at the tour company. Family Ancestry Tours. You are our test case, to see the work involved. If this works smoothly, we will think about how to market this. In fact, I will be back to the States this summer. Did you know the world's largest genealogical library is in Salt Lake City, Utah?"

"No. I didn't."

"I have spoken to genealogists there and plan to come back for two months to learn from them."

"And that means you'll be over here again."

"Yes. And the flight from Washington to Utah is short." His lids hooded and voice softened. "We won't have to cross an ocean to see each other."

Anna let it all sink in. "We'll have three weeks here. My trip to Poland and Germany. And then having you a short flight away for the summer. It's all too good to be true."

"Well, it is very real. Now tell me what we will do here in Washington. I cannot wait to see more."

While they sipped the champagne, she talked about all the things she wanted to show him. But she couldn't stop thinking about the tickets he'd given her, and about meeting the family overseas.

"You know, if my great-grandfather's parents came with to the US with their real name, I'd have spent my life as Anna Abraham. I'd probably have gone to Hebrew school and attended a synagogue and wouldn't even be celebrating Christmas. And I would've probably been able to have deep talks with Isaak about faith, because he was a very faithful man."

Josef reached for her hand, squeezed. "I never met Isaak, but I do know that he'd be very proud of you right now."

Josef always knew the right thing to say. Somehow she knew that their relationship and possible future together would have some big hurdles to jump. But it would be okay, because Josef always seemed to meet her halfway.

SHARE THE MOON

Sometimes trust is the toughest lesson to learn.

Sophie Shaw is days away from signing a contract that will fulfill her dream of owning a vineyard. For her, it's a chance to restart her life and put past tragedies to rest. But Duncan Jamieson's counter offer blows hers out to sea.

Duncan still finds Sophie as appealing as he had during boyhood vacations to the lake. Older and wiser now, he has his own reasons for wanting the land. His offer, however, hinges on a zoning change approval.

Bribery rumors threaten the deal and make Sophie wary of Duncan, yet she cannot deny his appeal. When her journalistic research uncovers a Jamieson family secret, trust becomes the hardest lesson for them both.

A Lyrical e-book available now.

Learn more about Sharon at
www.kensingtonbooks.com/author.aspx/31604

Chapter 1

New Moon: When the moon, positioned between the earth and sun, nearly disappears, leaving only darkness.

November

The sabotaged kayaks beckoned. Sophie Shaw trod a thin layer of ice pellets on the lawn as she headed to the lake's edge, where eight boats waited to be returned to the storage rack. The fickle New England weather had offered sleet-dropping clouds an hour earlier. Now, a wink from the sun reflected against Blue Moon Lake.

She dragged the first boat up a small incline, annoyed some bored teenagers had considered destruction of property entertainment. Growing up she and her friends had respected the local businesses.

A UPS truck screeched to a stop in front of a row of shops on Main Street. The driver hopped out and ran into Annabelle's Antiques with a box tucked under his arm. Sophie glanced both ways along the road for signs of Matt, whose new driver's license and clunker car played to every mother's fears. Fifteen minutes earlier, she'd texted him for help with the boat mess. He'd replied "k."

Sophie's flats glided along the slick lawn. She gripped the cord of a bright orange sea kayak and, using two hands, struggled backward up the slope. Her foot skidded. The heel of her shoe wobbled for security but instead, her toes lifted off the ground and flashed toward the clear sky. The burning skid of the cord ripped across her palms just as her other foot lifted and launched her airborne. *Thud!*

Air whooshed from her lungs. Pain coursed through her shoulder blades, neck, and spine. The ground's chilly dampness seeped into her cotton khaki pants, raising goose bumps on her skin. Seconds passed without breath before she managed to swallow a gulp.

Lying flat on her back, she stared at the cornflower blue sky and spotted a chalky slice of the moon. The night Henry died, a similar crescent had hung from the heavens, barely visible nestled among the glittering stars. She prepared for the scrape that threatened to tear the gouge of her scarred heart. Seven years. Seven painful years. She closed her eyes and after a few seconds, the weight of sadness lifted off her chest.

Tears gathered along her lower lashes. She pushed a strand of unruly long hair from her face. Footsteps crunched on the ice pellets and headed her way.

"Matthew Shaw…" Fury pooled in her jaw as she resisted the urge to yell at her son. "You'd better have a good excuse for taking so long."

A man with cinnamon hair, short on the sides with gentle waves on top, knelt at her side. She studied the strong outline of his cheeks and the slight bump on the bridge of his angular nose that gave him a rugged touch, but he wasn't familiar.

"Are you okay?" He searched her face.

The stranger hovered above. Tall treetops, clinging to the last of their earth-toned foliage, served as a backdrop to her view. A vertical crease separated his sandy brows. She couldn't pry herself from his vivid blue eyes, in part stunned from the fall, but also by her first responder.

For several long seconds she stared, and then mumbled, "I think so. Just a little shocked."

A whiff of his musk cologne revived her with the subtle charm of a southern preacher casting his congregation under his spell.

He frowned. "Does it hurt to move anything?"

"Sometimes it did before I fell."

The stranger's face softened and his lips curved upward. "A sense of humor, huh? That's a good sign."

"I suppose." His deep voice relaxed her like a cup of chamomile tea, the balanced and certain tone of his words easing her wounded spirit. Maybe this guy was a sign her rotten luck might change. "So, where's your white horse?"

"In the stable. Today I came in the white Camry." He motioned with a wave of his hand to a corner of the parking lot.

She pushed up on her elbow to look and a sharp pain jabbed her neck. "Ow!"

"Careful." His smile disappeared. "I was on my way over to help when you fell. You hit pretty hard."

The heat of embarrassment skittered up her cheeks. Not only had he witnessed her spastic aerobics, but she never played the distressed-damsel-on-the-dirty-ground card. A woman proficient at fly-fishing, who learned how to drive in a pickup truck and who, in her job as a journalist, had uncovered a corrupt politician, should be up and running by now.

"Go slow." His request suggested doling out orders came easy. "May I help?"

She nodded. He slipped a gentle hand into hers. The chill coating her skin melted against his warm touch. His well-groomed nails and thick fingers suggested he didn't work outdoors, rather the clean hands of a man who spent his days in an office. No wedding band either. He helped her sit and studied her as if a question perched on the edge of his thoughts.

"Can I call someone?" He blinked. "Your husband?"

"Oh, I'm not married." She caught the slight twitch of his mouth. "My son's supposed to be on his way to restack the boats."

Since her divorce from Mike, she'd concluded the available men in Northbridge were as predictable as the assortment at the dollar rental video store, filled with decade-old hits she'd seen so many times they held little interest. This man was a refreshing change.

"Ready to try to stand?" He took her by the elbow and she nodded.

Once on her feet, their hands remained together.

He glanced at them and let his drop. "You'll probably think this is crazy but—"

"Sophie?" The owner of Griswold's Café stood across the street and wiped his hands on a stained white apron. He'd placed the call to her father to alert them about the vandalism at Dad's boat shed. "You okay?"

"I'm fine." She waved. "Thanks."

She returned to the newcomer's gaze, as blue as the deep Caribbean Sea and as shiny as a starburst.

He raised his dirt-stained hands. "You might want to check yours."

Sure enough, her palms carried the same smudges from the impact of her fall. "Hold on. I have something to clean us off."

She trotted to her car, hoping the backside of her blazer covered any mess on the back of her pants.

After finding a package of wipes in the center console, she cleaned herself spotless and peeked in the rearview mirror. Her dark chocolate curls scattered with the freewill of a reckless perm. She neatened them with her fingertips then grabbed her cell and tried to call Matt but landed in his voice mail. The second she hung up, the phone rang. Bernadette's name showed on the display.

"Hey."

"Is your speech ready for tonight? You're our star speaker."

Bernadette always latched onto a crusade. The first was in third grade, a petition over the slaughter of baby seals for their skins. For tonight's public hearing, Bernadette had promised everyone the fight of her life. Her special interest group's concern about the large-scale development on Blue Moon Lake proposed by Resort Group International was a sore topic for many local residents, especially Sophie.

"Better find a new star speaker. There's a change of plans." Sophie readied herself for a negative reaction. "I'm covering the story for the paper now."

"You? Has Cliff lost his mind?"

"No. The other reporter can't do the assignment. Her father had a stroke earlier today. Cliff wanted to take the story himself, but I insisted he stick to his job as editor and let me do mine. I even made a five dollar bet I'd get a headline-worthy, bias-free quote from the company president."

"Do you think you can? I mean, RGI stole that land right out from under your nose. What was it…three days before signing the contract?"

Those were almost Cliff's exact words, along with some mumbling about how the paper's cheap new owner had cut his staff and he saw no other choice. "Two days."

"Honey, why would you want this story?"

"I have my reasons. This won't be the first time one of us needed to report on something close to us."

"Yeah, but wouldn't some public chastising against the corporate giant be good for your soul?"

"In a way." Sophie hesitated then decided to tell her best friend the truth. "Look, this is a chance to redeem myself. Prove to Cliff I really *can* stick to my journalist's creed after…well, you know, what happened with Ryan Malarkey."

"Mmm, forgot about him. He makes all us lawyers look bad." A long pause filled the air. "Guess that's a valid reason."

Sophie still harbored guilt from the last time a story got personal and she'd been fooled into violating her hallowed reporter vows. "Hey, on a lighter note, it's raining men over here at the lake."

Bernadette laughed. "What?"

"Some kids vandalized Dad's kayak shed. He asked for my help and this handsome guy appeared out of nowhere to help me. Fill you in later. He's waiting."

On her way back to the stranger, she studied his profile. Men this desirable didn't drop out of the sky around here. Why was he in town? Visitors to Northbridge weren't unusual in the summer, but not late fall. He faced the water, looking in the direction of the rolling hillside of Tate Farm, the property under discussion at tonight's controversial public hearing.

She neared the visitor and he turned around.

"Are you the owner of this place?" He pointed to the wood-sided shed with a sign reading "Bullhead Boat Rentals."

"No. My father runs it with my brother. Dad's too old to be walking around in this icy mess and my brother is gone for the day." She handed him a wipe. "They also operate the local tackle shop and Two Rivers Guided Tours, guided fly-fishing trips."

"I remember the tackle shop." He cleaned his hands and tucked the dirty wipe in his jacket pocket. "My family came here for a couple of summers. Close to thirty years ago."

Sophie studied him again. Summer vacationers passed through here with the blur of a relay race.

He brushed a dead leaf off the knee of his faded, well-pressed jeans. "Such a great little town." He scanned the main street, unhurried and relaxed, then took a deep breath, as if to savor a nostalgic moment. "Quintessential New England."

Although she'd lived all her forty-four years in Northbridge, she looked around with him. A few cars parked on the road near a long row of pre-WWI buildings, now housing retailers who had serviced the town's residents for countless decades, such as Handyman Hardware and Walker's Drugs. The retail stretch was sandwiched between her favorite place to eat, Sunny Side Up, a metal-sided, trolley car-shaped diner and the weathered façade of Griswold's Café. The popular hangout for waterfront meals had a karaoke night the locals rarely missed.

She examined his profile again. Surely she hadn't forgotten someone with such a sexy full lower lip and strong chin?

"I can't imagine anybody being unhappy here," he said, his tone quiet.

She held in the urge to retort with a cynical remark. Every time she stuck a foot out of town, circumstances jerked her back. "Too bad you picked today to return. Most of our visitors enjoy the warmer weather."

"I'm house hunting."

"Oh. Well, we have a lot of summer residents."

"I want a year-round place."

The absent wedding ring held renewed interest. "Where are you from?"

"Manhattan."

She adjusted her crooked scarf. "Living here will be a big change."

"I know. I've always loved this place, though." He reached out and tenderly brushed a leaf off Sophie's shoulder. His gaze flowed down her body like a slow trickle of water.

An unexpected burn raced up her cheeks.

He lifted his brows. "Hey, I never knew the lake went by another name. The town website said the original name came from an old Native American word."

She nodded. "Puttacawmaumschuckmaug Lake." The long name rolled off her tongue with ease, the pronunciation a rite of passage for anyone born and raised around the body of water. "It either means 'at the large fishing place near the rock' or 'huge rock on the border.'"

"What?" He chuckled. "Puttamaum…"

She shook her head and repeated the difficult word.

"Puttacawsch—"

"Nope. It's a toughie. That's why a reporter who visited here at the turn of the century suggested in his column we change the name. He said the water's beauty was as rare as a blue moon, and the phrase stuck."

He grinned, easy and confident. "My kids will love this place."

Kids? Sophie buried her disappointment. "Are you and your wife looking at the other towns bordering the water?"

"No. I like Northbridge. Oh, and I'm not married," he said matter-of-factly. His gaze arm-twisted her for a response.

She wanted to fan her hot cheeks but instead regrouped while pointing across the lake. "If you have a spare few hundred thousand and want to help the town out, take a look at Tate Farm. A developer wants to buy it to put up a large resort. Maybe you can outbid the guy."

"Oh?"

"Uh-huh. There's a public hearing tonight."

The hearing would be her first chance to meet the corporate vipers from Resort Group International face-to-face and she couldn't wait to hammer firm president, Duncan Jamieson, with some tough questions. With any luck the zoning board would vote down their request so the offer she'd made, along with her dad and brother, would be back in play.

The stranger's brows furrowed and he stroked his chin.

"Don't worry. I'm confident our zoning board will vote no on their proposal and keep the nasty developer away. By the way, I'm Sophie."

He dropped his gaze to the ground for a millisecond then looked back up. "I'm Carter."

If Nana were still alive, she'd have said in her thick Scottish brogue, "Verra good sign, Sophie. Carter comes from the word cart: someone who moves things." Nana held great stock in the art of name meanings.

He'd certainly moved Sophie.

Matt's rusty sedan whipped into the lot, ending the lusty thoughts. Her son hurried over, unease covering every corner of his face. "Sorry I'm late."

"What took you so long?"

"Grandpa called to make sure I helped you." He dragged his hand through his messy dirty-blond hair. "We were talkin'."

She had her suspicions about the topic but rather than ask, she introduced him to Carter.

He turned to Matt. "What do you say we let your mom take it easy and we'll finish this job?"

Matt nodded and trotted to the boats.

At her car, Carter opened the driver's door. "Better hop in." His tone lowered. "Your hands were cold before."

Sophie's knees softened and she tried to speak, but no sound came out. Turmoil reigned inside her body as he jogged away from her and caught up with Matt.

She tried to shake off the lost control caused by this stranger. This little incident had stolen some of her strength and lately every morsel was necessary to stay afloat. On the roller coaster of life, she had been taking a wild ride. First due to a chance to own the vineyards, giving her a helping hand from her inner grief and fulfilling a life-long dream. Then two weeks ago, RGI had barged into town and yanked her offer from the table.

Carter pointed to a kayak and said something. Matt laughed. The scene made her miss having a man in their household. Her heart softened, awed by the way this knight who'd arrived in a shiny white Camry galloped in and took charge…and how she'd simply let him. Was something good finally stepping into her life?

Disappointment skimmed her chest. Who was she kidding? Nothing would come of this.

Her cynical nature hadn't developed overnight. Rather, she had soured over time. Lost opportunities, gone due to circumstances beyond her control: Mom's cancer, Sophie's unplanned pregnancy, her subsequent marriage to Mike, even her lost bid on the land RGI now wanted.

Time to forget this guy and concentrate on her job. She'd have to work harder than ever to stick to her journalistic creed, but any teeny, albeit truthful, crumb of negative news about RGI or its president, Duncan

Jamieson, could sway the scale on the zoning board vote. Then the greedy developer would disappear from Northbridge forever.

Her family wanted that land. Land their ancestors were the first to settle back in 1789. Land where the winery plans of their dreams could come to life. The most important reason, though, was protecting the sacred place where her firstborn son, Henry, had died.

Chapter 2

A long line of cars pulled into the well-lit high school parking lot, higher than usual volume for a public hearing. Sophie grabbed her bag and hurried toward the entrance, hoping she could still get a seat up front.

As she neared the large regional high school, she passed a noisy group standing in a circle at the front of the building, chanting the plea "Save our Lake." Their signs bore the acronym "S.O.L.E." stacked on the left and the words, "Save Our Lake's Environment" extending from each corresponding letter. Protestors weren't the norm at these types of events and their presence added a thick cloud of tension to the cool night air.

Bernadette marched with the vocal group. Nana had liked to remind everyone how Bernadette was living proof her name theory worked. "I canna think of a better name for that lassie. She's named to 'be brave like a bear' and sure acts the part." There were times Sophie found *any* explanation about people's behavior to offer a measure of peace. After all, a wise person took heed in all the messages around her and her name meant "wisdom."

She waved to Bernadette, who yelled with more exuberance than any other protestor. A rosy glow highlighted her full cheeks and her large green eyes burst with equal excitement. She shook a defiant fist in the air.

"Nice boots," Sophie yelled over their noise. Bernadette had tucked her jeans into new boots, with razor thin heels and pointy toes, which crossed the border into sexy. Opposite of the sensible heeled style Sophie wore. "You're Northbridge's own *Che Guevera* in her Jimmy Choo's."

"You'd better start reading *Vogue.* These are from Target." Bernadette pushed aside her sable brown bangs, which always seemed due for a trim. "Grab a sign."

"I'm working. Remember?" Any public appearance of bias while covering a story could get back to her editor.

"Yeah, yeah. Same old excuse." Bernadette punched a follow-up fist of solidarity at the sky and resumed her chant.

The details about Carter would have to wait until after the hearing. Since Sophie's chance meeting with the handsome visitor, she couldn't shake her craving to learn more about him, a sensation that left her liberated and scared at the same time. Talking to the stranger was easy and comfortable, the way sliding into a pair of well-worn slippers let her know she was home, safe and exactly where she belonged.

She turned toward the entrance and slammed into a stiff body, making her stumble back a step.

"'Scuz me." Otis Tate dipped his bushy eyebrows in annoyance, his Adam's apple jutting out just beneath the scruffy edge of his white beard. As usual, his younger brother, Elmer, lagged several steps behind, shoulders stooped and taking away the extra few inches of height he held over the senior of the two septuagenarians.

"Sorry. I didn't see you." A cold breeze sent a chill through Sophie's wool skirt and tights, numbing her immediate reaction to scream "traitor." The mere sight of them made her blood boil. After they'd accepted Resort Group International's offer, they didn't even have the decency to give her a phone call. Bernadette had learned about the deal at her law office and called Sophie, adding to her humiliation. They probably hadn't given any consideration to the deep ties she held to the land. With no wives or children, their only goal was to sell to the highest bidder and retire near some friends in Florida, a consideration no self-respecting New Englander would utter aloud.

Otis cleared his throat. "Listen, we want you to know this isn't personal."

"I'd suggest you look up what personal means."

Both his brows arched. "Listen Sophie, we hadn't signed anything with you yet. Business is business. You'll find another spot for your winery." He elbowed Elmer.

Elmer flinched but didn't respond. Instead, he stared at the protestors, his downturned mouth giving away his sadness.

Otis leaned close enough for her to catch the warmth of his breath. "I heard Cliff gave you this story last minute. I assume you'll give it fair coverage."

The comment struck Sophie as hard as a kidney jab.

Her tone downshifted to a harsh whisper. "Nana was a friend of your dad's. She told me his name meant honorable. I wonder what she'd say about his sons."

Otis' face turned beet red and Elmer's froze like ice, as if her words cast a voodoo hex, Nana-style.

She raised her voice. "You don't have to fret over my coverage. I'll report on this with the unbiased dedication of an attorney defending a murderer." She turned to walk away then stopped and glared at both men. "Correction. Alleged murderer."

Elmer dropped his chin to his chest and it touched the ends of his flannel shirt collar. Sophie didn't care if she'd shamed the nicer of the two brothers. He, of all people, understood why she didn't want the land in the hands of strangers.

Two weeks after her son died, Elmer had paid Sophie a visit. Several people in town wished to set up a memorial garden for Henry, right on the spot where he'd passed away on the Tates' land. Elmer had requested her permission, admitting he wanted the memorial too. Henry had worked their farm every summer since turning fifteen and had grown close to Elmer, often calling the gentle old man his surrogate granddad. She'd agreed to the garden.

Now the place was hallowed ground. She visited there every year on the anniversary of Henry's death, his birthday or any other time she needed a tangible reminder of his life.

"If you'll excuse me, I have to get inside." The thick lump settled in her throat and tears burned in the back of her eyes.

Once inside the auditorium, she managed to get one of the last seats in the front row. On stage, members of the Northbridge Zoning Board had already taken their places behind a dais of two old rectangular fold-up tables with several microphones spaced along the tops.

She took a breath to relax. Attitude accounted for ninety-nine percent of any situation and regret over her backlash at the Tate brothers moments ago hit hard and fast. The wall clock showed three minutes before seven, so she used the time to scribble more questions for RGI on her notepad. A minute later, the group of protestors noisily filled the empty row behind her, where they'd left a few belongings to save their seats.

"How'd we sound out there?" Bernadette craned her neck to examine the crowded auditorium and slipped off her coat to reveal a white tee shirt with green letters spelling out S.O.L.E. printed across the bust line.

"Menacing. Only a fool would face you guys."

Bernadette pointed with her chin to the back of the auditorium. "Speaking of fools, here they are now."

A group of five men in suits had entered. Amongst town officials, she recognized the lawyer from Hartford representing RGI, who dressed fancier than the locals in his expensive-looking suit. She studied the two men to the attorney's side and stifled a gasp. The pitter-patter of her heart picked up speed.

Bernadette tapped Sophie's arm. "There's the head fool himself. Duncan Jamieson, president of RGI."

"Which one?"

"The hot tamale on the end, with wavy hair and wearing a navy suit."

"Are you sure?"

A puzzled expression flitted across Bernadette's face. "Absolutely. He came into the office two days ago to schmooze with one of the senior partners."

Sophie's mouth went as dry as dust. Bernadette had just identified Duncan Jamieson, head of RGI, as none other than Carter.

His presence begged for attention and separated him from the other men. Besides the expensive shine to his suit, assuredness permeated from every pore. He surveyed the crowd then leaned close and said something to his attorney, who nodded.

The group of men walked toward the stage. As he neared Sophie's section, his gaze met hers then dropped to the press badge dangling from her neck. He looked at her again and blinked. She held her breath, as much afraid he'd remember her as he'd forgotten her. After a negligible pause, his lip curled into a smile of clear delight. Before she could react, he winked and sealed the acknowledgement.

Sophie's pulse pounded in her ears as she neared code red. His cozy wink not only told others they'd met but dredged forth the lusty awareness of him which had consumed her body earlier. A sharp poke jabbed her back.

"What the hell was that?" Bernadette whispered. "Do you know him?"

"In a manner of speaking." She refused to turn around.

Carter, a.k.a. Duncan Jamieson, took the steps up to the stage and sat behind the long table with the other men. That guy had played Sophie more smoothly than a winning hand of poker, but she wasn't about to take his lies in silence.

Meet Sharon Struth

Sharon Struth believes you're never too old to pursue a dream. The Hourglass, her debut novel, was a finalist in the National Readers' Choice Awards for Best First Book. She is the author of the popular Blue Moon Lake series, which includes Share the Moon.

When she's not working, she and her husband happily sip their way through the scenic towns of the Connecticut Wine Trail, travel the world, and enjoy spending time with their precious pets and two grown daughters. She writes from the friendliest place she's ever lived, Bethel, Connecticut. For more information, including where to find her published essays, please visit sharonstruth.com or visit her blog, Musings from the Middle Ages & More at www.sharonstruth.wordpress.com.